T0018803

COCONUT DROP
DEAD

St. Martin's Paperbacks titles by Olivia Matthews

Against the Currant
Hard Dough Homicide
Coconut Drop Dead

COCONUT DROP DEAD

Olivia Matthews

St. Martin's Paperbacks

NOTE: If you purchased this book without a cover you should be aware that this book is stolen property. It was reported as "unsold and destroyed" to the publisher, and neither the author nor the publisher has received any payment for this "stripped book."

This is a work of fiction. All of the characters, organizations, and events portrayed in this novel are either products of the author's imagination or are used fictitiously.

First published in the United States by St. Martin's Paperbacks, an imprint of St. Martin's Publishing Group.

COCONUT DROP DEAD

Copyright © 2023 by Patricia Sargeant-Matthews.

All rights reserved.

For information, address St. Martin's Publishing Group, 120 Broadway, New York, NY. 10271.

www.stmartins.com

ISBN: 978-1-250-83908-4

Our books may be purchased in bulk for promotional, educational, or business use. Please contact your local bookseller or the Macmillan Corporate and Premium Sales Department at 1-800-221-7945, ext. 5442, or by email at MacmillanSpecialMarkets@macmillan.com.

Printed in the United States of America

St. Martin's Paperbacks edition / January 2024

10 9 8 7 6 5 4 3 2 1

To My Dream Team:

- My sister, Bernadette, for giving me the dream.
- My husband, Michael, for supporting the dream.
- My brother Richard, for believing in the dream.
- My brother Gideon, for encouraging the dream.
  - And to Mom and Dad always, with love.

CHAPTER 1

"Will we see you and Benny at the festival, Tanya?" My maternal grandmother, Genevieve Bain, sat at her dark wood folding table in Spice Isle Bakery, our family-owned business, early Friday morning. Her table stood between our customer service counter and the kitchen door, the busiest spot in the shop.

Her Grenadian heritage was in the cadence of the question she'd called across the waiting area to her longtime friend Tanya Nevis and Tanya's beau, Benny Parsons. The retirees were always impeccably dressed. And came to our bakery in the Little Caribbean neighborhood in Brooklyn, New York, at least once a day.

Tanya's dark brown eyes stretched wide. Her coral lips parted. "But Genevieve, how many years have you known me? You know I never miss a festival." Her Grenadian accent threaded her words. Her tone was warm with pride.

It was the day before the Caribbean American Heritage Festival. The annual celebration took place in Prospect Park the last Saturday in June, Caribbean American Heritage Month. The park came alive with sights, sounds, and scents reminiscent of the islands. It was a wonderful tribute to our West Indian culture and traditions.

Thinking about this year's event made my breath catch

with excitement—and nerves. For the first time, my family and I would be more than attendees. We would be event vendors, selling our pastries and finger foods. It would be the realization of another of my childhood dreams. I felt like I'd been waiting my whole life for tomorrow. But today, I had guests to serve.

The scents of confectioners' sugar, baked fruits, warm butter, nutmeg, ginger, and cinnamon floated out via the pass-through window between the customer counter where I stood and the kitchen where my parents were cooking. "Midnight Magic," one of the songs on the benefit CD by DragonFlyZ, a local, up-and-coming reggae/calypso/soca/ska band, spun from our speaker system. Several of our guests swung their hips and rolled their shoulders to the music's irresistible rhythms as they waited in line. A few lent their vocals to the chorus, making up with enthusiasm what they lacked in talent.

Benny looked at Tanya as though she were the only one in the bakery. His deep voice rumbled with his Trini accent. "I haven't missed a festival, either. And I'm looking forward to enjoying this one with you."

What a romantic. The petite woman's round brown cheeks darkened with a blush as she gazed up at him.

Beside me, my older brother, Devon Murray, smiled. He swayed to the music as he tallied Tanya and Benny's breakfast order of fish bakes and mauby tea. Dev and I were dressed in sea blue Spice Isle Bakery T-shirts and baggy shorts. His black chef's hat covered tight dark brown curls. Tall with a runner's lean build, my brother looked a lot like our father, Jacob. He had the same spare, warm sienna features and kind, curious dark brown eyes.

I favored our family matriarch. Looking at my grandmother was like seeing myself fifty-plus years into the future—if I was lucky. We were both petite, full-figured women. We had bow-shaped lips and wide dark brown eyes in heart-shaped sienna faces. My grandmother's long silver hair was wrapped into a tidy bun on the crown of her head. I'd tucked my long ebony braids inside my black chef's hat.

"All you holding up the line. Strups." Grace Parke's testy remark drained a bit of the joy from the room. Dressed in a pink top and ginger skirt with matching sandals, her tall, full figure was stiff with condemnation. I was certain the seventy-something-year-old woke up in a bad mood.

I added a few more wattages to my smile, hoping to take away at least some of the sting from Grace's comment. "Thank you so much for coming in today, Ms. Nevis, Mr. Parsons." I passed Benny the tray with their order. Having grown up in the United States, neither my brother nor I had a Grenadian accent.

Dev returned Benny's credit card with a receipt for his purchase. "We'll see you tomorrow."

"Yes, you will." Benny stepped back so Tanya could proceed him.

His words lifted my feet from the floor. My family and I were on a mission to encourage our customers to come to the festival tomorrow with their friends—and stop by our food truck. The event was an investment in our business. We needed to do better than break even.

Grace stepped up to the counter, pinning me with irritated dark eyes. Her annoyance sharpened her Jamaican accent. "I've said it before, all you shouldn't be at the festival. You should be here. Instead you're closing the shop and abandoning us. Is that how you repay customer loyalty? That doesn't make good business sense."

Beside me, Dev stilled. I sensed his temper stir at the

hint of criticism directed toward me. I hurried to respond to Grace before Dev said something I'd regret later. "Ms. Parke, you should come to the festival. It'll be fun."

"Listen to my granddaughter, Grace." Granny lowered the lavender-and-white afghan square she was crocheting. Her voice was tight with anger. "You need to get out more. And it's *free*."

Granny's afghan was for one of the many Christmas gifts she was making for family and friends. Yes, my grandmother was making Christmas presents in June. Between extended family, godchildren, and friends, she had an extensive list, and someone's feelings would be hurt if they didn't get one of her handmade treasures.

Grace kissed her teeth. "I don't like crowds, you know. Or standing in the heat."

"My friends and I go to the festival every year." D'André Greyson—aka the Knicks Fan—volunteered the information. He was two customers behind Grace in the line. Dev and I had finally learned his name from the credit card he used for his orders. "The parade, music, entertainment, and food make us feel like we're in the Caribbean."

"I know, right?" the Bubble-Gum-Chewing College Student, Carole Manor, called from the end of the line. "My friends and I always get there in time for the parade and stay until dark."

D'André flashed a grin. "We'll look for the mobile Spice Isle Bakery tomorrow."

Dev's tension seemed to ease. "Thank you."

Grace harrumphed. "You're making a mistake. Now, will you *please* take my order? I'd like a coconut bread and a mug of mauby tea. And, since you won't be open for business tomorrow, I'll take a loaf of hard dough bread today."

"Eh, eh." Granny cut her a look. "We'll be back Sunday, you know."

Grace gave Dev her credit card. Her voice was cool. "But I may not."

Oh, brother.

I added a couple of currant rolls to her bag. Witnessing my actions, Granny rolled her eyes. Grace's brow eased. Her lips softened. Her nod acknowledged the peace offering. She accepted her credit card and receipt from Dev before sweeping out of the bakery with her head high.

Granny returned to her crocheting. "How much d'you want to bet she comes to the festival tomorrow?"

"Despite everything she just said?" Dev gestured toward the space where Grace had stood. "What makes you think that?"

"Because Lynds gave her extra currant rolls." Granny glanced at me before returning her attention to her crocheting. "Despite what Grace said, our Lynds has exceptional business sense. She knows how to sweet-talk sour people."

Murmurs of agreement and good-natured chuckles rolled across the room. Embarrassment knotted my stomach muscles. Dev gave me a one-armed hug.

I raised my hands. "If Ms. Parke does come to the festival, will she allow herself to have a good time or will she be in a bad mood all day?"

Tanya spoke from her seat beside Benny. "How could anyone be in a bad mood during the festival?"

Granny shrugged. "There's always at least one bad apple in the bunch, you know. One who wants to ruin the event for everyone else."

"We can't let anyone or anything dampen the event for us." I already imagined my family in our food truck with a line of customers waiting eagerly to place their orders. "It's our first festival as vendors, Granny. We need to make it a day to remember."

Within a couple of hours, our breakfast crush had eased to a trickle of guests. A few female retirees and several young women on summer break chose to linger over their mid-morning treats in our dining area. Stray words from their easy conversations whispered across the shop. Both groups were talking about the festival, the latest gossip, and men.

Dev had joined our parents in the kitchen, preparing meals for our lunch customers. Granny remained at her table, humming and singing with the DragonFlyZ's CD as she crocheted.

The bell above the bakery's entrance chimed, interrupting me as I wiped the dining tables. Despite my best intentions, my heart leaped as New York Police Department Homicide Detective Bryce Jackson entered the shop. He located me in the dining area right away. How did he do that? His hazel brown eyes were like a Lyndsay Murray–seeking missile.

I'd had a crush on Bryce in high school. The lifelong Brooklynite had been handsome, intelligent, and kind. He still was. We'd overlapped two years when we'd attended Flatbush Early College High School. The ten years since then had been good to him. He'd replaced his braids with a conservative close-cropped haircut that emphasized his chiseled tawny good looks and deep-set eyes. His light gray suit, white shirt, and sapphire tie complemented his broad torso and lean hips. But looks were skin-deep. Bryce was attractive, but he and his senior partner, Detective Stanley Milner, kept trying to put me and my family behind bars.

Locking my shaking knees, I crossed to the checkout counter. "Good morning, Detective. What can I do for you today?"

"You can call me Bryce." His half smile was tempting. I slid him a look as I stepped behind the counter.

He addressed my grandmother. "Good morning, Ms. Bain."

"Good morning, Detective Bryce," Granny responded in a singsong cadence.

A chorus of greetings carried from the kitchen's pass-through window behind me, confirming my suspicion that my parents and Dev were listening to our conversation.

"Hello, there, young man." Daddy's greeting was that of an old friend.

"Good morning, Bryce!" My mother, Cedella Bain Murray, called in a cheerful tone.

"Hi, Bryce." Dev's voice sounded closest to me.

I closed my eyes and shook my head. The burden of having a loving, meddling family. But I wouldn't trade them for all the riches in the world.

"Good morning, everyone." Bryce's eyes sparkled with humor. He seemed obnoxiously pleased with himself. "Stan sent me to get mid-morning snacks. Can I have four currant rolls, please?"

Bryce's rumpled partner had a weakness for our pastries, especially our currant rolls. He claimed his wife, whom we'd never met, also was a fan of our baked goods.

"Of course." I took his credit card to process his order before gathering his purchases.

"Are you ready for the festival tomorrow?" Bryce's question didn't sound like idle curiosity. I appreciated his interest.

"I hope so." Did he hear the nerves in my voice? "Will you be there?" I cringed. Why did I ask him that?

The pastries warmed my fingertips through my black nitrile gloves as I placed them in the green paper Spice Isle Bakery bag. The aroma of baked currants, sugar, and butter wafted up to me.

"Yes, I will. Actually, this will be my first one. Do you have any tips for me?"

I turned from the prep counter and handed him the bag of currant rolls. "Wear comfortable shoes. You'll be doing a lot of walking."

Granny chimed in. "Make sure they're dancing shoes."

"Parking's impossible." Dev emerged from the kitchen. He held the door for my parents, who both wore black chef's smocks and matching chef's hats. "Take public transportation or be prepared to get to Prospect Park ridiculously early."

Mommy leaned her right hip against the back of Granny's chair. "If you do come early, eat a light breakfast. You're going to want to try all the good food and treats at the festival."

"Especially ours." Granny spoke over her shoulder. "And you'll need the energy for dancing. So saying, make sure you get a good night's sleep."

"And make sure you wear a hat." Daddy leaned against the wall beside Mommy. "You'll need the protection from the sun."

I glanced toward the entrance as the bell announced another guest. The attractive young woman who walked through the door looked familiar. She wore a loose-fitting black-and-white polka-dot summer shift. Thick dark brown curls framed her diamond-shaped brown face. Where had I seen her before?

A young man entered the bakery behind her. A smile curved my lips. "Manny!"

My cousin Manson Bain was the eldest of my uncle

Alrick and Aunt Inez's three children. Uncle Al was Mommy's older brother.

My eyes swept back to the woman beside him. I gasped. "You're Camille Abbey, DragonFlyZ's lead singer! I heard your band at Nutmeg's a couple of weeks ago. You were *amazing*!"

A member of DragonFlyZ was in our bakery!

Voices buzzed in the bakery as our guests expressed their awe at having a local celebrity in their midst. I'd gone to Nutmeg's with my cousin Serena, Manny's younger sister, and her boyfriend, Alfonso Lester. The audience had given DragonFlyZ two standing ovations.

"Thank you." Camille's smile was self-deprecating. Three younger women hurried from their table to ask for her autograph. The singer accommodated them while she responded to my remark. "We always have a good time performing there. The crowd really appreciates the music."

Manny smiled at her. "That's because you're an excellent performer."

I looked at my other family members, trying to read their reactions. From their wide-eyes and slack-jaws, they seemed as starstruck as I felt. But was I the only one who sensed the electricity arcing between Manny and Camille?

Granny set down her crocheting and considered the couple. "How do all you know each other?" She must have sensed their chemistry, too. Good.

I lowered my hands to my sides and crossed my fingers. *Please let them be dating. That would be* so *cool. I could tell everyone my cousin was dating the lead singer of DragonFlyZ.*

Manny dragged his eyes from Camille to Granny. "The studio's cut her band's last two albums and we're scheduled to do the next one. I thought Reena had told you."

Manny was an audio engineer with Caribbean Tunes,

an independent recording studio in Little Caribbean. And he was right; Reena had bragged that her older brother was recording DragonFlyZ's albums. But for Manny to bring the singer to the bakery was next level. Were they friends? Or something more?

I touched Bryce's forearm to get his attention before gesturing toward one of the speakers. "We're playing DragonFlyZ's CD."

The detective paused to listen to the music. "This is a great song."

"Thank you." Camille's eyes lingered on Manny's. "We're really excited about the work. And we're having a great time recording them with Manny's help."

Manny looked away from Camille. The effort seemed even harder for him this time. "I've told Camille so much about your bakery, she wanted to see it for herself. May we have two of your currant rolls and two glasses of sorrel, please?"

"Of course." Granny rose from her table. "And it's on the house."

"I appreciate that." Camille's ebony eyes were warm. "Thank you."

"Thanks, Granny." Manny escorted Camille to the counter.

As I turned to prepare their order, I noticed my grandmother walking toward the kitchen. "Granny, is something wrong?"

She waved me over and lowered her voice. "I'm calling your uncle. I want to know how long this has been going on." She sent a pointed look toward Manny and Camille, who were chatting with Dev and Bryce at the counter. "And why no one told me."

I shared Granny's curiosity. "I've never seen Manny so infatuated. Usually, women chase him."

My cousin was a good person. Everyone who knew him liked and admired him. But Manny was commitment averse. He preferred casual dating over relationship building.

"Exactly." Granny struggled to keep her voice low. "But you see how he's watching her? He's watching her hard, you know. This one could be Manny's soul mate."

"Let's not get ahead of ourselves, Granny." I squeezed her arm, silently urging her to slow her roll. "We don't even know if they're dating."

"That doesn't look like they're dating to you?" Granny waved a dismissive hand. "Don't mind, Lynds. I haven't started picking out names for my great-grands yet. I have to make a dress to wear to their wedding first." She disappeared into the kitchen.

The idea of Manny dating Camille was exciting. Dragon-FlyZ was going places. But knowing Manny's track record with relationships, I decided to wait until he admitted they were dating before choosing an outfit for the wedding.

CHAPTER 2

If I'm dreaming, don't wake me.

This year's Caribbean American Heritage Festival was perfect, from the cloudless blue sky to our assigned location toward the center of the activities to the reportedly record-breaking attendance. From our spot, we couldn't see the performance stage, but we could hear the steelpans and strong vocals of the calypso band entertaining the crowd. It amplified the party-like atmosphere for my grandmother, my parents, Dev, and me.

Having the opportunity to introduce new customers to our shop filled me with joy. I also was grateful to our regular patrons for stopping by to support us. In fact, Granny had been right; Grace Parke had made the trip. We'd served her earlier and, to everyone's surprise, she'd left in a good mood.

Due to space and preparation, we'd brought select items from our menu. They included dishes our regular customers most enjoyed like Tanya and Benny's fish bakes and fried plantains, Grace's coconut bread, and Bryce and Stan's currant rolls. It's not as though I were looking forward to seeing the detectives. But if they happened to stop by, I wanted to be prepared. It was what a good bakery manager would do for their loyal customers. We also had coconut drops, beef patties, and banana pudding. Our beverage list included sorrel, ginger beer, coconut water, and cold mauby and corailee teas.

"Your lines are even longer here than they are at your bakery." D'André grinned as he and his friends stepped up to our food truck's customer counter. They were all dressed in blue, orange, and silver Knicks fanwear.

"And we're loving every minute of it." I shared a smile with Dev beside me before turning back to take requests from D'André's group.

Dev processed their orders while Granny and I packaged their purchases in our special Spice Isle Bakery festival bags. They were designed to stand out in the crowd and, we hoped, attract additional customers to our truck.

The afternoon was hot and sticky, but our yellow-and-green food truck shielded us from the sun's intensity. The day's humidity multiplied the heat from our portable oven by at least a factor of ten. Beads of sweat collected at my hairline and trailed down my back. The weather didn't detract from my excitement over being a vendor at this community event, though.

The Samba dancers who'd performed in the parade that had opened the festival this morning roamed the park in their jewel-toned costumes. Vendors literally called attention to the inventory in their booths, including jewelry, clothing, and souvenirs. Local calypso, reggae, and soca bands took turns on the performance stage, playing favorite classics as well as new songs. My parents, brother, grandmother, and I watched as the revelers—including toddlers; so cute!—swung their hips and shook their shoulders as the music carried across the park. The scents of sharp jerk smoke, savory curry dishes, spicy meats, fried fish, and rich sauces wafted from the refreshment trucks, including ours.

Joymarie Rodgers stepped forward with several friends. I welcomed them before addressing her. "Good morning, Joymarie. You look lovely. Doesn't she, Dev?"

She grinned. "You're sweet, Lyndsay."

Dev's face brightened when he saw her. His brown eyes glittered with pleasure. "She always looks lovely. What can we get for you today, darling?"

He took my place at the register. Dev and Joymarie had known each other for years. He'd come to his senses and asked her out just after we'd opened Spice Isle Bakery. They'd been dating for a little more than two and a half months.

Joymarie blushed. "Good afternoon, Dev. My friends and I would each like a coconut bread and a large sorrel, please."

During a lull in customer traffic later, I brooded over the nearby booths and trucks. Our competition. One of the vendors had an order line that wrapped around itself. Our line had been long, but nothing like that.

Envy furrowed my brow. I spoke over my shoulder to my family. "Are we drawing as many patrons as other food trucks?"

"Whaddayou?" Granny considered the vendor with the extensive customer line. "How do you know those aren't the first customers they've had all day? Or that they're as efficient as we are at serving our guests? We've been working hard, hard since this morning, eh."

I gave her a dubious look. "Come on, Granny. You don't really believe that."

Always the fashionista, my grandmother refused to wear either the black chef's smock and matching hat or one of our colorful Spice Isle Bakery T-shirts. For the festival, she'd dressed in a turquoise-and-emerald brush-patterned, sleeveless blouse and knee-length shorts. She protected her outfit with one of our Spice Isle Bakery aprons with the yellow, green, and red flag of Grenada in the lower right corner. She'd tucked her long silver hair under a turquoise head wrap.

"I do believe it." Granny arched an eyebrow as though daring me to question her again. I didn't.

"Lynds, don't mind, nuh." Mommy waved a cloth-and-plastic folding hand fan alternately in front of herself and Daddy as she led him away from the portable oven. "We're getting as many customers as we can handle."

Dev took a deep swallow from his black container of ice water. "That's true. This is our first time at the festival. We should treat this as a learning experience, not a competition."

With the exception of Granny, we all wore black chef's hats to keep our hair out of the food. But instead of the usual black chef's smocks, we wore light wicking T-shirts under the bakery's apron.

Daddy took the fan from Mommy and waved it in front of both of them. His eyes were warm with pride. "Try to relax and enjoy yourself, Lynds. We're doing well."

Turning to my father, I forced a smile. "If you're all happy, then so am I." I wasn't, not really.

"Yes, I!" Uncle Roman's greeting from behind me made me jump. "The party sell off, oui."

Romany Murray was my father's oldest brother. His declaring the festival to be a success was high praise. Uncle Roman had attended Caribbean festivals across the United States and Canada.

He'd met us at our home early this morning to help transport our equipment and supplies to Prospect Park. Many hands make light work. He'd even helped us locate our assigned space and set up our food truck. As soon as the truck was functioning and the festival music started, Uncle

Roman had disappeared. Now he was back, and his brick-red-and-sea-green floral shirt was damp with sweat both front and back. I hurried to pour him a glass of ice water.

"Uncle Roman, be careful you don't get heatstroke." I shoved the full glass at him.

He chugged half the glass before coming up for air. "You think that's what I have?"

Granny passed him one of the folding hand fans. "You have something. You're not a young man anymore, Roman. Mind you don't pass out."

"Excuse me, Lyndsay." Sheryl Cross, president of the Caribbean American Heritage Festival Association, stepped up to our truck.

After approving my family's vendor application for this year's festival, the older woman had tried to rescind our invitation last month when Bryce and Stan had suspected my mother of killing her former boss. Cray, right? But our bakery was reinstated thanks to an intense community campaign Reena had organized.

"Good afternoon, Ms. Cross." Her long-sleeved pink blouse seemed limp from the heat. "Everyone's raving about this year's festival. My uncle thinks this is the best one yet."

Sheryl gave Uncle Roman a pleased smile. Beneath her wide-brimmed canvas hat, her dark eyes glinted with interest and curiosity. "Oh, that's your uncle?" She dragged her attention back to me. "Well, I'm glad he and his wife are enjoying themselves."

Subtle much? "My uncle isn't married."

In fact, Uncle Roman had been granted a divorce from his third wife almost six months earlier. Daddy had suggested, instead of continuing the cycle of marriage and divorce, his older brother take up draughts. The board game was cheaper.

"Oh, he's single?" Sheryl looked at Uncle Roman. According to Granny, the association president was also divorced.

I could understand her interest. All the men in my family were attractive. I wasn't biased. It was a fact.

"Is there something I could do for you, Ms. Cross?" *Please, God, don't let her ask for my uncle's phone number.*

"Please call me Sheryl." Pulling her business card from her matching pink purse, she presented it to me. "My daughter's getting married in January. Her fiancé is an up-and-coming member of the state's assembly with aspirations for a federal position. Perhaps you've heard of him, Delford Lawrence?"

"Yes, I have. He's very impressive." I'd even voted for him. I wasn't keen on his personality, but I supported his policies and his voting record.

"Of course he is." Sheryl preened a bit, perhaps envisioning herself moving into the White House with her daughter and soon-to-be son-in-law. "My ex-husband and I are paying for their wedding. His mother claims not to like West Indian food. I don't think she's ever had *good* West Indian food. That's why I want to hire Spice Isle Bakery to cater my daughter's wedding reception. But first I want you to serve a few sample dishes to reassure his mother that the reception menu will be of the highest quality."

My breath left me. My mind went blank. We were being asked to cater a high-profile wedding. The publicity alone would broaden our customer reach. I felt faint. "Yes, of course. I can provide you with a bid by—"

"No, no." Sheryl waved a dismissive hand. "You don't need to bid. I'm hiring your family."

I was going to faint. "We would be honored. I'll contact you Monday to work out the details of the tasting. Thank you for considering us."

Sheryl gave me a pleased smile. "I've tried several of your dishes. It's as your grandmother's always saying. Your food is exceptional." She disappeared back into the crowd.

I turned, slack-jawed and wide-eyed, to my family. From their stunned expressions, I could tell they'd heard my conversation with Sheryl. "Well, now I don't feel so bad about the other trucks attracting more customers than us. We just got hired for a catering job."

Granny glowed with joy and perspiration. "Let's hope this one ends better than the last, nuh?"

My smile faded, but only slightly. "Granny!"

"Is the festival everything you'd hoped it would be?" Bryce removed his sunglasses as he came to a stop in front of our customer counter Saturday afternoon. Stan was with him. Both men wore sunglasses and baseball caps. Bryce must have shared my father's tip with his partner.

As I looked at Bryce, a pulse fluttered at the base of my throat. I could hear it echoing in my ears. A black cap covered his tight curls. A snug cream cotton T-shirt molded his muscular torso. Sky blue straight-legged shorts hugged his lean hips and fell to just above his knees, exposing powerful calves. Detective Fine didn't skimp on leg days.

I swallowed to ease my dry throat. "We're managing. Thank you. And thank you both for stopping by."

Stan was a few inches shorter than Bryce. A blue, orange, and white New York Mets baseball cap covered his shaggy salt-and-pepper hair. A black, bronze, and white plaid shirt hung loosely from his broad shoulders. Baggy gray shorts covered the knees of his short, stocky legs.

A smile creased Stan's comfortable features as he rocked back on his heels. "Bryce and I have been looking forward to the festival for weeks."

Stan's warmth was disconcerting. Only a few weeks ago, he and his handsome partner had investigated my mother for a murder she hadn't committed. They may have forgotten, but I hadn't. I'd never been so frightened, not even when, a month and a half before that, they'd done the same to me. Those were two strikes against them. Then why couldn't I get Bryce out of my mind?

I found a polite smile and pasted it onto my lips. "What can I get for you, gentlemen?"

Stan considered our shortened menu offerings. "I'll have two of your Old-Fashioned Coconut Drops. I've never had those before."

Granny smiled. "One for you and one for your wife?"

Stan chuckled. "You know me so well, ma'am."

Bryce pulled his wallet from his shorts pocket. "I'll have one, as well."

Old-Fashioned Coconut Drops were like weirdly shaped, delicious cookies. Their ingredients included coconuts—of course—raisins, cinnamon, and nutmeg. The scents of those ingredients combined with the savory aromas of curried meats and jerk smoke from nearby vendors and the fresh foliage from the park create the odd but enticing fragrance unique to the festival.

Granny prepared their order, wrapping the drops in parchment paper and securing them in two Spice Isle Bakery bags.

I collected their payment and gave them their change. "Thank you for your business. Enjoy." My smile was stiff but still polite.

Bryce's eyes darkened with disappointment as he took his bag from Granny. Stan gave him a concerned look.

Beneath the counter, Granny dug her index finger into my thigh beneath the hem of my denim shorts. I gritted my teeth against the knifelike pain and sent her a sharp look.

She scowled at me before giving Bryce and Stan a bright smile. "Don't be strangers. We hope to see you again soon."

I waited until both men wandered away before turning to her. My voice jumped four octaves. "What're you doing?"

"That man was looking at you hard, you know." Granny feigned a longing look.

"He did *not* look at me like that." *Did he?* "And even if he did, I've told you before, I'm not interested in someone who could so easily see me and my family as ruthless killers."

"All you talking about Bryce Jackson?" Daddy escorted Mommy from the stoves in the back of the truck to join us at the counter. Dev followed.

Granny glanced at my parents over her shoulder. "Lynds's giving him a hard way to go."

"Bryce seems like a nice person." Mommy gave me a chastising look. "He made a mistake, Lynds. Show a little forgiveness and give him a chance, nuh?"

"You mean *another* chance? I already gave him a chance after he tried to throw *me* in jail. Then he came after *you,* Mommy." I ripped a disinfectant wipe from the container beside me and used it to clean off the counter and cash register. "He even tried to prevent us from doing the investigations that would clear our names."

Just thinking about those experiences stirred feelings of annoyance and confusion. How could I trust someone who didn't trust me—or my family? Besides, I didn't have time for romance. I was building a business.

"I agree with Mom." Dev wiped sweat from his forehead beneath the band of his black chef's hat. "Bryce and Stan were following the evidence. They never arrested either of you, although I'm sure their higher-ups were pressuring them to bring someone in."

My sudden cleaning spree ended. His words eased some of my resentment. "I hadn't thought of that."

Granny leaned toward me. "Do you think you can stop being vexed with him now?"

I looked from her to my parents and Dev. I flexed my shoulders to ease my irritation. "Why's it so important that I give Bryce a chance?"

Daddy shrugged. "Bryce and Stan seem like good people. And I can tell they're trying to make amends. Why else do you think they come to the shop almost every day?"

Granny gave him a wide-eyed look, part shock, part consternation. "Because our food is exceptional."

I snorted. "If they want to atone for their sin of suspecting Mommy and me of being killers, they can start by saying 'sorry.'"

"Lynds." Mommy folded her hands at her hips. "I've forgiven them."

That didn't surprise me. Mommy never could hold a grudge. "They weren't investigating your mother for murder."

"No, but they were investigating my daughter." Mommy's lips curved in a trace of a smile. She briefly cupped the side of my face. "Your father and I have tried to teach you and Dev that holding on to anger and resentment isn't good. Those burdens do more harm to you than the other person."

My mother's words were familiar. They should be; I'd heard them most of my life. It was valuable advice, but I still struggled with it.

"I'll try harder, Mommy." I sighed my surrender. "I promise."

Mommy's smile blossomed into a grin. She met Daddy's eyes before turning back to me. "Thank you, darling."

Maybe the detective and I could try being friends. I frowned. Was that something I wanted? More crucially, was a friendship with Bryce something I could risk? Or would getting close to the detective turn my life upside down?

CHAPTER 3

"You're crushing it!" Reena gave me a side hug with her right arm as we followed Granny and Dev to the festival's concert area Saturday afternoon. Her left fingers were entwined with Alfonso's, her boyfriend of two months. "I've seen at least a hundred of your Spice Isle Bakery bags. They're all over the park. It's brilliant!"

I wrapped an arm around her waist and squeezed her back. "Thank you, Cuz."

Manny had sent Reena and Alfonso to get Granny, Mommy, Daddy, Dev, and me. DragonFlyZ was performing soon. We couldn't leave the bakery's food truck unattended, though. What had Manny been thinking? Fortunately, we'd found a solution to the dilemma. Granny, Dev, and I were taking a break to enjoy the band's concert while Aunt Inez and Uncle Al helped Mommy and Daddy at the truck. Once DragonFlyZ's set was over, Granny, Dev, and I would return to the truck so Mommy and Daddy could take a break and enjoy the festival.

Despite the humidity of the early summer day, Reena wasn't sweating. Of course. Her warm brown skin wouldn't dare to be anything but perfect. She was stunning in a lemon yellow jumpsuit that nipped her small waist and showed off her long dancer's legs. She'd used the same shade of yellow for the highlights in her thick dark brown braids, which swung above her shoulders. Her heart-shaped face was expertly made up. We arrived at the location, which wasn't far from the food vendor trucks. Reena went straight to Manny, who stood just a few yards from the center of the stage. One band had just completed its performance. DragonFlyZ was setting up for theirs. The band members' smiles seemed to reflect back the crowd's positive energy and excitement.

Camille stepped up to the microphone and wrapped both hands around its stand. "Good afternoon, everyone! We're having a bacchanal up in here! Are you having fun?" A wave of agreement rolled across the park and crashed onto the stage. The festival was indeed one big party. Camille threw her head back and laughed. "Are you ready to have some more?" The shouts were even louder this time. "All right then! Let's get to it!"

The song started with a strong chord from the lead guitar. The rhythm and bass guitars and drummer added their sounds. I was certain it was an original piece. The beat was more syncopated than I remembered from the one she'd played at the nightclub. It pulled at me, grabbing my hips and shaking my shoulders before I realized I was moving. Beside me, Reena's feet appeared to have a mind of their own as they followed the music. Alfonso spun her around. I smiled at Dev and Granny dancing next to each other, seemingly lost to the rhythm. Beside them, Manny moved with the music as his eyes mooned up at Camille. A besotted smile curved his full lips.

I leaned closer to Reena and jerked my chin toward the stage. "It looks like Manny's fallen hard. He can't take his eyes off Camille. And she's looking back at him the same way."

Camille stood at the mic as she interpreted her song, spreading her arms, lifting her hands, and rolling her shoulders. Her eyes kept drifting back to Manny's as though she couldn't help herself.

"I think those two have fallen hard for each other." Reena raised her voice. "They barely noticed Al and me when we were with them earlier. It was like they were on a different planet." She rolled her eyes with a laugh.

I listened to the song's lyrics as I danced:

I'm taking my heart. I'm moving on.
When you come back, you'll find I've gone.
The sands may shift beneath my feet,
But I won't fall; I'll still stand strong.

The power in her words added to the excitement in the crowd. The audience picked up her chorus and sang with her. The other songs the band performed were received with the same enthusiasm. By the time their set ended almost an hour later, the crowd had doubled in size. People were chanting their name.

"DragonFlyZ! DragonFlyZ! DragonFlyZ!" The cheers and applause were thunderous. Manny shouted, cheered, clapped, and whistled along with them.

"Camille's very talented." Granny gave him a sly look from the corners of her eyes. "But you know that. How long have you had a crush on her?"

Reena, Dev, and I stepped closer to catch Manny's answer. I looked up at the stage. Camille was helping her bandmates pack their instruments and equipment, preparing to carry them offstage as another band arrived. And still she kept glancing over at Manny.

"What do you mean? We're friends." His eyes bounced around the area as though he couldn't hold our gazes.

Granny pressed. "But you like her as more than a friend."

Manny shrugged, still avoiding eye contact. "She's nice. She's incredibly talented like you said. And she's always doing good things for the community. She just did a charity album—"

My poor cousin must have forgotten who he was dealing with. Granny had ways of getting answers from her children and grandchildren.

Her hand on Manny's shoulder ended his nervous chatter. "Manson Christopher Bain, I know you're a well-educated man. Don't insult my intelligence by asking me to explain my meaning." She let her hand drop. "You and I both know you understand me."

Reena, Dev, and I exchanged wide-eyed looks of fear. Alfonso seemed frozen in shock. *Full name and both barrels.* Manny had nowhere to go.

Reena rubbed her older brother's back through his light-weight palm green T-shirt. "Just tell Granny what she wants to know and she'll go easy on you."

Manny cut her a look before letting his eyes drift back to the stage. Camille tossed him a smile and a casual wave. He waved back with a goofy grin; at least it was goofy for him. I hardly recognized this man.

Manny had started dating in high school. That pattern had continued over the years. He'd go out with someone for a while, but if she tried to hold his hand, he'd start complaining about feeling smothered, trapped, caged like an animal. A couple of months later, we'd be introduced to someone new.

I nudged his left shoulder. "Why didn't you tell us about her?"

Manny spread his arms. "There's nothing to tell. We're just friends."

We all heard the lie. Granny was the only one who called him on it.

"'Just friends?'" She kissed her teeth. "Then why're you staring at the girl like this?" She did a credible impersonation of Manny's besotted look. I smothered a giggle behind my hand. Reena laughed out loud. "And why's she looking at you like this?" She copied Camille's sultry look so well, we all gasped.

Grinning, Dev shook his head. "Gran's got your number, man."

Granny turned to lead us back to the truck. I started to follow when a movement about a yard into the crowd claimed my attention. I only saw her back, but there was something familiar about the tall, auburn-haired woman whose cerulean blue blouse bared toned arms and whose turquoise short-shorts showcased sculpted legs.

"I'll catch up with you," I told Granny before squeezing my way through the crowd. I tapped the person's shoulder. "Excuse me."

Roxanne Stewart turned to me. Rocky, as she preferred to be called, was a member of my local gym, Parish Avenue Fitness. It was walking distance from my home. Many years ago, we'd taken an adult beginner kickboxing class together. Since that time, she'd progressed to the advanced track. I was still hanging around the intermediate-advanced group. But it had been Rocky who'd convinced me to enter the gym's fall kickboxing exhibition in September.

"Lyndsay! What're you doing here?" Rocky's Brooklyn accent was strong. Her dark eyes sparkled with pleasure in her warm brown diamond-shaped face. Her deep auburn close-cropped hair—compliments of a professional dye job—shaped her head, curving to the back of her neck.

I jerked a thumb over my shoulder. "My family has a

truck here. Did you come to watch your boyfriend perform?"

Rocky was dating the DragonFlyZ's drummer, Earl Lees. An image of the tall, lean man in a black T-shirt, baggy cream shorts, and an oatmeal Belfry hat flashed across my memory. Very handsome.

"Yeah. They just finished their performance." She winked at me. "I have a thing for drummers."

"I hope you mean you have a thing for *this* drummer." A deep voice joined our conversation. Earl's teasing correction came with the hint of a Dominican accent. He wrapped an arm around Rocky's tight waist and kissed her forehead.

"Of course." Rocky grinned up at him. "Lyndsay, my boyfriend, Earl Lees. Earl, this is Lyndsay Murray, my friend from the gym I've been telling you about. I've brought you currant rolls from her bakery."

Earl's eyes widened. "Oh, yes. They're fantastic."

I never grew tired of the encouragement from satisfied customers. "Thank you so much. My family and I love your music."

"Thank you." He lowered his dark eyes with modesty as he smiled.

I turned to Rocky. "I'd better get back to the truck. It was nice to see both of you."

Wait until I told my family that DragonFlyZ's drummer loved our pastries. *Scream!* I was walking on air. Becoming a vendor for the festival had to be one of the best decisions we've made to date.

I returned to our food truck late Saturday afternoon to find Granny, Dev, Manny, Reena, and Alfonso staring off in the distance. Concern tightened their features and dragged down the corners of their mouths. Manny's eyes were narrowed. His eyebrows were knitted. Dread knotted my stomach muscles as I hurried toward them.

"What's happening?" The hot early-summer sun beat against my head. Tendrils of perspiration traced my hairline. Coming to a stop beside Manny, I followed their gazes.

Camille stood several yards away with an angry-sounding woman. They were in the shade of a large, old maple tree yards from the food area. I could see how the width of the aged tree and the distance from the event would give someone a sense of privacy. In fact, the other woman was partially blocked by the thick trunk. All we could see were her arms as they made wild, angry gestures. At one point, Camille stepped back as the stranger jabbed a finger toward her. The singer slapped the offending finger away and the other woman pushed her. Manny lurched forward as though he was going to intervene. My eyes widened. *Oh, no.*

Reena's hand shot forward. It landed on her brother's shoulder. "No, Manny. You'll only make the situation worse."

Manny's tension eased, but only slightly. "You're right."

I exhaled. "Who is she?"

"It sounds like Karlisa Trotter." Manny sounded like he was chewing glass. "She's DragonFlyZ's manager."

"Oh-ho." Granny nodded as though his response helped make sense of the scene playing in front of us. "Do they often argue like this?"

"Pretty much." Manny dragged his hand over his hair. He stared at the distant scene as though he couldn't look away. "She acts as though the band works for her, not the other way around. The group's talented and charismatic. They should've gotten a record deal with a bigger label long before now. Camille thinks she should be doing more for them."

Granny returned her attention to the argument. "Do you think that's what they're arguing about now?"

Manny sighed, shrugging his broad shoulders. "I have no idea. Things have been tense between Karlisa and Camille for a while. I've noticed it as they've been in the studio, recording their album."

Why were the two women arguing in public? Did they think we couldn't hear them? Camille's voice was louder, but every now and then, a word or phrase from both of them carried toward us. I wasn't certain what I was hearing, but it sounded like:

> *You* knew!
> . . . *borrowed* . . .
> *And take care of it* . . .
> . . . *listen* . . .
> . . . *cheated us!*

I shook my head. "It sounds like Karlisa made a bad deal for the band and now Camille wants her to fix it." But I was only guessing. The few words I'd heard hadn't been clear and were only fragments of their conversation.

As we watched, Camille turned to storm away from the manager. Karlisa caught Camille's arm as though to stop her. Camille shrugged out of the older woman's hold and marched away. Her angry strides took her on a path parallel to the festival's gathering. Karlisa hurried after her, disappearing from view.

Reena turned to Manny. "Lynds is probably right. They're having a business disagreement. She's probably going to talk it over with her band."

Manny rubbed his forehead as though trying to erase his frown. "Yeah. I'll catch up with her later." His tone was troubled.

Granny patted Manny's shoulder. "Don't mind, nuh? If you're still worried, you can ask her about it later. For now, let her and her bandmates figure it out."

I gave Manny a reassuring smile before following Granny to the truck. But like him, I was curious. What had the band manager done that made Camille angry enough to confront her in the middle of the festival?

CHAPTER 4

Customer orders at our food truck returned to their brisk pre-concert-break pace late Saturday afternoon. Mommy and Daddy were with Aunty Inez and Uncle Al, enjoying the festival music and activities while Granny, Dev, and I served our customers.

"I'll have seven more of your coconut drops." A middle-aged father pulled out his wallet. He was shepherding three children under the age of ten who appeared to have hit their sugar limit—but it was a celebration.

"Seven, Daddy?" The youngest son's eyes grew to half the size of his head. "Are the extras for me?"

Smiling at the little boy's greed, I turned to the counter where the treats stayed warm in the baking pan. The scents of warm coconuts, baked raisins, brown sugar, and nutmeg rose to greet me. I wrapped the requested amount in individual pastry sheets before securing them in a Spice Isle Bakery bag. Turning back to the generous parent, I exchanged the bag for his credit card.

"No, they're not all for you." He spoke patiently with a strong Trini accent. "One is for your sister." He put his hand on the shoulder of his oldest child. The girl appeared to be eight or nine. "One is for your brother." He rested his hand on the tight curls of a six- or seven-year-old boy.

"One is for you." He paused to cup the youngest one's cheek. "And two each for your mommy and me."

His youngest gaped at him. "You get *two* each? Why do you get so many?"

"Because she's the mommy and I'm the daddy." He retrieved his card and receipt from me. "We haven't had coconut drops this good since we were home. My wife and I will be sure to stop by your shop."

I pressed my hand to my heart. I knew by "home" he meant his birthplace. "Thank you so much. We look forward to seeing you and your family again."

Another customer stepped up to the counter before I could share his compliment with Granny and Dev. "Welcome to the Spice Isle Bakery food truck. How can I help you?"

The woman was about my age. She looked cool and comfortable in a lightweight cotton sleeveless dress. The blue-green abstract print was at the same time bold and soothing. It floated around her full figure. Her dark brown mane framed her round brown face and lay on her shoulders.

"I thought I knew until I heard the child talking about the coconut drops." Her accent represented Jamaica at the festival. Her brown eyes twinkled. "You know what? Give me two drops and a pattie, please."

"My pleasure." I turned to wrap the coconut drops and beef pattie in individual sheets of wax paper.

"I've seen so many people around the park with these Spice Isle Bakery bags." She gave a shy giggle. "I thought, let me see for myself why everyone's coming here."

"We're glad you did." I placed her purchases in one of our red, green, and yellow bags.

In addition to her payment, she handed me a business card. "I'm Belle Baton, chair of the West Indian American Relief Fund. You've heard of us?"

I offered her the bag and her change. "Yes, I have."

"I'm flattered." Her face glowed with pleasure and per-spiration. "I've heard of *you,* Lyndsay Murray. You're the Grenadian Nancy Drew."

My cheeks warmed with embarrassment. I really wish the community hadn't adopted D'André's nickname for me. "That's an exaggeration."

Belle waved her hand dismissively. "I admire you, you know. You're confident and fearless. You opened your own business and you're solving murders for the police."

Confident? Fearless? She was talking about me? My mind went blank. I never imagined anyone using those words to describe me. I wouldn't use them to describe my-self.

"My family's helped me every step of the way." I swept an arm behind me to draw her attention away from me and toward Granny and Dev. "I couldn't do any of this on my own."

Belle wagged a finger at me. Her lips curved in a half smile. "I don't believe you. You'd have to be assertive and courageous to track down not just one but two killers. You're amazing."

Tension tightened my back. She was making me uncom-fortable. My eyes dropped to the counter. "No, really. I couldn't have done that without my family's help. And we were highly motivated. The first time, we had to prove my innocence. The last time, we had to prove my mother's."

"I suppose the motivation does make a difference." The bag crinkled as though she'd shifted her hold on it. "Any-way, do you have a business card? I'd like to discuss your catering an event for us. We're co-hosting a holiday recep-tion with the festival association."

Her words brought a rush of adrenaline. I'd known the festival would boost our profile, but I hadn't expected immediate results. Two catering requests in one day. First Sheryl, the president of the festival association, had asked us to cater her daughter's wedding. Now Belle wanted us to cater a holiday reception. And several customers, like the father of three, had promised to come to the bakery. Incredible! In my mind, I saw our bank loan balance shrinking. I looked over my shoulder to exchange grins with Granny and Dev. Their grins were bright with excitement.

I turned back to Belle. "We'd be pleased—"

"Oh-ho." Sheryl appeared from nowhere, stopping beside Belle. "We're co-hosting a holiday reception? And how is it that I'm the last to know when I'm the *president* of the festival association?"

I looked from Sheryl to Belle. What had just happened?

Belle's discomfort was like a presence sitting on our customer counter. She didn't meet the older woman's eyes. "Isn't that a question for your staff, Sheryl? They should be keeping you better informed."

Sheryl's eyes shot daggers at Belle. "My *staff* doesn't have a *problem* keeping me *informed*. *You're* the one who makes promises you never keep. As long as you're part of the West Indian American Relief Fund, our organizations will *never* work together on *any* events. No, sir. Not while I have anything to say about it. It will be over my dead body."

A blush stained Belle's cheeks. "All right, Sheryl. You've made your feelings very clear." She faced me. Her voice trembled. "Lyndsay, I'll contact you Monday with the details. I hope you're still interested in catering the event."

"Of course." I think. "Thank you, Belle."

Without another word or glance in Sheryl's direction, Belle disappeared into the festival's crowd.

Sheryl's features were stiff with anger. "A word of advice." She adjusted her purse strap on her ample shoulder before jabbing a finger toward Belle's retreating figure. "Get everything in writing with that one for when you have to take her to court to get your money, eh. *Everything.*"

Sheryl spun on her heel. The crowd seemed to part, clearing a path for her as she marched away.

My jaw dropped. My eyes stretched wide. I turned to Granny and Dev. "What. Just. Happened?" I addressed Granny. "What's the story with Sheryl and Belle?"

Unfazed, Granny flipped the fish bakes she was frying on the steel gas griddle plate. "Competition."

Her one-word answer didn't clear my confusion. "But their groups do different things."

Dev's sienna brow creased in bewilderment as he pulled a fresh batch of currant rolls from the stainless-steel countertop convection oven. "The Caribbean American Heritage Festival Association supports cultural events. The West Indian American Relief Fund organizes charitable drives and awareness campaigns for causes that support Caribbean countries."

"Not competition between the organizations, you know." Granny pressed the fish bakes against the griddle plates. "Sheryl respects strength. Belle, she only has mouth."

I nodded my understanding. Sheryl believed Belle was full of talk but never put in the work. That didn't explain her next-level vitriol, though. "I'm not going to let her displeasure influence us. We decide who we do business with. Sheryl Cross doesn't pay our bills."

"No, she doesn't." Granny inclined her head in acknowledgement. "But it doesn't hurt to take advice from someone who has more experience than you. If we work with Belle, let's make sure to get everything in writing. All right?"

"That makes good business sense." Dev sliced the fresh currant rolls. Their sweet, buttery scent blended with the fish bakes' spicy aromas.

"I agree." I looked in the direction Sheryl had disappeared.

Perhaps Granny was right and Sheryl was hostile toward Belle because she thought Belle was unprofessional. That was an understandable reason not to want to work with someone. But I sensed something more had happened between those two. Or maybe my experience with murder investigations had left a mark on me. I now saw misdirection, half-truths, and subterfuge behind each word and every action.

"Can I get two more sorrels and two patties, Cuz?" Manny's voice interrupted my speculations.

He'd returned with Camille. The singer seemed distracted. Was she thinking about her argument with the band's manager? I still wondered what it had been about.

"Of course." I turned to get the refreshments.

Camille accepted the sorrel and beef pattie. She turned to Manny. "I'm glad we had a chance to hang out today. I had a great time with you."

"I enjoyed your company, too." Manny smiled as though he wasn't aware of anyone but her.

It was like watching a romance movie. My heart sighed.

Camille gave him a shy smile. "I'd better get back to my band. Call me later?"

Manny grinned. "Count on it."

"It was nice meeting all you." Camille saluted us with her recyclable plastic cup of sorrel before leaving.

Dev waited until she'd disappeared before speaking. "You want me to remind you to call her later?"

Granny smiled as she came to stand beside me. "You think he'll need reminding?"

"Whatever, fam." Manny rolled his eyes, then climbed into the truck.

I put a hand on his arm as he stopped beside me. "Camille seems really nice, Manny. I'm happy for you."

"Thanks, Lynds." He took the chef's hat and apron I offered him. "What about you? What's next for you?"

"For me?" I brought to my mind where I stood now in relation to my three-year personal and professional plan. A warm sense of joy and well-being wrapped me like one of Granny's afghans. "I'm actually way ahead of my goals. I hadn't imagined our vendor application for the festival would've been accepted this year, for example, or that people would've already hired us to cater their events."

"Although that first dinner didn't turn out so well," Granny grumbled.

I gaped at her. "You know that was due to circumstances beyond our control." Granny shrugged in response. Shaking my head, I turned back to Manny. "Anyway, what's next for me is to continue to grow the bakery, to annually participate in the festival, and to cater more events."

Opening a West Indian bakery with my family had been my childhood dream. After earning my MBA from Brooklyn College, I'd stepped out on faith—and with a supportive family—to make my dream come true. My parents each own 25 percent of the business. Granny and Dev have 5 percent each. I held the remaining 40 percent.

Manny joined Dev in the food prep section of the truck. "What about your personal life?"

"Yeah, Sis." Dev's voice carried from his station in front of the portable oven behind me. "You can't work twenty-four/seven/three-sixty-five."

"I do have a personal life." My voice had risen several defensive octaves. "My kickboxing exhibition is in September. I expect all of you to attend, by the way."

Manny's sigh was loud and gusty. He must think he stood on the other side of the park instead of right behind me. "What about something relaxing? What're you doing for fun?"

"Kickboxing is fun." I bristled at his question. "But remember, the bakery's only three months old. We're still working on its processes and schedules."

"But as you said, love, it's growing faster than we'd expected." Granny's words were somber. "We might need to bring in help sooner than we'd planned."

I paused, considering Granny from the corners of my eyes. Why was she suggesting we bring in help? Was she concerned about me—or the business? Then I remembered this was Granny. If she was worried about the bakery, she'd tell me.

My neck and shoulder muscles relaxed. "I'm fine, Granny. I don't need help. But thank you."

Once I got into a routine with the bakery, I'd be able to establish a proper work-life balance, especially since we were done investigating murders. I was pretty sure the NYPD wouldn't put us on any more suspect lists. I mean, how unlucky could one family be?

Customer buying patterns at our festival's food truck were similar to the traffic at the shop: brief lulls and long rushes. Granny and Manny were using this latest lull to rest in the bit of shade outside our truck. They were seated on the folding chairs we'd brought with us, laughing and chatting as they drank ice water from large colorful sports bottles. Our festival space was open, but the breeze was no match for the heat from the griddle and convection oven.

"What's on your mind?" Dev stood beside me at the counter.

I gave him an apologetic smile. "I'm sorry. I was thinking about our new catering jobs."

Dev bumped his shoulder against mine. "Don't apologize. They're exciting opportunities for us."

Granny and Manny joined us in time to hear Dev's comment.

Granny stopped beside me, patting my back. "Dev's right. Business was exceptional today. And all these people who found us here will come to the shop and bring their friends."

I crossed my fingers. "From your lips to God's ears, Gr—"

The clamor of frightened screams and racing feet cut me off. "What's happening?"

I followed Manny, Dev, and Granny from the truck. Dev and Manny kept Granny between them. Were they protecting her from the commotion or preventing her from joining it? A score of festival attendees raced past us. Fragments of shouted words trailed behind them.

"We have to see . . ."

". . . Eastern Parkway entrance . . ."

"An accident . . ."

". . . DragonFlyZ . . ."

I stepped around my brother and reached out to an adolescent girl running past me. The teenager wore denim cutoffs and a hot pink "I Left My Heart in Haiti" T-shirt.

I wouldn't normally have the confidence to call attention to myself, but the crowd's panic got to me. "What's happening?"

She pointed ahead of her. "Someone fell."

"Thank you." I released her and turned to Dev, Granny, and Manny.

Granny looked concerned. "It must've been quite a fall, oui."

"I wonder who it was?" I felt a stirring of unease. I'd heard someone say DragonFlyZ. I was sure of it. "Do you think—"

"All you come!" My father's voice boomed out from behind me.

We turned as one to face him. He, Mommy, Uncle Roman, Aunt Inez, Uncle Al, Reena, and Alfonso jogged toward us from the opposite direction of the human stampede. They stopped beside Manny.

Aunty Inez put a hand on his arm. Her eyes were wide in her diamond-shaped face. Her warm brown eyes were dark and clouded. "There's been an accident."

Granny swung an arm behind her. "We just heard. Somebody fell."

Uncle Al stopped in front of his son. He squared his shoulders. "Manny, they're saying it was Camille."

"What?" Manny stepped back, breaking contact with his mother. "Who's saying that?"

Reena laid her palm on her brother's shoulder. "The festival officials who found her body. They said it's the lead singer of DragonFlyZ. She fell down some stairs."

"No!" Manny shook off Reena's hand. His words were rough with anger. "That's a lie!"

In the blink of an eye, Manny spun and sprinted into the crowd. Dev and I exchanged a look before chasing after him. Dev followed Manny. Their greater height and broad shoulders cleared their path through the mass of bodies surging toward the accident site. I didn't think I could make it through. Instead, I raced alongside the group, sidestepping trees and bushes, dodging playing children, curious adults, and oblivious couples making out. The uneven path rose up and rolled down. It curved along the walking path. Beneath the late-afternoon sun, I felt as though I were running in a vat of molasses. I took even, deep breaths, catching the scents of rich spices, fresh foliage, and dry dirt.

Please don't let it be Camille. Please let her be safe.

I silently chanted those words with every footfall that hurried me to the Eastern Parkway entrance. I'd rather no one was injured or, worse, killed. But if I could wish away heartache for my cousin, I had to try.

The crowd created a bottleneck once everyone reached the park stairs. I did a visual scan of the curious group. Dev and Manny were a few strides behind me. The mass of fans surging around them hampered their movements. Since I was outside of the crowd, I could more easily maneuver the accident site. I made my way off the grass. My smaller frame allowed me to slip between and slide around people as I maneuvered around the bushes.

"Excuse me. Pardon me. I'm sorry." With a few gentle nudges and subtle hip bumps, I made my way to the front of the gathering. People around me shook their heads and whispered words of grief as they drifted back into the crowd. A few made the sign of the cross, touching their index and second fingers to their forehead, chest, and both shoulders.

In front of me, barred by park officials and event staff, were six steps carved out of gray stone. They led to a lower-level path. Metal handrails angled down, following the stairs. Emergency personnel were already on the scene. They'd roped off the area at the bottom of the steps. Beyond the ropes, EMTs packed their kits. Sorrow hovered over them like a thick, dark canopy.

A body lay barely an arm's length from them, twelve feet from where I stood at the top of the stairs. I knew her loose-fitting purple blouse and her wide-legged olive green pants. A knot closed my throat. My eyes stung. Shocked and horrified, I stumbled back.

"Lynds, what's going on? Can you see anything?" Manny's voice slashed through the drumming in my ears.

He crashed into my back. "Is it . . . Camille!"

Dev snatched him before he could race down the steps. "Manny. Don't."

The sound of my cousin's sobs broke my heart. Dev and I stood on either side of him. Dev held his shoulder. I wrapped an arm around his waist.

As the EMTs covered Camille's body, two men who'd been beside her straightened and stood back. My mind cleared, bringing them into focus. Bryce and Stan. As though sensing my presence, Bryce raised his head and met my eyes. The pain in his was all the confirmation I needed: Camille Abbey was dead.

CHAPTER 5

"Tragedy Hits Caribbean American Heritage Festival."

I winced at the headline on the front page of Sunday's *Brooklyn Daily Beacon*. "I'm sure Sheryl Cross isn't happy about this. She worked so hard on the event all year. Now the tragedy of Camille's death is the only thing everyone's going to remember about it. God rest her soul."

My family and I stood around the long, rectangular blond wood center island in Spice Isle Bakery's state-of-the-art commercial kitchen. It was the last Sunday in June, the day after the festival. We didn't open the bakery until 10:00 AM on Sundays. The later start allowed us to attend the early Mass before beginning our day. I started reading aloud the news story on the untimely death of DragonFlyZ's lead singer. In Camille's honor, the reggae band's benefit CD played softly in the background.

The newspaper's crime reporter, José Perez, must have interviewed Bryce and Stan at the scene.

Standing on my left, Granny looked over my shoulder. "They're not saying yet that it was an accident, you know. This is a quote from your friend Bryce."

"He's not my friend, Granny." I wasn't surprised when she ignored me.

Granny deepened her voice and affected her version of a Brooklyn accent in an attempt to imitate Bryce for her dramatic reading. "'We have to wait for confirmation from the medical examiner before making an official statement. But it appears Ms. Abbey tripped on some steps in the park and fell, hitting her head when she landed.'"

"What a tragedy." Daddy was on my right at the center island, preparing the coconut bread. "She was so young and so talented."

"God rest Camille's soul." Mommy stood beside Daddy. She set down the serrated bread knife she was using to portion the most recent batch of currant rolls. Each slice freed the scents of melted butter, confectioners' sugar, warm fruit, and cinnamon. She made the sign of the cross.

Granny continued skimming the article as I held the paper. "Oh, yes. There's a quote here from the band's business manager, Karlisa Trotter." She cleared her throat, preparing to read her lines. "'I believe this is a tragedy, not just for Camille's family and friends, including me, but for her fans and the entire music world.'"

Dev spoke from behind me where he was frying the fish bakes. The sharp notes of the hot pepper and salted codfish competed with the sweet pastry smells. "She seems a little melodramatic."

Was he referring to the band manager or Granny's re-enactment of the reporter's interview? In fairness, my grandmother's reading was much more entertaining than mine.

Granny continued in the clipped, fast-talking speech she'd given the manager. "'I had just negotiated a contract with a major music label for DragonFlyZ. With Camille on vocals, the band would've taken the music industry by storm. Now it will be a struggle to replace her.'"

"'Replace her'?" Mommy's gasp interrupted Granny. "But she's not even in the ground yet, oui."

"Della, please let me finish." Granny looked at Mommy from beneath her eyebrows before completing Karlisa's quote. "'This is business. It's not personal. My job is to look after the best business interests of the entire band, not just one member.'"

Mommy snorted. "It may be business to her, but to a lot of people, it *is* personal." She placed the sliced currant rolls on a tray to be transferred to the display case in the bakery's customer service area when we opened. "Al and Inez said Manny was inconsolable last night. They tried calling him, but he said he didn't want to talk."

After putting away the newspaper, I moved to the sink to wash my hands before returning to my currant roll dough. Granny went back to making coconut drops. My family and I had agreed to make the menu items that were most popular at the festival: coconut drops, currant rolls, coconut bread, and fish bakes. If the customers we'd met during the event stopped by the shop today, we wanted them to see their favorites in our display case.

"I texted Reena this morning." My mind went back to my conversation with my cousin as I sprinkled flour over the clean, dry surface in front of me before removing the dough from the mixer. "She said Manny wanted to be left alone."

Mommy's sigh was heavy with empathy. "Inez said he's wandering around." She shrugged. "What could she do? He's grown. If he wants to walk around the neighborhood all day, she can't stop him."

"I doubt he's walking aimlessly." I shaped the currant roll dough into a smooth ball about twice the size of my hand. "He's probably gone back to Prospect."

"I'm sure you're right." Granny added eggs and vanilla

extract to the dough mixer. "He must have gone back to where Camille died. The poor child."

I wrapped the dough with a clear plastic sheet. It had to cool in the refrigerator for at least half an hour. Now that I'd mastered the art of making the flaky crust, I could store my dough in the fridge beside everyone else's. It felt good to contribute to our product inventory. I transferred my bundle to the refrigerator shelf and exchanged it for one that had been sitting overnight.

"I can't even imagine the heartache Manny's feeling." I heard the pain in Dev's voice.

Neither could I.

A heavy silence blanketed the kitchen as we slipped into our own thoughts about Manny, Camille, and the uncertainty of Fate.

I blinked back tears as I rolled out the dough. Camille's death was a terrible tragedy. Its effect on Manny was an added blow. I'd seen how much he'd cared for her. It was in his eyes when he looked at her, his face when he smiled at her, his voice when he spoke with her.

Granny exhaled, shattering the brief pause. "Well, Manny knows that when he's ready to talk, the family's here for him. That's all we can do. Be with him when he needs us."

She was right. We were a family. We'd be there for him whenever he was ready for whatever he needed from us.

When Granny opened the bakery, there were almost half again as many customers as our usual Sunday breakfast crowd. The line was down the block. A few of the new customers were people we'd met during the festival, including the father of the three young coconut drop lovers, and a woman who might be their mother. I pictured the sheet of coconut drops we'd made this morning. We might need more. They were followed by the couple who'd kept coming back for fish bakes and sorrel. And the friends who'd placed several orders of currant rolls and mauby.

The weekends were always hectic at the shop, especially Sundays. It was as though customers were squirreling away pastries for Mondays and Tuesdays when the bakery was closed. The air was swollen with the scents of cinnamon, ginger, nutmeg, confectioners' sugar, and warm butter. DragonFlyZ's benefit CD bounced through our sound system. Customers were rolling their shoulders and swinging their hips to the hypnotic rhythms. A few accompanied Camille in low voices. Still the mood was solemn. The community would grieve the fallen star for a while.

"So how did it go at the festival?" Tanya led Benny to the order counter. She lowered her voice to a conspiratorial whisper. I could barely hear her above the music.

I smiled, lowering my voice, too. "Good morning, Ms. Nevis and Mr. Parsons. It went well, until Camille's death, of course."

Beside me, Dev nodded. "Thank you for coming by yesterday and telling your friends about our bakery."

Tanya glowed. "It was my pleasure, darling. I'm glad it went well." She shared a brief look with Benny. "We're just coming from church. The congregation prayed for Camille, her family, and the band."

I pressed her hand where it lay on the counter. "That's lovely."

Tanya's smile trembled. She took a breath, seeming to steady herself. "We'll have our usual fish bakes and hot mauby tea, and a few other things, too."

She went through a long list of baked goods, including her favorite hard dough bread. I wrapped everything securely and packaged them in our green, yellow, and red

Spice Isle Bakery bag while Dev tallied her order. Benny carried their breakfast tray to the dining area. Tanya walked beside him with their bag of goodies.

A tearing sound directed my attention to Grace Parke. The seventy-something-year-old stood in the middle of the line with her arms crossed, kissing her teeth. "The line's longer today than it was at the festival." Patience wasn't one of her virtues.

From her powder pink skirt suit and matching wide-brimmed hat, I guessed Grace had attended her church's early service. How long had it taken her to get into a bad mood? A frown marred her pretty, round brown face. She looked like she'd sucked a lemon.

"You make that sound like a bad thing, Grace." Granny didn't look up from the lavender-and-white afghan square she was crocheting.

Joymarie was next in line. Dev moved away from the cash register and leaned over the counter to kiss his girlfriend. The public display of affection startled Joymarie. It surprised all of us. Joymarie's astonished expression warmed into a pleased smile. Cheers and applause erupted around us. The noise brought Mommy and Daddy out of the kitchen.

"What's happening?" Daddy looked around.

Granny chuckled. "Your son's kissing his girlfriend instead of minding the customers."

"Oh, yes?" Mommy's voice bounced with amusement. "Well, let's see, nuh?"

With a grin, Dev complied. This time, Joymarie cupped his face. Laughter mingled with cheers and applause. Even Grace clapped them on. Granny and I smiled at each other, but it was a bittersweet delight. Manny's heartache wasn't far from our thoughts. Did our cousin's unexpected tragedy have anything to do with Dev's uncharacteristic exhibit of affection? Whatever the reason, I was happy for him and Joymarie. We served her coconut bread and corailee tea.

As I packaged Joymarie's order, I caught sight of Bryce in the line. The detective was making our bakery part of his morning routine. Despite my efforts to remain cool toward him—and they were strenuous—I couldn't deny a rush of pleasure every time I found him in the line.

Bryce wore iron gray knee-length shorts and high-top black sneakers. His tan T-shirt stretched across his broad shoulders and flat stomach. Not for the first time, I wondered what he did to stay in shape: running, cycling, swimming, all of the above? His hazel eyes danced and his full lips curved into an irresistible smile at Dev and Joymarie's kiss, and our guests' cheers and whistles in reaction.

The pulse at the base of my throat fluttered. That happened a lot when Bryce was around. It was annoying.

Our eyes met. Bryce raised his hand in a brief wave. I lifted mine in reply. My fingers continued upward, brushing against my black chef's cap. My braids were tucked under it. Like Dev, I wore a red apron over my sea blue Spice Isle Bakery T-shirt and khaki shorts. I was presentable, but I wasn't at my best. Oh, well. It's not as though he's never seen me like this before.

Carole, the Bubble-Gum-Chewing College Student, cracked a bubble, cutting short my private exchange with Bryce. I hadn't recognized her without her overburdened backpack. "That was the best festival yet. Or at least it was until the DragonFlyZ's lead singer died."

Grace grunted. "Their album sales are going to go through the roof now for sure, boy."

My head shot up. I pinned her with wide, disbelieving eyes. What a tactless thing to say. Granny waved her hand as though dismissing Grace's words. The crowd booed their displeasure. Their voices rose above the sound of DragonFlyZ's "Love Is Like Rum."

Undeterred, Grace doubled down on her prediction. "All you know I'm right. How many of you are planning to buy their album now when you weren't before?"

The room quieted. Customers' eyes dropped to our blue-tiled flooring in shame.

Grace grunted. "Oh-ho! Now we see."

D'André waited behind Joymarie. He was in full New York Knicks regalia: blue, orange, and silver team T-shirt and black team shorts. He looked over his shoulder at Bryce. "Detective Jackson, when do you expect to get the medical examiner's report?"

"I'd like to know that, too," José Perez, the *Beacon*'s crime reporter, called from the middle of the line. A chorus of agreements rolled across the room.

José and I had had a couple of tense run-ins in the past, but we were coming to an uneasy truce. Our first conflict occurred days after we'd opened the bakery and police suspected me of killing a rival baker. The second was when my mother was suspected of murdering her former boss. Both times, I'd accused José of trying to convict us in the court of public opinion. He claimed he was just doing his job. Funny that I knew so many people whose job it was to put me and my loved ones behind bars.

Bryce's features stiffened when he looked at José. He returned his attention to D'André before answering. "I wish I could tell you. The medical examiner's office is pretty swamped, but we'll release the report as soon as we receive it."

Seemingly satisfied, D'André nodded, then turned to

me. "I heard the defense and prosecution still haven't come to a deal in the trial for Emily Smith's murder. Do you think you'll have to testify?"

Large cubes of ice filled my gut every time I thought about Granny and me being called to take the stand during a murder trial. That's why I tried hard not to think about it. But someone was always asking.

Principal Smith had been Mommy's boss when she'd taught math. They hadn't gotten along, which was the reason we'd been stunned when Emily had asked us to cater her retirement dinner. The event had ended in tragedy. The principal had died at the hospital and Mommy had been suspected of her murder. Because my family and I had helped solve the case, I might be called to testify if it went to trial. But my biggest fear was that the defense would try to once again cast my mother as a suspect.

"We're hoping the two sides can reach a plea deal." I struggled to keep the tension from my voice. "I think the prosecution has enough evidence to win the case otherwise."

"I agree." D'André nodded to Dev, then placed his order.

Bryce stepped forward, giving me a half smile that made my toes curl inside my sneakers. "Good morning, Lyndsay, Dev." He called over to my grandmother, "Good morning, Ms. Bain."

I braced my hands on the counter and struggled to sound brisk and businesslike. "Good morning, Detective. How can I help you?"

His smile wavered before settling back into place. "I'd like two coconut breads and to take you to lunch tomorrow."

I blinked. "I can get you those coconut breads, but lunch is not on the menu."

Bryce was undeterred. "How 'bout dinner?"

I glanced at Dev. His eyes were glued to the cash register as he processed Bryce's credit card. But his lips trembled with barely contained humor.

I turned back to Bryce. "I'm working tomorrow."

Bryce shrugged. "You've still gotta eat."

Standing behind Bryce, Grace sighed. "Could you please just go out with him so we can keep the line moving? It can't be easy for him to ask you out in front of your whole family. Your parents are behind the window. Your big brother's standing right in front of him, and your granny's over there at the table."

The other guests weighed in on Grace's judgement.

"She has a point."

"Yeah, that takes guts."

"I couldn't do it."

"And he's not hard to look at." This last comment came from Carole as she smacked another bubble.

Bryce's eyes gleamed with the anticipation of victory. His voice was swollen with amusement. "What d'you say?"

I expelled a breath of irritation as I wrapped the two coconut breads securely and put them in a Spice Isle Bakery bag. "As much as I appreciate everyone weighing in on my dating life—"

"Or lack thereof," Granny grumbled.

I ignored her. "I'll make up my own mind. Thank you. And thank you for your order." Avoiding Bryce's eyes, I handed over his bag. "As for dinner . . . I'll think about it."

"You have my number." Still smiling, he turned to leave the bakery.

Granny grunted. "That one's not going to wait forever, you know. You'd better make up your mind soon."

Granny was speaking the truth. Bryce was smart, charming, and attractive. He also was gainfully employed. Why was he pursuing me? Was he really interested—or was I just a challenge?

CHAPTER 6

The lunch rush left us breathless. It had lasted even longer than usual, another example of our festival success bearing fruit. We were tidying the customer service area and the kitchen late Sunday afternoon when the bell above the door chimed.

"Manny!" I stored the bottle of sanitary wipes I was using to clean the counter and display case and turned to the pass-through window behind me. "Manny's here."

Mommy, Daddy, and Dev joined us from the kitchen.

Granny had set down her crocheting and stood to wrap her arms around her oldest grandchild. "How are you managing, love?"

Manny returned her embrace. "Not so well, Grandma."

My heart tore a bit. For Manny to admit to any discomfort meant he was in a really bad spot.

Granny looked as stricken as I felt. The faint lines tracing across her brow deepened. She stepped back to search his face. "You want some lunch?"

Manny found a smile for our matriarch. It was barely a shadow of his usual joyful expression. "No, thank you, Grandma." He turned to me. "Lynds, can I speak with you in private?"

"Of course." I grabbed a hairnet from one of the storage drawers behind the customer counter. No one was allowed in the kitchen without one. I wouldn't risk even one strand of hair getting into our food.

Manny gave the hair covering a dubious look but put it over his tight dark brown curls without complaint. I led him to the office, but he stopped me with a hand on my shoulder. I looked up at him. Like Dev, my cousin was almost a foot taller than me.

He jerked his chin toward the back door. "Can we walk?"

"Sure." I led him into the rear parking lot.

Three cars were parked there. Granny rode to the bakery with my parents in their bronze SUV. They were the first to arrive each morning. Dev drove from his apartment in his silver SUV and arrived about the same time I did. We usually closed the bakery together. The twelve-year-old orange compact sedan was mine.

I stopped outside the bakery's back door. Humidity was thick enough to pour into a bucket. The late-afternoon sun was strong. The asphalt beneath my feet seemed to absorb its heat, then blow it onto me. Perspiration trickled down my spine as beads of sweat popped onto my hairline and upper lip. I dabbed at them with the back of my wrist.

The spicy, savory aromas from the dishes we'd cooked teased me as they escaped through the kitchen vent and fanned out onto the street. They were all that remained of the jerk chicken, stew beef, curried goat, rice and peas, and fried plantains.

Manny paced back and forth in front of me. His strides were long, his movements jerky. I waited for him to speak. The air was still as though it listened for his words, too.

After several long moments, Manny stopped and turned

to me. "Lynds, Camille's death wasn't an accident. She was pushed."

I blinked. I don't know what I'd expected, but his declaration wasn't it. "Why do you think that?"

His features were tight. Waves of anger and frustration rolled from him, battering against me like a boat in a storm. "The way she fell. It doesn't make sense. I tried to tell those detectives. They wouldn't listen to me. *You* have to tell them."

Whoa! What now? "Tell them what, Manny? You haven't told me. What do you mean the way she fell doesn't make sense?"

Manny paced away, then returned to me. "The band was recording their next album. They've been at the studio for weeks. The whole time, there was tension between them. A lot. You could feel something was wrong, but no one said anything."

He seemed to think his statement explained everything. It didn't. I pushed gently. "What does that have to do with Camille's fall?"

"Why won't you believe me?" His dark eyes were clouded with betrayal.

My heart shredded a little more. "Manny, no one wants to believe someone they know has been murdered."

"I'm not making this up." His voice was sharp.

"I didn't say you were." I ignored his impatient tone. He was in pain. "But if I'm going to tell Bryce we suspect Camille was murdered, I have to give him something concrete. Help me understand why you're suspicious about the way she fell."

The muscles in his jaw clenched and released. His frustration tried to force us apart.

I held his eyes. "Please, Manny. Let me help you. Tell me what you're thinking."

"She was on her back." The words ripped from him. His voice was thick and barely recognizable. He scrubbed the heels of his palms against his eyes as though trying to get rid of the image of Camille's body. "I'm *never* going to forget seeing her like that."

My heart finally shattered. Blinking back tears, I reached up to cup his shoulder. "Manny, I'm so sorry. Camille seemed like a wonderful person. It's unfair you didn't have more time with her. I can't imagine the pain you're feeling. But, Manny, do you really think someone would kill her? Maybe that's just the way she landed."

He lowered his hands. His brown eyes were pink. His cheeks were damp. "Lynds, how do you fall *backward* on your own?"

That gave me pause. How indeed? I let my hand fall from his shoulder and lowered my head to think about that.

Manny jerked his chin toward the parked cars. "Walk with me. When you trip and fall, you fall forward." He pretended to stumble. The action pitched him forward before he caught himself. "See? If I were to fall, I'd fall forward." He turned to face me. "Now push me. Hard."

"Umm . . ."

"Don't worry. I'll catch myself."

I arched an eyebrow. "I'm stronger than I may look." I waited a beat, then shoved him. But not too hard. He rocked backward before catching himself.

Triumph gleamed in his eyes. "See? If Camille had tripped, she would've landed on her face. But she landed on her back. Someone pushed her. I'm sure of it. This has been bothering me all night and all day. That's why I came to ask for your help."

Even without Manny's demonstration, his theory made sense. If she'd been walking forward and tripped, she would've naturally fallen forward and landed on her stomach. If she'd been standing at the top of the stairs, talking with someone—arguing with someone?—and they shoved her, she would've fallen backward and landed on her back.

"Wait here." I started to jog back to the bakery.

"Where're you going?"

I called over my shoulder, "To get Dev." I hurried through the kitchen.

"Everything OK?" Mommy asked.

"I'm not sure yet," I responded without stopping. At the customer service area, Dev was waiting on a short line of customers. I hated to interrupt him, but we had a situation. I sensed Manny wouldn't wait. I turned to my grandmother, who sat serenely crocheting another afghan square. How many of those had she completed so far? "Granny, would you mind taking over the counter, please? I need to speak with Dev."

She didn't hesitate. "Of course, love." She put down her crocheting and came to the counter.

I gave her a grateful smile as I tugged Dev behind me. "Thank you, Granny."

"What's going on?" Dev allowed me to drag him through the kitchen.

"What're all you doing?" Daddy called after us.

"We'll explain everything shortly." I led Dev through the back door into the parking lot. I brought him to a stop with his back to Manny. "Manny and I need your help."

I nodded to my cousin. It took him a second to get into position. Then I shoved Dev. Hard. His arms shot up in reflex. Camille's arms had been raised above her head.

Manny caught my brother, then looked at me. "You see? She was pushed."

Dev straightened. "Lynds, what the—"

I jogged back to the bakery. "I'll call Bryce."

* * *

"Have you changed your mind about having dinner with me?" Bryce's voice carried through the speaker on the bakery office's phone late Sunday afternoon.

My face burst into flames. I threw a wide-eyed look at Manny, seated on the other side of the desk in the tiny office. His attention remained on the phone.

"Good afternoon, Detective." I managed to choke out the words. "I have you on *speaker*phone. I'm here with my cousin, Manson Bain, and my office door is open."

Translation: My family's in the kitchen, pretending to cook and bake while listening to every word we say. The sounds of cooking utensils, pots, pans, and plates were muted, a sure sign my grandmother, parents, and brother were straining to hear us.

"Hi, Manson." Bryce didn't miss a beat. Was he capable of shame? "We met yesterday."

"Call me Manny. And yes, we did." Manny leaned into the desk, bringing himself closer to the phone's speaker. His tension vibrated between us. "That's when I told you I didn't think Camille's fall was an accident."

"I remember." Bryce's voice sobered. His words were soft with empathy. His consideration for my cousin eased the knots in my muscles.

I cleared my throat before continuing. "Bryce, this morning, you said you didn't know when you'd receive the medical examiner's report. I don't think we have time to wait for it."

I sensed confusion in Bryce's hesitation before he spoke. "Why not?"

"Because I agree with Manny." I looked at my cousin. Having the police department give this case their attention was important to him, so it was important to me. "Based on the way Camille landed, it's obvious she was pushed."

My grandmother raised her voice to be heard in the office. "Tell him how you experimented on Dev to test your theory!"

My jaw dropped. Manny and I exchanged an irritated look. Dev had tattled on us. Oh, well. We'd've done the same.

"We will, Granny." I gave Bryce a concise description of our experiment. He didn't seem impressed.

Mommy's voice was fretful. "All you shouldn't be shoving Dev around so, you know. He could've been hurt."

Dev's response was too low to hear, but he must have been embarrassed. He was an adult, after all. He shouldn't need his mother for protection, especially from his younger sibling.

I drew a breath and caught the scent of jerk spice and sweet fried plantain among the aromas baked into the office walls. "We'll talk about that later, please, Mommy. Right now, Manny and I are on the phone with Detective Jackson." I turned back to the phone and lowered my voice. "Sorry about that, Detective. If you had to guess, when do you think the medical examiner's report will be ready?"

Bryce blew a heavy breath that made my knees weak. *Focus. Focus.* "As I said this morning, the ME's office is slammed. It's hard to speculate when they'll complete Ms. Abbey's examination. It could be next Monday—at the earliest."

Manny's heavy black eyebrows stretched almost to his hairline. "A *week* from *tomorrow*?"

"At the earliest." Bryce gave us no hope.

"That's too late." Manny looked to me. He seemed to be asking for a solution.

"Bonjay!" Granny's exclamation blew into the office. "Sounds like they need to hire more people."

Manny spread his arms. "The killer could get rid of any evidence. Even leave the city. Their trail will have grown cold."

"That's ridiculous for sure." Daddy added his agreement.

Mommy sighed. "They can't keep people waiting so long."

Manny dragged his hand over his tight dark brown curls. "We need justice for Camille now."

"Is your family in the office with you?" Bryce sounded puzzled. He'd seen our office several times during his police searches. He knew how small it was. No doubt, he wondered how we were all able to fit.

My tone was dry. "They may as well be." They were also right.

I couldn't bear to see my cousin in so much pain. We couldn't wait more than a week. Manny needed answers now. Had Camille fallen or had someone pushed her? If she'd been pushed, by whom—and why? He couldn't grieve Camille until he had closure on her cause of death. I could understand that.

I sat back on my chair, struggling to convey my thoughts. What magic words would best convey our urgency? "Bryce, we should consider the possibility Camille was attacked and begin the investigation now."

Even through the phone, I sensed Bryce measuring his words. That was his way. He and Stan kept everything secret: their cases, their strategies, their thoughts. "Stan and I are *homicide* detectives. We took control of the scene yesterday because we were closest to the location. However, based on our years of experience with crime scenes, we're reviewing all of the evidence before deciding whether to open an investigation. The ME's report is an important part of that evidence. We don't want to get

ahead of it. But please know Stan and I are very sorry for
your loss."

I frowned at the phone. There was something he wasn't
telling us. I knew Bryce and Stan were trained, experienced
professionals. I also knew they were extremely cautious in
the way they approached their cases. If they wanted to wait
for the ME's report before investigating what to Manny
and me was an obvious homicide, we weren't going to
change their minds. At least not today, not with the flimsy
argument we presented.

I rubbed my eyes with the thumb and first two fingers
of my right hand. This wasn't a surrender. It was a par-
tial retreat. "We appreciate your condolences, Detective.
Thank you. Could you let us know what the ME's report
says?"

"That depends." Amusement returned to Bryce's voice.
"Will you have dinner with me?"

Manny arched an eyebrow. Laughter rolled in from the
kitchen.

I closed my eyes as my body flooded with embarrassment. No, Bryce Jackson wasn't capable of shame. "I've
got to get back to work."

"Lunch tomorrow, then." He was undaunted.

"Have a good afternoon, Detective." I disconnected the
call.

Manny scrubbed his face with his hands. His palms
muffled his voice. "I can't believe this. They wouldn't even
consider what you said."

My heart sat like a rock in my chest. "I'm so sorry,
Manny."

He dropped his hands. Grief and frustration hardened
his dark eyes. "Don't apologize. I appreciate your trying."

I had a sense of foreboding as he pushed himself to his
feet. "Where—"

Manny turned toward the office door. Granny, Mommy, Daddy, and Dev had gathered just beyond the threshold.

Granny stepped forward to wrap her arms around him. "Let me fix you a plate, love."

Manny bent over to return her embrace. "No, thank you, Grandma. I'm not hungry."

Granny stepped back. "I didn't ask if you were hungry. You skipped dinner last night and you haven't eaten all day. I said I'd fix you a plate. Come."

She led him by the hand to the kitchen's center island. My parents, Dev, and I followed. Manny took a seat, gracefully accepting defeat at Granny's hands. It was telling that he didn't ask how our grandmother knew he hadn't eaten since yesterday. He must have realized his food consumption had been observed and analyzed through multiple family texts and phone calls.

The bakery was closing in a few hours. I propped my right hip against the counter below the pass-through window so I could monitor customer traffic with one eye and my family with the other. "Manny, what are you going to do now?"

He watched Granny as she stood at the stove across the room, fixing him a plate with stew chicken, sweet fried plantain, and rice and peas. "I'm going to talk with Camille's bandmates. I told you I'd sensed tension between them during our recording sessions. I want to know what that was about."

Exclamations of dismay rose up in the kitchen.

I gave him my full attention. "You can't do that on your own."

His lips curved into a half smile. "You did. Twice."

I shook my head even as he spoke. "Not on my own."

He scrubbed his face again. "I can't wait two or even

three weeks to know what happened to Camille. I need to know now."

"We understand that." Granny set his plate and a glass of iced mauby tea in front of him. "We're not asking you to wait. We're saying let us help you."

Manny looked at Granny, Mommy, Daddy, Dev, and me in turn. He shook his head. "No. It could get dangerous. You've already risked your lives with the last two investigations, especially you, Lynds. A third investigation would be pushing your luck. You didn't even know Camille."

I crossed my arms. "Manny, we love you. Stop arguing and accept our help."

His eyes widened in shock. "Reena's right. Opening the bakery's changed you."

"Yes, man." Mommy grinned. "It's changed her for the better."

Daddy winked at me. "I barely recognize her, oui."

Dev chuckled. "Reena warned you."

"She's come into her own." Granny's eyes shone with pride as they settled on me.

"Thank you." Manny looked at us again. "I'd be grateful for the help." He turned to Granny. "And thank you for the meal, Grandma."

"You're welcome, love." She patted his shoulder, then turned to me. "Where do we start?"

I checked on the bakery via the pass-through window before facing my grandmother. "Where we always start, with a family meeting."

CHAPTER 7

"At least this time, no one in the family's a suspect." Uncle Roman's voice was wry as he sat back on his chair. "But mind the investigation doesn't make the bo-bo suspicious and draw attention to us, eh."

Despite the heat, Uncle Roman nursed a mug of hot mauby tea. He sat on the far side of one of the two tables we'd pushed together for our family meeting Sunday evening. Except for the beads of sweat collecting at his hairline, he looked comfortable in a bright blush short-sleeved cotton shirt with white-and-green images of palm trees and crashing ocean waves. He wore it with baggy sand-colored shorts.

Granny, Mommy, Daddy, Dev, and I had made stew chicken, macaroni-and-cheese pie, and tomato-and-cucumber salad for dinner. The air was still swollen with the scent of hot, sweet spices, sharp cheese, and vinegar and olive oil. Uncle Roman, Aunt Inez, Uncle Al, Reena, and Manny helped clean up afterward.

"But we haven't agreed to do an investigation." Aunt Inez sent a pointed look to Manny beside her. "You remember during one of those investigations, your sister and cousin were almost killed."

Reaching diagonally across the table, she lifted Reena's

glass of iced mauby tea. Her movements were jerky as she used her paper napkin to wipe the condensation ring that had formed on the table before setting her daughter's glass on it.

Aunt Inez's temper was like an ocean wave rolling to the opposite end of the table and breaking over me. Her scarlet sleeveless cotton blouse matched the angry color slashing her cheekbones. Her brown eyes snapped. Her heart-shaped lips tightened.

Granny nodded, acknowledging Aunt Inez's point. "And Lynds and I were threatened with a screwdriver. Yes, there's danger involved. But in the end, we caught the killers both times."

"It's too risky." Seated at the foot of the table beside Aunt Inez, Uncle Al looked at Manny with clouded ebony eyes. "We don't even know if there's a murder. The police called it an accident."

"No-o-o." Manny drew out the word. Dressed in a plain black short-sleeved shirt and black lightweight slacks, he was almost lost beside the pageantry of Reena's amethyst cap-sleeved dress. "They said it *looked* like an accident. They're waiting for the medical examiner's report for confirmation."

"Then we should wait for the report as well." Mommy sat beside Daddy at the head of the table. Her hand cupped his as it rested between them. Both still wore their black chef's smocks. Like Dev and me, they'd set aside the matching hats. "It could turn out to be an accident."

Granny kissed her teeth, rolling her eyes from her spot diagonally across the table from me. "The report won't be ready for at least a week. Manny wants answers now."

My grandmother sat on Mommy's left. Reena was beside her. Granny's pink, tourmaline, and jade dress competed against my cousin's.

Reena rested her hand on her brother's shoulder. "So would I. If I were in Manny's situation, I'd need answers to help me get closure, too."

"I can't wait any longer." Manny gritted the words through his teeth. Reena rubbed her brother's back.

Uncle Roman set down his empty gold porcelain mug. "They say when there's a homicide, the first forty-eight hours are the most important. You have to jump on the case and what and what."

"But these investigations are dangerous, you know." Daddy turned his hand over to entwine his fingers with Mommy's. "We can't rush into them. We need to practice patience. We have to take the time to think things through."

Dev still wore his sea blue Spice Isle Bakery T-shirt, like me. "Uncle Roman's right. The first forty-eight hours are the most important. We've already lost half of that time. We need to get started."

Uncle Roman shrugged. "But it's one thing to risk our lives for family, you know. It's another thing to risk our lives for strangers."

Granny scowled at him. "So whose side are you on now? Do you think we should investigate or not?"

Uncle Roman sat forward, cradling his empty tea mug between his large palms. "A wise monkey knows which tree to climb, eh?"

His words brought a smile to my face. Yes, we had to choose our battles—or in this case, our investigations—wisely. I listened as my relatives' debate continued around me. I could see both arguments. On the one hand, these investigations weren't to be taken lightly. As Aunt Inez and Uncle Roman had pointed out, we're putting our lives on the line. On the other hand, someone my cousin cared for very much may have been murdered. Could we really walk away from that?

Dev looked around the table. "We should put this to a vote."

He was met with murmurs of agreement. My brother used to be the youngest junior partner with a Brooklyn-based international law firm. Sometimes it showed, like now.

Manny extended his hands, palms out. "Just so we're all clear, you're voting on whether you're going to help me. Whether the family gets involved or not, I'm still going to investigate."

Aunt Inez shook her head. "It's too dangerous, I said."

Manny sighed. "Mom, I'll be careful."

Uncle Al wrapped an arm around his wife's shoulders. "Manny, we know you cared for this woman—"

"Forgive me for interrupting, Uncle Al, but I think we may be missing the point." I gestured toward my mother's older brother. "We've gotten involved in murder cases in the past to help our family. First I asked for help and then Mommy." The room was so quiet, I thought I'd hear a pin drop. "Now Manny's asking for our help. Camille was his friend. He wants to find the truth about what happened to her. Are we really going to tell him no?"

Granny's eyes shone with approval at my words.

Uncle Roman nodded. "She's talking sense."

Aunt Inez's brow furrowed with remnants of concern. "But, Lynds, we already know the truth. The poor woman fell."

I spread my arms. "If Camille's death was an accident, we aren't in danger. But Manny senses there may be more to it, and I agree with him. We should at least take a look."

"It's what I'd want if I died unexpectedly." Granny pointed a finger around the table at each of us. "I'm putting all you on notice from now. If I die other than in my sleep, I want a full investigation."

Weak chuckles released some of the tension in the room.

I couldn't laugh off the statement. "Granny, you're going to outlive us all."

Uncle Al squeezed Aunt Inez's shoulders. "All right, Manny, we'll help with the investigation, but we all have to be careful. Right?"

I waited until the murmurs of agreement ended. "Manny, we'll get started tomorrow."

Jab! Cross! Hook! Uppercut! Body blow! Front right kick! Squat! Front left kick! Squat! Again!

With each punch I threw in Parish Avenue Fitness's weight room, my thick yellow vinyl gloves made a satisfying thump against the heavy foam-filled body bag's high-density surface. The force of the blow caused the freestanding six-foot black vinyl bag to snap back on the round sand-filled base that anchored it.

As usual, there were only a few people at the fitness center so early on a Monday morning. It was coming up on a quarter till six. The sun was only now starting to rise.

The neighborhood gym was old. As I paused to catch my breath, I drew in the stench of sweat that had fused with the beige walls and fog gray cement flooring. The equipment was in excellent condition, though, and the rooms were spacious enough that members weren't working out on top of one another. The best part was that the facility was walking distance from my family's home where I lived with my parents and Granny.

Using my forearm, I wiped the warm sweat that collected on my upper lip and dripped from my chin. I'd already stretched, run three miles on the elevated track, and did a circuit of upper-body weight training. My workouts were taking a little longer now that I'd committed to a training regimen for the local gym's annual fall kickboxing exhibition. I was getting to the facility even earlier to make sure I still arrived at the bakery in time to help prepare the food and open the shop. With Rocky's help, I'd structured my routine to focus on improving my strength, reflexes, agility, and speed. I tried not to think about the fact that the event was less than three months away.

Why did I let Rocky talk me into this?

I closed my eyes and focused on my breathing rather than the panicked voices screaming in my head. If I could confront killers, I could train for a skilled fitness exhibition.

Jab! Cross! Hook! Uppercut! Body blow! Front right kick! Squat! Front left kick! Squat! Again!

"Your jabs are clean and sharp. Good for you." Rocky's comment came from behind me, breaking my concentration.

I turned to her. Her unitard hugged her dancer's figure from her shoulders to just above her knees and left her sculpted arms bare. The solid black material was interrupted by a hot pink stripe down the left side.

"Thank you." I smiled at her encouraging words and the admiration in her voice. "My intermediate kickboxing instructor said the same thing. She thinks it's time for me to take the advanced class."

"Ha! It's past time." Rocky lifted her well-shaped arched eyebrows. Her expression screamed, *I told you so!* "Are you going to take our advice?"

I let my eyes slide away and focused on pulling off my gloves. "I'm thinking about it. I appreciate the tips you've given me, although I don't know why you're helping me since we're going to be competing against each other."

Rocky stretched her arms above her head, beginning her warm-up. "I told you, we're not competing against each other. We're competing against ourselves. One way to get more women to enter the exhibition is to show them how much fun it can be and how well other women like us do in the events."

I hunkered down beside my green nylon gym bag, dropping my gloves inside. "Have you convinced any other women to enter the competition?"

"You're the only one I've asked." Rocky paused in her stretches. "Do you see any other women practicing kickboxing here?" She swept her arm to encompass the weight room. Her words were thick with amusement. "Most women come here to stay in shape or get fit. They aren't training for events or learning a skill like we are."

My eyes followed her arm past the body bag down the aisle to the rows of weight benches, elliptical machines, and treadmills. There were more women than men in the room. To Rocky's point, I didn't recognize any of them from my kickboxing class and I never noticed other women using the bags placed around the room.

I looked up at her. "We need to make sure a lot of women attend the exhibition if we want them to start participating."

She frowned. "You're right. We should make sure to tell all the women in our classes."

Lightbulb! "There're flyers at the guard desks. We should hand them out during our classes."

Rocky snapped her fingers. "Of course!"

I dug my rose-colored cell phone from my bag and checked the time. It was a quarter to six. I needed to leave. Since the bakery was closed Monday, I could take a little longer to get to work, but not much. There were accounts to balance, marketing to schedule, promotions to plan, supplies to order, and my hard dough bread baking skills needed work. But before I dealt with any of that, I wanted to know what Rocky could tell me about DragonFlyZ and whether anyone involved with the group would have a motive to kill their lead singer.

"I was so sorry to learn about Camille Abbey's death." I stood with my bag. "Earl and the rest of the band must be devastated. Have you met the other members?"

"Yes, Earl introduced me to them. We've hung out with them a couple of times, usually after performances or recordings." Rocky's sorrow was like a coat surrounding her. "Earl's really upset. They're all in shock. They've been friends since before they started the band."

"Oh, I'm so sorry. I didn't know." My heart broke a little more for Camille and her friends. "How did they meet?"

Rocky's brow furrowed. The look in her dark eyes grew distant as though she was trying to remember. "Earl said they lived in the same neighborhood and went to the same high school. Camille wasn't only the lead singer. She also cowrote songs with Miles Tosh, the lead guitarist. They used to date."

Used to? That caught my attention. "He must be very upset. Did they break up recently?"

Rocky bent her right arm behind her head and pulled her elbow with her left hand, stretching her right triceps. "It was a couple of months ago, I think."

Why hadn't Manny told me this? Had he known? He must have.

"Hmm-m." I struggled to sound only vaguely interested while I really wanted to pepper Rocky with even more questions. "That must've been awkward, not only for them but for the rest of the band. I wonder whose idea it was to break up?"

Rocky altered her pose to stretch her left triceps. Her eyes glinted with suspicion. "What's with all the questions and what-have-yous? Usually, you're rushing to get to work."

My acting skills must need work. I wondered if Granny could give me tips on that as well as baking. I wasn't ready to tell anyone, not even Rocky, that my family was investigating Camille's death.

I doubled down on my I'm-Just-Curious cover. "The bakery's closed Mondays." My smile faded as sorrow and confusion swept over me. "Camille's death is a tragedy. It was so sudden. And she was only a couple of years older than me. It's a reminder that we shouldn't take anything for granted."

"You're right." Rocky's voice was low. I strained to hear it. "Camille was only a couple of years younger than me." She hesitated. "Miles told Earl that Camille broke up with him. She said he was arrogant and controlling. And yes, their breakup made things awkward with the band."

I nodded. That could explain the tension Manny sensed during the band's recording sessions. If Miles didn't want Camille to leave him, was he arrogant and controlling enough to try to change her mind? Or to push her down a flight of stairs? Only Miles could answer that question. And I needed to find the courage to ask it.

CHAPTER 8

Camille had looked just like her mother perhaps twenty years younger. The Abbeys were an attractive family. Her siblings—two sisters and a brother, all younger than her—were a perfect blend of both parents, which made seeing their grief so much harder because it was multiplied five times.

Their dark brown eyes were red rimmed and swollen from so many tears. Manny and I joined them in their spacious living room early Monday afternoon. They seemed to be looking through us rather than at us. I swallowed the lump in my throat and tried not to think about how shattered I'd feel if I were in their position.

"We're so very sorry for your loss." Manny's voice was low as though we were at a church service.

Manny had called and gotten their permission to give them our condolences in person. I wasn't looking forward to questioning grieving loved ones again. I'd learned during the previous investigations that uncovering the truth meant putting oneself in difficult situations and asking uncomfortable questions like: Do you have any idea who'd want your daughter dead?

The Abbeys' living room was dark and heavy with heartache. Manny and I sat beside each other on an overstuffed sky-blue-and-white-polka-dot sofa. Beeswax and linseed oil scented the air. Beside the jewel-toned area rug, I could almost see my reflection in the polished hardwood flooring.

Camille's parents, John and Lynne, sat on the matching love seat to our right, holding hands. On our left, their daughters, Viola and Gwen, had carried two chairs from the dining room. Viola appeared to have wrapped her anger around herself. Gwen's head was bowed as though in prayer. John and Lynne's son, Benedict, stood behind his sisters. He'd propped his narrow right shoulder against the wide archway between the living and dining rooms. He looked tired and lost.

John stared at us. Grief had dulled his eyes and sapped his energy. "How did you say you knew our daughter?" His words had a Haitian flavor.

Manny pressed back against the sofa as though he needed its support. "I'm an audio engineer with Caribbean Tunes. It's a recording studio. A lot of independent labels, including Camille's, use us. DragonFlyZ recorded its last two albums with us."

"My sister told us about your studio and what have you." Benedict appeared to be the youngest of the four Abbey children. His Brooklyn accent was awash in sorrow. "She enjoyed working with you. Said you were really talented and professional."

Manny lowered his eyes. His voice was strained. "I'm glad. I—we—enjoyed working with her. And the band." He cleared his throat.

Viola directed her question to me. "How did *you* know my sister?" Her voice was numb. She cradled what appeared to be a mug of hot tea between her palms.

"I was just a fan." I winced inwardly. As painful as it was, I needed to get the family to talk. "Camille had such a beautiful, strong voice. She could make you feel the song."

A sob broke across the room. I turned my head to see Camille's mother wiping her eyes.

"Yes-s." Lynne choked out the word. "Cammie was very talented. She'd started singing in the church choir, you know. She used to get solos all the time."

"That's how Miles Tosh *discovered* her." Viola used air quotes with the word "discovered." Contempt darkened her brown eyes and thickened her Brooklyn accent.

Lynne waved a dismissive hand. "Viola, Miles is done now. Drop it, nuh?"

"Miles is the band's lead guitarist, right?" I jumped on the opening Camille's sister had given us. "You don't like him?"

Viola's narrowed eyes cooled. She stared at me and Manny as she wiped her nose with a well-used tissue. "Why're you asking? Are you a reporter?"

My jaw dropped. "No. I'm a baker."

My spontaneous utterance, as Dev would call it, didn't impress Viola or her siblings. She and Gwen looked between Manny and me with growing skepticism.

"You're a baker?" Benedict straightened from the threshold. His creased brow eased as his dark brown eyes widened with recognition. "You're Lyndsay Murray the Grenadian Nancy Drew. I've read about you in the *Beacon*."

Urgh. That nickname! José and I needed to talk. "Well, I—"

Gwen broke her silence. "I thought I recognized your name." She examined me as though looking for my cloche hat and matching handbag. I said I didn't want to be compared to Nancy Drew, not that I hadn't read the books.

I shook off my irritation. "We wanted—"

Benedict swept his right arm toward the sofa, drawing his family's attention to Manny and me. "She and her family solved two murders in Little Caribbean before the police did." His frown abruptly returned. His eyes clouded with confusion. "Why are you here? I—we—thought Cam's death was an accident."

The hesitation in his voice shredded me. I glanced at Manny. His cheeks were flushed. His eyes were pinkening. He seemed shattered. I took his large left hand and squeezed it between both of my smaller ones.

A deep breath eased the tightening in my chest. "We don't mean to cause you more pain, but there's some question as to whether Camille tripped—or whether someone pushed her."

Viola fisted her hands. Her words shook with temper. "Who's questioning Cam's death? You?"

Viola's reaction was a volatile mix of sorrow and anger. Staring into her eyes, I felt like I was standing in the middle of a storm. "Yes, Manny and I." I released his hand. "The detectives are waiting for the medical examiner's report."

Gwen's words were thin with shock. "The police haven't said anything to us about Cam's death being suspicious. Why would they tell *you* before *us*?"

Manny rubbed his eyes with the fingers of his right hand. "We called them. Yesterday." He looked to Camille's parents. "I'm sorry if we were out of line. But Camille was my friend. If someone hurt her, I don't want to wait to find out who. I want answers now."

"So do we." The response exploded from Viola.

I held her eyes. "Then tell us about her relationship with Miles and the other band members. Can you think of anyone who'd want to harm her?"

Viola still held back. I understood her hesitation. She didn't know us. Why should she trust us?

"You seem to have cared about my sister." Gwen's voice broke the impasse. She stared at Manny as though trying to determine whether his grief was real. She must have decided it was. "Cam dated Miles for almost a year."

Viola crossed her arms and legs. Temper simmered around her. "None of us liked him."

Lynne frowned. "Vi."

Gwen continued. "He recognized her talent as a singer and a songwriter. He wanted to showcase her to help raise the band's profile. I think he was also jealous of Cam's talent. It made her stand out. She commanded attention on the stage. She was also the better songwriter and he knew it. I think he felt threatened by her."

I frowned. First the breakup and now the jealousy. More and more, Miles sounded like someone we needed to speak with.

Benedict shifted his stance. His restlessness carried from across the room. "It wasn't until *after* my sister became DragonFlyZ's lead singer that anyone even knew who they were."

Gwen nodded, turning her attention from her brother back to Manny and me. "Miles told everyone he was co-writing their song lyrics, but he wasn't."

"That's enough." John's command was abrupt. "Maybe all you are right. Maybe Miles could've been a better boyfriend, but he wasn't a murderer. I wouldn't let my child date a killer." His words cracked with pain and uncertainty.

Lynne wrapped her arms around her husband. Silence dropped into the room. I exchanged a look with Manny.

Should we leave?

His eyebrows knitted. *Maybe.*

I started to stand, but Viola's words stopped me.

"She was my big sis." She took a shuddering breath. "Was there something I should've done to protect her? I don't know. But I do know that I want to do everything in my power to get justice for her."

"Vi's right." Benedict's voice had thickened. "I don't want to believe Miles is a killer, but I know he's a lazy fool who took credit for Cam's work. That wasn't right. I'm glad they broke up."

"Do you think their breakup was the reason for the tension in the band?" Manny turned to Camille's parents. "During recording sessions, the group wasn't as comfortable with each other as they'd been with their last album."

"That may have been part of it." Gwen contemplated the hardwood flooring as she spoke. "But it wasn't the only reason. Things changed after the benefit CD and Cam decided to leave the band."

"What?" Manny's eyebrows leaped up his forehead. "Why?"

Lynne sighed. "Our daughter didn't want to sing secular music. She never did. She wanted to be a gospel singer. She'd written a few songs for herself. They're very good. Miles tried to persuade her to change some of the lyrics to make them more secular, but she refused."

John's eyes were haunted. "Miles was pressuring her to change her mind. He said secular bands made more money. But it wasn't about the money for Cammie. It was about the music."

Gwen folded her hands on her lap, clenching her fingers together. "Cam told me Miles was determined to change her mind. He'd even told their manager, Karlisa Trotter, about her plans, hoping Karlisa could talk Cam into staying."

Viola's jaw dropped. She caught Gwen's eyes. "Cam never told me that."

"She knew you'd be angry." Gwen spoke without inflection.

To Viola's credit, she didn't protest Gwen's response.

I recalled Camille and Karlisa arguing at the festival. "Did Karlisa convince Camille to stay?"

Gwen shook her head. "Once Cam made up her mind about something, it was impossible to get her to change it."

Faint chuckles rose from the other side of the room. Camille's parents exchanged their first smile since Manny and I had arrived.

"That's the truth." John covered Lynne's hand with his. "She was born hardheaded."

Both Miles and Karlisa knew Camille was planning to leave DragonFlyZ. But why would they kill her if they wanted her to stay? Karlisa probably wouldn't, but as the jilted boyfriend, Miles had a second motive.

Happy memories seemed to have eased the sorrow in the room. I had one last question before Manny and I left the family alone with their thoughts. "Do you know whether the other band members were worried about losing their lead singer?"

Viola jerked as though I'd startled her. "I don't know. I wouldn't think so. I mean, my sister had put the band on the map, but she wasn't their first lead singer. Ena was."

I exchanged a look of surprise with Manny. Had we identified a second suspect? It was time for another call to New York's finest.

CHAPTER 9

"At least two members of DragonFlyZ may have had motive to kill Camille Abbey." I locked eyes with Bryce from across the table in the bakery's dining room early Tuesday afternoon. Manny was seated beside me. Stan was on Bryce's right. He looked like he'd pulled his tan suit and white shirt from a pile of laundry he'd neglected to fold. Reena would pass out.

After meeting with Camille's family yesterday, I'd suggested to Manny that we invite the detectives to lunch. The shop was closed Tuesdays, so we'd have the place to ourselves. I'd made stew chicken, and macaroni-and-cheese pie. The rich aroma of sharp cheddar cheese and the savory scents of thyme, onions, ground ginger, and caramelized brown sugar surrounded us.

Bryce paused with a forkful of stew chicken halfway to his mouth. "Are you investigating this case?"

I arched an eyebrow. "Are you admitting there is one?"

Bryce set down his utensil. "Where did you get this information?"

I gestured toward Manny. "We spoke with Camille's family yesterday."

Bryce's lips parted. He stared at me in silence for a beat.

"I can't believe you did that. You told the victim's family you thought their daughter had been murdered?"

It sounded superbad when he said it. "They have a right to know." I couldn't think of anything else to say to explain my seeming insensitivity.

Stan swallowed a mouthful of pie. "This is wonderful. Thank you." His comment diffused the tension between Bryce and me.

Stan took a healthy drink of sorrel. "We haven't received the final report from the medical examiner, but we also have concerns about the cause of Ms. Abbey's death."

Bryce forked up more pie as he considered Manny. "Which two band members do you think had motive to kill Camille Abbey?"

The empathy in his voice erased the last remnants of my defensiveness. At least he and Stan were willing to listen to us. I shifted toward Manny, waiting for his response. He hadn't touched his food. I'd made his favorites. I blamed his lack of appetite on his emotional state and not my cooking.

"Her ex-boyfriend, Miles Tosh, for one." Manny took a deep drink from his tall, thin glass of sorrel. "He's the lead guitarist. They broke up six months ago."

"Was he abusive toward her?" Stan shifted his now-empty plate aside. As a chef, I felt my heart lift at the evidence of how much he enjoyed the meal.

"Not that we know of." I rushed to correct any misperceptions. "They'd dated for less than a year. A couple of people said he was controlling, but no one said he was physically abusive."

Bryce lowered his drink. "If he doesn't have a history of abuse, why would he start now?"

"Because she broke up with him." Manny was adamant. An edge of frustration entered his tone.

Bryce exchanged a look with Stan. I wished I could read their silent communication. Did they agree Miles was a valid suspect or not?

"What does her family think?" Bryce asked.

Manny lifted his arm toward the detectives in a jerky, impatient gesture. "They think Camille's death was an accident because that's what you're saying in the press."

Hoping to calm my cousin, I put my palm over his hand as it lay between us on the table. His muscles eased slightly. "Camille's family doesn't want to believe they stood by while she dated a killer. They also said the band's relationship has been strained since they recorded their benefit CD."

Manny nodded, taking another sip from his glass. "I'd noticed it, too. And it's not just the band members. Their manager has been more agitated and impatient than usual."

Bryce split a look between Manny and me. "What caused the tension?"

Manny slid his still-full plate aside and leaned into the table. "They think it has something to do with Camille's plans to leave the group."

Stan's bushy brown eyebrows shot up his forehead in surprise. "Why was she leaving?"

Manny shook his head. "She wants—wanted—to move her career in a different direction."

"OK. The ex-boyfriend is a possible suspect." Bryce put his knife and fork on his empty plate and set them aside. "Who else do you have?"

I searched his face for some signal that he'd enjoyed the meal. I found nothing. "Ena Sorter. She was the band's lead singer, but when Camille arrived on the scene, she became the backup."

DragonFlyZ had produced two recordings in addition

to the fund-raising project with a small record label that used Manny's recording studio. Ena had a beautiful voice. She'd been the lead singer with the first release, but I could understand why the band had made the switch to Camille. Camille's voice had more emotion and a greater range, which allowed them to do more things musically.

Bryce spread his hands. "If Camille was leaving Dragon-FlyZ, why would Ena need to kill her?"

Manny shook his head. "Ena didn't know Camille was leaving. Outside of her family, the only person Camille told was Miles. Then he told Karlisa Trotter, the band's manager."

"Well, isn't that interesting?" Stan drained his glass of sorrel. "I can understand why Little Caribbean's amateur sleuth would have Ms. Sorter on her suspect list."

Stan had given me a nickname. I was momentarily shocked into silence. At least it was better than the one José insisted on using. "My family and I are serious about looking into Camille's death, Detectives. Camille deserves justice and there are too many unanswered questions."

Bryce scowled. "Lyndsay, Stan and I have suspicions about Camille Abbey's death, too. The ME's final report will give us additional insights for our investigation. We've asked them to put a rush on it. We should have it by tomorrow, Thursday at the latest. That's only two days from now. We've got it covered. All right?"

I exchanged a look with Manny. The report would come five days after Camille's death. That may seem quick to the detectives, but it felt like an eternity to me. I'm sure Manny had the same reaction. "All right."

Bryce's eyebrows met above the bridge of his broad nose. "Why do I have the feeling you're not listening to us?"

I shrugged. "I have no idea, Detective. Why do you?"

With a sigh, Bryce stood, pulling his wallet from his front right pocket. "How much do we owe you for lunch?"

I stood, shaking my head. "No, please. Lunch was on us."

Stan rose from the table. His gray eyes twinkled as he handed me his credit card. "Oh, no, ma'am. That wouldn't be ethical. We need to pay our own way."

Bryce offered his card as well. "And could you add three currant rolls to my order, please. One each for Stan and me, and one for his wife."

Stan patted Bryce's shoulder. "Thanks, partner. That's very decent of you."

I crossed to the checkout counter to ring out our guests. Manny followed and packaged their currant rolls.

I returned their cards with their receipts. "Thank you both for your time."

Bryce returned his wallet to his pants pocket. "We'll be in touch to let you know the results of the ME's report."

"Thank you. We'd appreciate that." I locked the door after them.

"They're going to wait another two days before they even get started?" Manny's frustration snapped around him like an electrical storm.

I expelled a breath. "I think they've already started investigating. They admitted they have questions about Camille's death, too. But that doesn't mean we have to wait for them to catch up. We should continue our investigation."

The frown lines on his face eased. "So you're still going to help me?"

"Of course! On one condition."

Manny arched an eyebrow. "What?"

I jerked my chin toward the dining area. "Clean your plate."

His shoulders sagged. "I'm sorry, Lynds. The food smells delicious and looks great, but I'm not hungry."

I crossed my arms and pinned him with a stern look. "Want me to call Granny?"

Manny's lips parted in surprise, but he returned to our table at the dining area without another word.

Sometimes our love for our family drives us to make difficult choices, like ratting them out to our matriarch and investigating a murder.

"The medical examiner's report confirms our suspicions." Bryce's words weren't as satisfying as they should've been.

In fact, confirmation that someone had pushed Camille Abbey down a flight of steps to her death four days ago at Prospect Park broke my heart. My parents and Dev stood around the bakery's checkout counter with me and the detectives. Through their silence, I could tell they felt the same way.

It was just after the breakfast rush Wednesday. We'd already started preparing for lunch. The spicy, savory aromas of stew, curry, and jerk meats mingled with the rich smells of fried plantain and sweet scents of fresh pastries. A handful of customers dallied over mid-morning snacks in our dining area. Some were older, perhaps retirees. Others wore hospital or transit uniforms as though they'd stopped in on their way home from their overnight shifts. All were openly eavesdropping on my family's conversation with the New York Police Department's homicide detectives. How long will it take for the news to spread across the neighborhood? I estimated less than ten minutes after the first guest left.

Granny sat at her table, crocheting. I couldn't see her expression, but her words were seasoned with impatience and regret. "Did you think my granddaughter would be wrong? She's already cracked two murders you couldn't solve."

A blush warmed my cheeks. I slid a look toward Bryce under cover of my eyelashes. He was photo-session ready in a gray linen suit and magenta tie. He smelled nice, too. A hint of his woodsy cologne drifted beneath the ginger, onion, cilantro, nutmeg, and pepper scents coming from the kitchen. I took another breath.

"Granny, the detectives suspected Camille had been murdered, too." My tone was a mild chastisement.

She snorted. "I thought they got paid to be suspicious."

Granny wasn't going to give the detectives any credit. I left her alone and switched my attention to Stan. The older detective's sand-toned jacket hung limply from his shoulders as though he'd machine washed a suit meant to be dry-cleaned only. I fisted my hands to keep from adjusting his left shirt collar, which was overlapping his jacket. "Did the medical examiner find anything that could help identify the killer?"

"Not much." Stan rocked once on his heels. "Ms. Abbey didn't have any defensive wounds. The push must've caught her off guard. She didn't have time to fight back. We did find a piece of blue linen cloth in her left fist. Ms. Abbey may have grabbed at her assailant's clothing and torn it as she fell backward."

I searched my memory, trying to recall whether I'd noticed anyone at the festival wearing a blue linen blouse, shirt, or dress during the festival. I'd seen a lot of people, but no one stood out.

Dev lowered his voice, obviously aware of our dining

room audience. "Since the two of you will be in charge of the investigation, will you update us on your progress?"

"We can do better than that." Bryce's eyes settled on mine. "Lyndsay, we'd like your help."

I blinked at him. "*My* help?"

A collective gasp came from the direction of the dining area. When I glanced toward our guests, everyone seemed to be looking in other directions. I shook my head. Granny could teach them a thing or two about subtlety.

My family threw a series of tense responses to Bryce's request. They spoke over one another, no longer caring that our customers could hear them.

"Why?" Daddy demanded.

"What for?" Mommy set her hands on her slim hips above her pale yellow slacks.

"What can my sister do that you can't?" Dev sounded like he was cross-examining the detectives.

Granny left her table and came to stand with me behind the customer counter. Her small hand was light and warm against my left shoulder blade. She pinned the detectives with a look. "Whaddayou?"

Stan and Bryce exchanged a look of confusion.

"You've repeatedly told me to leave the investigations to you." I folded my arms beneath my chest and scowled. "Why are you asking for my help now?"

Granny would accuse me of putting on a puppy show—being silly—but I felt some kind of way that the detectives were asking for my help now when they'd blown me off in the past. Maybe I shouldn't hold a grudge. We wanted the same thing: justice for Camille.

"I understand your concern, Ms. Bain." Stan inclined his head toward Granny. "But your granddaughter knew the victim. And we can tell by the way your customers react that she's well-known and well regarded in the community."

"I'd only met Camille for the first time the day before she died." I let my arms fall to my sides. "You should speak with Manny. He's known her for months."

"We will." Bryce leaned against the counter. His posture brought him—and his distracting cologne—closer to me. "But your cousin would be more comfortable speaking with me if you were there, too. You may not have known Camille Abbey well, but you're familiar with her band. The members of DragonFlyZ will speak more freely if you're with me."

"He's right." The affirmation came from an elderly gentleman, lingering over a cup of bush tea as he unabashedly weighed in on the discussion. He was dapper in a white shirt and tan jacket. He'd set his hat on the empty chair at the table he shared with an elderly lady. His accent identified him as a Trinidadian. "Most people don't want anything to do with the bo-bo, but they'll speak with you. They like and respect your family, and admire the way you've handled yourself with those other murders."

"Well, if he can speak, I can, too." A full-figured, middle-aged woman in a transit uniform flung her arm toward the older man. "How're you *not* going to help the bo-bo solve Camille Abbey's murder?"

I wasn't surprised that our customers were weighing in. What surprised me was that they'd waited so long. "My family and I have solved the other cases on our own. Why should we work with the detectives?"

Granny rubbed my back. "Because you're looking for a killer and the detectives carry guns."

My eyes reflectively dropped to the waists of Bryce's and Stan's jackets where slight bulges indicated they were both packing weapons. Granny had a point.

Bryce shrugged. "We both know you're going to continue your investigation. Why shouldn't we work together?"

Daddy scowled at Bryce. "Before I let my daughter help you, I need your promise that you'll keep her safe."

"That's right." Mommy nodded. "I don't want her to be shot at, followed, threatened, or otherwise harassed again."

Dev's features looked like they were carved from stone. I understood my family's concern. When I was investigating with them, I knew we had one another's backs. We'd do everything within our power to keep one another safe. Yes, Bryce and Stan were trained for dangerous situations, but they weren't family. Were they as motivated as my relatives were to keep me safe?

Bryce's eyes darkened. Straightening from the counter, he looked from my grandmother, brother, and mother before meeting my father's eyes. "I give you my word Lyndsay will be safe with me. I won't let *any* harm come to her."

Well, he had me convinced.

Stan cleared his throat, shattering the moment. "I won't actually be involved with this investigation. I'm working one of our cold cases. But if I were on this case, I'd protect your daughter as though she was my own. You're all good people. I wouldn't let anything happen to any of you."

Mommy, Daddy, and Dev still hesitated.

Granny gave a nod of encouragement. "We can believe them."

Dev turned to me. Waves of tension rolled off him and battered me. "Lynds, what do you think?"

I think I wasn't sure it would be a good idea for me to spend long hours alone with Detective Fine. Aside from that, it would be more efficient to work with the police for once instead of running competing inquiries.

Straightening my shoulders, I turned to Bryce. "We should start with Miles, the band's lead guitarist."

CHAPTER 10

I heard the relief and excitement in Manny's voice when I called late Wednesday morning to tell him I was working with Bryce to find Camille's killer. I promised to keep him and the rest of my family in the loop. Manny gave me the numbers and addresses for all the Dragon-FlyZ members. Our first stop would be Camille's ex, Miles Tosh.

Miles was a real estate attorney with Becker & Chastain Attorneys at Law, PLLC. Their offices weren't far from the bakery. We drove Stan back to the precinct first. On the way, I told the detectives about Camille's family and what Manny and I had learned from them. Then Bryce and I drove to Miles's office.

Standing beside Bryce in the law firm's reception area, I felt like a country mouse to his city slicker. It hadn't occurred to me how ridiculous we'd look together with him in a suit and me in a sea blue Spice Isle Bakery T-shirt, cream knee-length shorts, and white sneakers. At least I'd taken off my chef's hat.

Tension tightened my grip on my black handbag. Since I didn't have a time machine that would allow me to change before arriving at the firm, I tried hiding behind Bryce, matching my steps to his as we approached the receptionist. He spotted me anyway. His nameplate read: "Gage Becker." Any relation to the firm's primary named partner?

Gage's puzzled blue eyes bounced from Bryce to me, then back. I'd been dismissed. "Good afternoon. May I help you?" The burly young man sounded like he'd traveled into the firm from Queens.

Bryce shifted his jacket to display his badge. "I'm Detective Bryce Jackson. This is my colleague, Lyndsay Murray. Miles Tosh's expecting us."

Gage slid another curious look my way before returning his attention to Bryce. "One moment." He picked up his receiver, pressed four buttons, then waited. "Mr. Tosh, Detective Jackson and his colleague, Ms. Murray, are here. They said you're expecting them." He paused again. "All right. Thank you." He cradled the phone. "Mr. Tosh's on his way. You're welcome to have a seat while you wait."

Bryce inclined his head. "Thanks."

With his hand on the small of my back, he moved us back toward the waiting area's wide red faux leather armchairs. I sank onto one of the butter-soft seats. Bryce took the one beside me.

Miles arrived before I could get comfortable. He gave my T-shirt a curious look before facing Bryce. His Jamaican accent rolled through his words. "I'm Miles Tosh. What can I do for you?"

Bryce stood. "I'm Detective Bryce Jackson. This is my associate, Lyndsay Murray."

I rose from the seat. *The* Miles Tosh, lead guitarist with DragonFlyZ. Fandom battled with suspicion. I strove to find middle ground. "Good afternoon."

The short hairs on the back of my neck stirred. In my peripheral vision, I caught Gage shooting quick looks between us and his computer. So our bakery's patrons weren't the only ones with a weakness for eavesdropping.

Miles's eyes were clouded with confusion. "Let's continue this in my office." He turned to lead us from the waiting area.

Bryce stepped aside so I could precede him. I smiled at Gage as I walked past his desk. He pretended not to see me.

Oh, brother.

The firm's wide hallway entertained a mixture of natural sunlight that streamed in from the receptionist's area and a fluorescent glow from the recessed lighting in the high ceiling. The fixtures were strategically placed to highlight the framed photos of the firm's legal team. The company had diverse representation: men, women, young, older, and BIPOC partners and associates.

This space wasn't as nice as Dev's former law firm. Not for the first time, I wondered if my brother regretted walking away from his position as junior partner with a prestigious international firm. Did he miss working in an imposing building in downtown Brooklyn? He'd had a large private office on the nineteenth floor with a sweeping scenic view through a floor-to-ceiling window. At the bakery, the five of us shared an office the size of a boot box. We could peek out at the side alley from a window that wasn't much bigger than a mail slot. Dev seemed happier now, though. In the month he'd been working full-time with the shop, I'd heard him laugh at least three times as much as he'd laughed in the two months before he'd left his firm. And he and Joymarie were spending more time together. But was this what he wanted for his future? His childhood dream had been to be a lawyer.

Miles gestured for us to enter his office first. He closed the door, then circled his desk to settle onto his black faux leather executive seat. "You said you had some questions about Camille's death. I don't know if I can help you. I wasn't there when she fell."

Bryce pulled out a notepad. "You and your band performed during the event. Is that correct?"

Startled, I put my hand on Bryce's left forearm. His muscles tensed beneath my fingertips. He couldn't just jump into an interrogation. Miles may have grown up in New York, but based on his accent, he was born and had spent most, if not all, of his formative years in Jamaica. We had to build a rapport with him first.

I leaned forward and let him hear my genuine enthusiasm for his music. "The festival isn't the first time I've seen your band in a live performance. I saw you at Nutmeg's. You and your band were fantastic that night, too. The audience gave you several standing ovations."

"Thank you. That's nice to hear." Miles's dark features brightened with pleasure. His full lips curved and parted to reveal perfect white teeth. A dimple creased his left cheek. I could see why Camille had been attracted to him.

I searched my mind, trying to channel my inner Reena. My cousin could charm a fish from the water. "You slayed at both the club and the festival. Your original songs have all the feels. I can hear the islands in them. You and Camille wrote them together. Is that right?"

Miles grinned with pride. "Yes, we did. We were a great team, you know. The songs featured our heritage—calypso, reggae, and soca—but we put some hip-hop vibes in there for the market, you understand."

I nodded, sliding a look at Bryce.

Picking up on my signal, Bryce drew a pen from his inside jacket pocket. "You and Camille were also dating until recently. When did the two of you break up?"

Miles's smile faded and his confusion returned. He shifted his attention to Bryce. "It was a couple of months ago, *Detective* Jackson. Why?"

Bryce ignored the question. "*She* broke up with *you,* right? Why?"

Miles sat straighter on his chair, regarding us closely. His brow furrowed and his tone became more formal. "I don't understand. You're a policeman. Why are you here, asking me questions about Camille? She fell."

"No, Miles." My voice was gentle. "Camille was pushed."

Blood drained from his face. "No-o-o." The single syllable lingered.

The pain on his face stole my breath. "I'm so sorry, Miles. Can you think of anyone who'd want to hurt her?"

"No!" Miles swung his chair to the side, putting his profile to us. He rubbed his eyes with his fingertips, wiping away his tears.

I felt a punch to my heart. Digging through my purse, I pulled out a small, open packet of tissues and reached across his desk. "Here. What happened that day, Miles?"

"Thank you." He took the tissues from me and used one to dry his face. "Nothing. Nothing happened." He drew a shaky breath. "We did our performance. We were sharp. And then we packed up. I didn't see Camille again. She'd come to the festival with that audio guy."

My back tensed. I didn't like his dismissive tone. "You mean Manson Bain."

Bryce covered the fist I'd clenched on my lap. His hand was large and warm. I felt mine relax.

Miles continued. "Yes. That guy. Following her around the park like a lovesick puppy."

I leaned forward. Bryce squeezed my hand in another warning. Clenching my teeth, I sat back.

"Did seeing them together make you angry?" Bryce asked.

Miles swung his chair to face us. "Not angry enough to push Camille. I might have pushed Manson."

My temper snapped. I ignored Bryce's increasing pressure on my hand. What was he thinking? That I'd just sit there like a stump while someone insulted my family? No, sir. Not even as a joke. The Murrays and Bains weren't built that way.

I surged from my chair to tower over a startled Miles. "Manson Bain is my cousin and if you make any more comments like that one, you and I are going to have problems."

Miles raised his hands in surrender. "My apologies. I didn't realize Manson was related to you."

I nodded my acceptance of his apology and reclaimed my seat.

Miles shrugged. "Yes, it bothered me to see Camille with your cousin—but not enough to kill her."

Bryce scanned Miles's features as though trying to decide whether Miles was lying. The lead guitarist didn't flinch. I wondered what both men were thinking as they took each other's measure. Could Bryce read anything from Miles's body language? Did Miles have anything to hide?

Bryce broke the short silence. "You and Camille shared credit for DragonFlyZ's original songs, but she was the one with all the talent."

Miles frowned. "Who told you that?"

"Do you deny it?" Bryce's tone was almost baiting.

I didn't have the confidence to pull off that kind of interrogation technique.

"Of course I deny it." Miles tossed a hand. "Those songs were as much mine as they were hers. And they were getting top downloads on the streaming services. We were getting signed to bigger venues. Even that charity CD we did raised our profile. That was Camille's idea, though. I didn't want to do it."

Bryce frowned. "Why not?"

"Because we wouldn't make any money." Miles's eyes stretched wide. He seemed shocked that Bryce would even ask that question.

His answer didn't surprise me, though. I'd met people like Miles before, many while working for a marketing firm in Brooklyn after earning my MBA. All they cared about were the three Fs, fortune, fame, and fortune, by any means necessary.

I remembered what Tildie Robinson had said about the large preorder sales and stores selling out of the album the day it dropped. "Did it bother you that it was selling so well since you weren't making any money from it?"

Miles waved a hand at my question. "It was a good marketing investment. Those sales boosted our other albums and drew the attention of top, top record companies. It was hard work, and Camille and I fought the whole time. She said I was controlling like that was her favorite word." He kissed his teeth. "Well, if 'controlling' means I'm going places, then I'm guilty as charged. Once we signed with a big record company, we were all going to quit our day jobs and focus on the band full-time."

"You were going places with Camille's songs and Camille's voice." Bryce cocked his head. "But she wanted to leave the band. Could you have signed with a top record company and quit your day job without her?"

The way he slipped in that question was impressive. I waited eagerly for Miles's response.

"Not many people know Camille wanted to leave DragonFlyZ. You must've spoken with her family." Miles paused. He pressed back against his seat, bracing his elbows on its black vinyl arms. "They think *I* could've killed her?" His face was expressionless, but his voice cracked with pain.

A lump formed in my throat as though in empathy. I swallowed to dislodge it.

Continuing his cat-and-mouse game, Bryce shrugged. "Camille was a big reason for the band's success. For *your* success."

"That's true." Miles inclined his head, still masking his emotions. "So why kill her? If she was our ticket to the big time, wouldn't I need her alive?"

"But she was determined to leave." Bryce watched Miles as though trying to see beneath his mask. "Maybe you didn't want her starting a solo career. Maybe you were afraid she'd take your fans with her. Instead her death has increased DragonFlyZ's album sales."

Miles flinched as though Bryce's accusations hurt him. "We're a reggae band, Detective. Camille wanted to sing gospel. She wouldn't have been our competition."

I couldn't argue with his point. "What did you do after DragonFlyZ's performance?"

"I helped the band pack our equipment back into Earl's van, then we went back to the park." Miles frowned. "Camille caught up with your cousin. The others went their separate ways. I went back to the stage to meet up with a reporter. She wanted an interview." He paused and cleared his throat. "She was taking some photos of me when I heard about Camille."

"I'm so sorry for your loss." The words were ripped from me.

Miles dropped his eyes to the surface of his faux cherrywood desk. "We were all friends, you know. If Camille wanted to leave the band, we would've supported her."

Miles gave a short, shaky laugh. "Ena would've been ecstatic."

"That's right." Bryce's eyes narrowed. "She was your lead singer before Camille replaced her. If Camille had left, would Ena be your lead singer again?"

Miles cocked his head in consideration. "Probably. At least for a while."

Bryce and I exchanged a look. We definitely needed to speak with Ena.

"This wasn't what I pictured when I imagined taking you to lunch." Bryce's embarrassed smile made my toes curl.

I dragged my eyes from his mouth and glued them to my hamburger. "This is all I have time for. I need to get back to the bakery."

It was early for lunch, but I'd skipped breakfast to get to the bakery on time and wouldn't have a chance to eat before guests started arriving in about half an hour. As a solution to our dilemma, we'd agreed on a fast-food drive-through and parked in its lot to eat late Wednesday morning. Yes, it was lame and Granny would lose her mind if she caught me rushing through a meal, but my emphasis was on speed, not quality.

"I understand." Bryce adjusted his driver's seat. He pushed it even farther back from the steering wheel, giving himself more room to eat. "I just didn't want you to think this is what I usually do on a date."

My frown tightened the muscles across my forehead. "Why would I think that? This isn't a date."

"No, I know. I just . . ." He didn't sound like himself. His words were rough and choppy. He turned the engine on to lower the windows. "It's hot in here." He grasped his soda from the cupholder and took a deep drink.

"Yes, it is." I pulled a French fry from its carton. This wasn't a date. Then why did I feel so awkward?

His dark four-door sedan was quickly filling up with the smell of greasy fried food. We'd stopped at a restaurant about a mile or two from the bakery. The commercial neighborhood was similar to Parish Avenue. There were beauty salons, restaurants, clothing boutiques, shoe stores, and specialty shops up and down both sides of the congested street. Pedestrians crowded the sidewalks as they flowed in and out of the businesses. Sitting in an unmarked police car, we attracted quite a bit of attention. In the past, those stares would've made me uncomfortable. Today, eating burgers and fries with Bryce, I found the strange looks from passersby amusing.

"How long has your family been attending the Caribbean American Heritage Festival?" Bryce's voice was calmer now.

That helped me relax. "Since the very first one in June 2002. I was seven. I ate so many coconut drops, I made myself sick. We've gone back every year since."

Bryce's warm laughter made me smile. "I've lived in Brooklyn my whole life. I don't remember Caribbean American Heritage Month being so popular when I was a child."

I swallowed another bite of my hamburger. "The celebration didn't become official nationally until 2006." I shifted on my seat to face him. "It's a big deal to my family, to our community, because it celebrates the contributions Caribbeans and people of Caribbean descent have made to our new home."

Bryce's grin showed off his perfect white teeth. "I know. I've seen the play *Hamilton*. Our first Secretary of the Treasury was from Saint Kitts."

"You smile, but did you know after the revolution, the

United States was being crushed by its war debts? By the time Hamilton left office, the country was fiscally sound."

Bryce raised his eyebrows. "You know your history."

I took a drink of my soda. "I saw the play, too, and read the book. But it's not just Alexander Hamilton. Shirley Chisholm, the first Black woman to be elected to Congress and to run for President, was of Caribbean descent. Her father was Guyanese and her mother was Bajan. Colin Powell, Kamala Harris, Eric Holder. I can give you more names. I'm really proud of my heritage. Being West Indian American is the best of both worlds. I love having the chance to share that history."

"And I appreciate learning about it." His dark eyes glinted with admiration. "Your parents, grandmother, aunt, and uncles have accents, but you, Dev, and your cousins don't. Why is that?"

I swallowed the last of my burger. "The best explanation I've heard is from an elementary school teacher. She said when a young child hears one accent at home and another at school, the two cancel each other out and often the child doesn't speak with any discernible accent. However, I have cousins who have very strong Brooklyn accents. Maybe they're exceptions to that rule." I shrugged.

"I like Caribbean accents. They're almost musical. I don't always understand your uncle Roman, though." His charming half smile made another appearance.

I laughed. "Sometimes I think Uncle Roman doesn't want to be understood."

We finished our meal, threw the wrappings in a nearby trash can, and got back on the road.

Bryce signaled to turn onto Parish Avenue. "So what do you do besides work long days at the bakery?"

I smiled at his profile, which was just as compelling as

the rest of him. "I work long nights and weekends at the bakery."

He chuckled, a soft, low sound that made me wish I didn't have to work so much. "You can't work all the time. You've got to find at least a couple of hours to have fun and relax."

"What do you do to relax, Detective?" To my surprise, I really wanted to know.

"Are we back to 'Detective'?"

"Bryce."

He pulled into the lot behind the bakery and stopped his car near the rear entrance. He put his car in Park before shifting to face me. "Lyndsay, I'm truly sorry for the pain I caused you and your family with my previous homicide investigations. I went where the evidence led me, but I didn't read it carefully enough. In my rush to judgement, I focused on two innocent people, and I really regret that. I'm going to apologize to your family as well."

"I know they'll appreciate your apology as much as I do. Thank you, Bryce." My heart was beating so hard and fast, I could barely hear myself. That apology was more than I could've hoped for.

He climbed out of the car to open the passenger door for me. I was grateful for his gallantry since my mind went blank and I couldn't remember how to operate the lock.

He waited to speak until I was standing beside him. "I bowl."

It was as though he'd spoken another language. "Excuse me?"

"You asked what I do to relax. I bowl." He closed the passenger-side door. "I'll call you later to schedule our next interview."

"Thank you." It took all of my meager acting skills to

look confident and composed as I waited for him to drive off. Locking my knees, I turned stiffly toward the bakery's back door.

Detective Bryce Jackson was flirting with me. If I was going to help him investigate Camille's murder, I'd have to ask him to stop. Between the demands of the bakery, the stress over the trial of Emily Smith's killer and how it might affect my mother, and the anxiety over Manny's grief, I had enough distractions. I couldn't add another thing, especially not Bryce's flirtations.

At least not until after we solved Camille's murder.

CHAPTER 11

The bell above our shop's entrance chimed late Thursday morning, heralding Tildie Robinson's arrival. She was smart in a warm gold cotton cap-sleeved dress. A seashell necklace settled just above the scooped neckline.

Tildie was the owner of Lester's novelty store, which was walking distance from our bakery. She also was Granny's nemesis. That didn't stop her from coming to our shop several times a week. Granny claimed Tildie wouldn't come if I stopped giving her free coconut bread and mauby tea. Although my grandmother claimed not to have any charitable feelings toward the other woman, there was something about Tildie that I liked. And I had a sense Tildie wanted to heal whatever rift had come between these former friends.

"Good morning, Ms. Robinson," I called to her from the customer counter where I cleaned the display window. "Would you like a coconut bread and mauby tea?"

Granny didn't give me the evil eye this time. Progress.

"Good morning, Lyndsay." Tildie hung her red faux leather handbag from the back of the chair opposite my grandmother before settling onto the seat. "I would love some of your wonderful coconut bread and delicious tea.

Thank you." She turned to Granny. "Good morning, Genevieve."

"Tildie." Granny's voice wasn't as frigid as it had been in the past. She set aside the lavender-and-white afghan squares she was crocheting.

In the kitchen, Mommy, Daddy, and Dev were baking pastries and getting ready for the lunch rush. If it was anything like the breakfast orders, we were in for a crowd. Confectioners' sugar, warm fruits, cinnamon, nutmeg, and vanilla aromas wafted forward into the customer service area from the pass-through window. Thyme, onion, cilantro, curry, jerk, and caramelized brown sugar followed.

Tildie gestured toward the crocheting project. "That's lovely. Did all you have a good festival?"

"Yes, we did, although Camille Abbey's death was a tragedy." Granny paused and bowed her head as though thinking of poor Camille. "And you?"

At Granny's table, I served the two ladies each coconut bread on a pale gold porcelain dessert plate and hot mauby tea in a matching mug.

"Thank you, darling." Tildie smiled up at me before returning her attention to Granny. "I moved a lot of inventory. It was a good day until, as you said, Camille's tragic accident. It's so sad. I carry the band's benefit CD and their latest release, *DragonFlyZ 4 the People*."

"I know them." Granny stirred in four packets of sugar. Like me, she had a wicked sweet tooth. "Della bought them for me."

Tildie stirred her hot drink. The silver metal teaspoon pinged as it tapped against the porcelain mug. "Yes, she bought them from my store."

Granny's eyes sprang up to meet Tildie's. "She got them from you?"

Tildie nodded as she sipped her tea. "That's right. She

preordered six copies of the benefit CD and one copy of the other release. She picked them up the same day they came out." She paused as Granny grumbled something. "What was that, Genevieve? I didn't hear you."

"The band's donating all the proceeds from their benefit CD sales to the West Indian American Relief Fund." Granny held Tildie's eyes. That wasn't what she'd said.

I rushed to fill the suspicious void. "You're right, Granny. And I'm glad to know it's been selling well, Ms. Robinson. Mommy had purchased a copy for each of us." The band had released the CD May 1, in advance of Caribbean American Heritage Month. Mommy had gotten one copy each for her and Daddy, Granny, Dev, Uncle Al, Uncle Roman, and me. "We've been playing it for weeks. So have the shop owners on both sides of the street."

Tildie narrowed her eyes with suspicion at Granny, but she didn't challenge her. "There were a lot of preorders, you know, and sales were brisk. But we shop owners are donating our commissions to the relief fund, too."

"That's very generous." Granny hummed. "And it was smart marketing to release the album before Caribbean American Heritage Month."

Tildie swallowed a bite of coconut bread. "It was Camille Abbey's idea. That way, the aid organizations would receive the first donations June 1. You know sales were brisk all month, but after the tragedy they really picked up. The record company's having trouble keeping up with orders."

Granny's eyebrows lifted. "Woi. Then the relief fund's getting a lot of money to help the people back home."

My heart was heavy as I sipped my mauby tea. "In addition to her beautiful voice, her big heart will be her legacy. May she rest in peace."

Our brief silence was thick with grief.

"I heard you're investigating Camille's death, Lyndsay." Tildie gestured toward me with her mug of tea.

Granny snorted. "Where'd you hear that?"

Tildie's confusion deepened the wrinkles across her brow. "Are you saying word on the street isn't true?"

Granny shrugged. "I'm asking where you heard it."

Little Caribbean's rumor mill strikes again. Impressive.

I set my empty mug beside the cash register behind the customer counter. "Have you heard of any conflicts Camille may have had with anyone, perhaps other members of the band or someone else?"

The bell above the bakery's door demanded my attention. Sheryl Cross, president of the Caribbean American Heritage Festival Association, strode into the shop.

Tildie spoke again before I could greet my latest customer. "Oh-ho. So you are investigating Camille's death? But I'd heard it was an accident. She tripped and fell, poor thing. What is there to investigate?"

Sheryl's lips parted in surprise. "But wait. Are you spreading rumors that Camille Abbey was murdered at the festival?"

Granny and I exchanged a wide-eyed look before she responded to the association president. "Who said so?"

"She just did." Sheryl pointed at Tildie.

"I never did." Tildie rose to her feet. She took her bag from her chair and settled the strap over her shoulder. "Genevieve Bain's family does not spread rumors. They are dedicated to the truth. Why else would Lyndsay risk her life to investigate murders?"

Sheryl's blunt features darkened with outrage. "She investigated them because she and her mother were suspected of those murders."

Tildie kissed her teeth. "And you think someone who's

been the target of malicious rumors would spread them?" She rolled her eyes and strode out of the bakery.

Sheryl's loose-fitting silver pantsuit was the perfect costume for her storm cloud impersonation. Her movements were jerky as she marched toward me, clenching the black faux leather straps of her handbag. Her voice trembled. "Are you telling people that Camille was killed at my festival?"

Her festival? I thought it was the community's festival.

Swallowing a sigh of frustration and impatience, I squared my shoulders and met her eyes. "Ms. Cross, Camille's death wasn't an accident. She was murdered."

Sheryl harrumphed, glaring at me. "Ms. Murray, Camille Abbey's death was an unfortunate accident. That's what the police said."

Granny grunted. "Sheryl, don't you read the news? The bo-bo changed their mind and they've asked Lynds to help them solve the case."

I heard the pride in my grandmother's voice. Sheryl wasn't impressed.

Her face flushed almost purple. She set her fists on her full hips. "This is all your fault. This investigation's going to damage the event's reputation. No one will come to the festival if it's connected to a murder."

I shook my head. "Prospect Park is a public site. You can't control whether a crime has happened there."

"No, I won't let you do this to me." Sheryl waved her arm. The motion was abrupt and angry. "If you're going to ruin me, *I* will ruin you. I'll find someone else to cater my daughter's wedding. *And* the association's holiday reception. *And* I'll make sure no one I know has you cater their events. Even if the festival survives your treachery, you will never be a vendor at the event ever again."

Sheryl Cross was off the rails. My face burned as blood flooded my cheeks. "Ms. Cross, with all due respect, the Caribbean American Heritage Festival isn't *your* festival. It's the *community's*. Camille Abbey was a beloved member of our community and a dear friend to my cousin. If I have to choose between catering your daughter's wedding and getting justice for Camille, I'll choose justice for Camille every time."

"That's because we raised you well." My father's voice came from behind me. He put his arm around my shoulders.

Surprised, I jumped. Looking around, I found him standing with Mommy and Dev. Granny rose to join us. No one looked happy.

Granny stood on the other side of me. "This isn't about you, Sheryl. It's about standing up for what's right."

Sheryl stiffened as she glared at each of us in turn. Her eyes landed on me. "You do what you think is right. And I'll do the same."

She turned on her three-inch black heels and stomped from the bakery.

"That could've gone better." Granny's voice was dry.

"Is Sheryl concerned about the festival's reputation or her own?" My attention remained on the door even after the association president had disappeared. Was there another reason she didn't want the police investigating Camille's death?

CHAPTER 12

"Tildie should never have opened her big mouth." Granny set her hands on her hips and glared toward the door as though she could still see her nemesis.

The anger in her words caused my muscles to tighten. "She did defend us to Ms. Cross, though."

"Chutz!" Granny waved her hand as though swatting an irritating bug. Her movements were stiff with temper as she sat to return to her afghan squares. These latest chains, double crochets, and slip stitches would need to be redone.

I exchanged a look of concern with Mommy, Daddy, and Dev. Granny was upset about something more than Tildie's offhand comment. Had our confrontation with Sheryl and Tildie's inadvertent role in it triggered an unhappy memory?

With a heavy heart, I filled five pale gold porcelain mugs with ginger tea from the white thermal carafe behind the customer counter. The black one held hot mauby. The corailee tea was in the stainless-steel carafe. Dev and I avoided that one. I offered a mug each to Mommy, Daddy, and Dev, then carried mine and Granny's to her table.

I set her tea in front of her, then took the chair Tildie had occupied. "Granny, will you tell us why you and Tildie had a falling-out?"

"I'd like to know, too, Mommy." My mother's voice was soft and tentative, a blend of concern and confusion.

Granny's hands stilled. She straightened on her seat and exhaled. "Thank you for the tea."

"You're welcome." I blew across the top of my mug to cool the drink.

As predicted, Granny pulled the last few stitches from her afghan square. Her movements were slow and measured. In the silence, I sensed everyone's strained anticipation. Would Granny finally share the origin story of her conflict with Tildie? Or would she change the subject as she had before? The suspense was killing me. I knew my grandmother, though. The more you let her see your excitement, the longer it took for her to get to the point.

Granny's attention remained on her crocheted square. "All you want to know what happened between Tildie and me? I'll tell you."

Without comment, Mommy, Daddy, and Dev brought chairs from the relatively empty dining section. Daddy placed Mommy's and his chairs beside Granny. Dev sat next to me. Expectation hovered around us.

Granny laid what was left of the afghan square on the table in front of her and smoothed her palm over it. Her hand tensed, then relaxed. "Tildie and I had been friends since childhood."

Mommy shook her head. A puzzled frown creased her brow. "But the whole time Al and I were coming up, you two never spoke."

Granny blinked. "Della, let me tell the story, nuh?"

Mommy squeezed Granny's forearm where it rested on the table. "All right. I'm sorry, Mommy."

Satisfied, Granny settled back against her seat and started over.

"Tildie and I had been friends since childhood. We both

grew up poor, you know." Her tone held an edge of defensiveness as though her childhood still bothered her despite everything she'd accomplished. "We weren't able to go to university. So when we received our secondary certification, we applied for jobs at the post office. My parents said government jobs had strong benefits. By then, Winnie already had her government job and was helping the family financially. I wanted to do the same thing."

My grandmother had worked for the Grenville Post Office for more than forty years, longer than Dev and I had been alive. Her older sister, my great-aunt Winnifred, also had worked for the government for more than four decades. They'd each retired one year apart, with full benefits.

"The test was hard, you know." The look in Granny's eyes grew distant as she sank into her memories. "At first, Tildie and I had studied together, but she was restless. My father told me Tildie was a distraction and I should leave her to study on my own. So I did. She didn't like that."

Mommy harrumphed. "I'm sure she didn't, but Grandad was right. You needed to concentrate on the test."

"Oh, yes." Granny nodded. "My father was looking out for me."

Mommy squeezed her mother's forearm again. "Just as you always look out for us."

Granny blessed her with a smile. "The day of the test came and I felt good, you know. Prepared. I'd studied hard. My parents had quizzed me. After the test, I thought, 'I got this,' as the cool kids say today." Her smile faded. "Tildie looked as if she'd seen a ghost. But when the scores came back, Tildie had gotten perfect marks and I'd failed badly, oui."

Daddy gaped at her. "What?"

"Bunjay." Shocked, Mommy covered her mouth with her hand.

Dev leaned forward on his chair. "There must've been a mistake."

My eyes grew wide. "How was that possible?"

"Dev's right." Granny shook her head. "A mistake had been made. But you know, if it doesn't come out in the rinse, it will come out in the wash."

Granny was right. The truth always comes out in the end. I thought of Camille and prayed the same would apply to the investigation of her murder.

"What happened, Gran?" Dev prompted. He seemed as eager as I was to learn how the truth made it into the wash.

"Don't be so impatient, nuh." Granny took another sip of her tea. "The person who'd given the test was a friend of Tildie's family. I was sure she'd switched the scores."

"Oh, my goodness." Mommy shook her head in disgust. "So the woman lied for her."

"I couldn't prove it, but what other explanation could there be?" Granny spread her arms. "I made such a fuss, carrying on. I refused to leave until I received justice. Finally, the office agreed to have Tildie and me take the test a second time, and one of the postal directors would monitor it personally. Tildie was furious, but so was I. It was the same test. I made a hundred percent. Tildie failed."

"Oh-ho!" Daddy applauded. "And what did Tildie have to say to that?"

Granny's sniff was the sound of disdain. "She tried to make excuses. In the end, the truth was she'd been too lazy to study and instead had tried to take my place. She lied to me and about me, and for that, I told her I'd never speak to her again."

"You just walked away?" I asked.

"That's right." Granny shrugged. "I didn't speak with her again until I came to the States." She hesitated, lowering her eyes to the mutilated afghan square. "But we're older now, you know. Maybe it's time to let go of the bitterness and resentments of the past and make peace with her."

The idea lifted a weight from my shoulders. I didn't like to see my grandmother upset. "If you're ready, Granny. Ms. Robinson seems to be making an effort, too."

Mommy sighed. "I never knew any of this. I never even thought to ask."

Daddy stood, helping Mommy to her feet. "Desperation is a strong motivator."

As I watched Daddy and Dev return the chairs to their respective tables in the dining area, my mind drifted back to Manny, Camille, and our homicide inquiry. Daddy was right. Desperation was a powerful motivating force. It's been known to lead to murder, which prompted me again to wonder who had been desperate enough to kill Camille.

CHAPTER 13

We'd needed all hands on deck to serve the lunch custom-ers Thursday afternoon. In addition to online and phone orders, we had guests lining up outside the store. Mommy and Daddy had kept the meals moving with a kitchen cho-reography they'd perfected over decades of marital bliss. They were used to cooking for large groups, feeding family and friends for holidays, birthdays, reunions, and other get-togethers.

Since no one could read Dev's handwriting, Granny transcribed the requests coming over the phone while Dev printed those generated online. I took care of the patrons in the bakery and processed the pickup orders.

Like many of the shopkeepers in the neighborhood, Spice Isle Bakery was playing DragonFlyZ's benefit CD continuously. The bakery was fragrant with the aromas of steamed vegetables; fried plantains; and stew, jerk, and curry meats. There'd been a lot of familiar faces from the festival, including the father whose children had a weak-ness for coconut drops and the couple who'd kept coming back for more beef patties. The afternoon had been hectic and I'd loved every minute of it. We'd kept up with the orders, and our customers had left happy.

A warm glow of success surrounded me as I wiped the

plastic jar of paper butterflies with an antiseptic towel. The display did seem to be bringing us luck. Finally. If our bakery continued to do this well, we may need to add more butterflies.

The bell above the door chimed. Thrilled by the possibility of even more patrons, I looked up with a bright smile. It dimmed when I recognized the *Brooklyn Daily Beacon* crime beat reporter.

"José, what brings you in this afternoon?" I'd begun to identify the differences in his expression when he wanted food versus information. The look on his face pointed to the latter. I set down the container of butterflies and braced myself.

"Good afternoon, Ms. Bain." He tipped his head toward my grandmother, who was working on another lavender-and-white afghan square at her table.

Granny glanced up. "Hello, José."

The reporter turned his charm on me. "Yo, Lynds."

I wasn't impressed. "It's still 'Lyndsay.'"

He feigned a wince as he approached the counter. "I'm not there yet?"

"You used your *news* stories to try my mother in the court of public opinion." I used air quotes when I said "news." "You will *never* be there."

"Really?" He brushed his Superman curl off his forehead. "Then how're you able to work with the detective who investigated your mother for murder?"

I returned his smug look with narrowed eyes. "What makes you think I'm working with the police?"

Granny's snort of derision didn't help protect my cover.

José's smile grew. "Your bakery's a great place to get news tips. Your regulars are plugged into the community and they enjoy sharing their knowledge with an attentive audience. I've got to make sure none of my competitors find out about this place."

That wasn't the worst thing a person could say about our bakery. Our guests were well informed. That was because they were nosy. Their interest was driven by concern, though. They cared about my family because we were a part of their community.

"You know the rules, José. No loitering in our bakery." I stepped back from the counter and gestured toward the menu on the wall above the pass-through window. "Either place an order or go home."

The reporter flashed a smile at my parents on the other side of the window. "Good afternoon, Mr. and Ms. Murray."

Daddy inclined his head. "Afternoon."

Mommy smiled. "Hello, José. What can we get for you today?"

José made a quick review of the bakery's offerings. "I'll take a banana pudding. Thank you." He pulled his wallet from the back pocket of his sandstone slacks. He'd paired them with a cool blue short-sleeved shirt and silver tie. "So who do you and Detective Jackson like for Camille Abbey's death?"

I wrapped his banana pudding in a green Spice Isle Bakery bag. "I can't talk about an open investigation." I'd wanted to say those words for a long time.

As an innocent suspect, I'd been devastated each time my name had appeared in an article about a homicide case. Based on that experience, I didn't want to be the one to put an innocent person in the center of the murder inquiry.

José sighed. "You've got to give me *something*, Lyndsay. DragonFlyZ is a really popular group with a lot of local fans. Their audience is growing up and down the East Coast—and in the Caribbean. Their fans all want to know what happened to their lead singer. What *can* you tell me?"

I shook my head. "I'm sorry, José, but I don't know if I can tell you anything. You should speak with Bryce."

José handed me his credit card as I gave him the bag. "What about the tall Black man who was walking around the park with Camille right before she died? Are the police questioning him?"

"You mean my grandson?" Granny's words were cool. "No, they're not."

I turned from the cashier and handed José his credit card and purchase receipt. "For once the detectives aren't investigating anyone in my family."

"Is that because Jackson's trying to get on your good side?" José placed the bag on the counter while he pocketed his receipt and returned his card to his wallet.

"Oh-ho." Granny chuckled.

I ignored Granny and glared at José. "No, it's because my relatives aren't murderers. My cousin Manny couldn't have killed Camille. He was with Granny and me when Camille was attacked. And Manny was the first person to raise the alarm that Camille's death wasn't an accident."

"I did some research on DragonFlyZ." José collected his purchase. "Camille Abbey's family said she was going to leave the band to start a solo career."

"We knew that." Granny's comment sounded more like a boast than an agreement.

I swallowed a sigh. "Manny and I spoke with them the other day. They know the detectives are investigating Camille's death."

José and Granny exchanged a look. It was as though they were competing with each other to see who knew more about the case. "Did you know Camille and Miles Tosh, the lead guitarist, recently broke up?"

"Yes, we did." Granny's eyes glinted with satisfaction.

I shook my head at their antics. "His grief over Camille's death seems genuine." ·

José arched an eyebrow at Granny. "All right. Did you know Camille wanted to get rid of the band's manager?"

Granny exchanged a look with me before responding. "No, we didn't."

José's dark eyes gleamed with victory. "One of our entertainment reporters told me Camille didn't think Karlisa Trotter was doing enough to promote DragonFlyZ. The final straw was when Karlisa tried to talk the band out of doing the charity CD."

I frowned. "Why? Because she wouldn't get paid?"

The album was raising a lot of money for the islands, many of which were still struggling in the wake of floods, hurricanes, and other natural disasters. The funds would support local food banks, and help pay for repairs to the countries' infrastructure, hospitals, and schools. It was a wonderful way for the community to support their birth countries. In addition, the CD was giving the band a lot of exposure with strong sales nationally and internationally.

"That's right." José nodded. "Every cent was going to various nonprofit organizations. When Karlisa tried to block the project, Camille wanted to fire her right then and there."

"Woi." Granny's eyebrows leaped up her forehead. "So what stopped her?"

"Karlisa did." José flashed a grin. "At the last minute, she had a change of heart. I guess supporting the benefit project was a better option than losing an up-and-coming client on the verge of becoming the next big reggae sensation."

Granny and I watched José leave the shop.

Granny broke her silence first. "Remember, with Ca-mille's death, it's not just the charity CD sales that are spiking. Their other albums are selling through the roof, too. Do you think Karlisa would kill for money?"

"Maybe. Maybe not." My mind raced with the possi-bilities. "But she might kill to keep her job. And with Ca-mille out of the way, she has a better chance of doing that. I think it's time we asked DragonFlyZ's manager where she'd been at the time of Camille's death."

"All you think Camille was pushed?" Ena Sorter, Dragon-FlyZ's backup singer, frowned. A trace of impatience threaded through her Trini accent. "Camille was clumsy. She probably tripped over her own feet and fell."

Bryce's eyebrows bounced up his broad sienna forehead. "A New York State–certified medical examiner disagrees with you."

Bryce and I sat with Ena at her kitchen table late Fri-day morning. Bryce had picked me up at the bakery right after our morning rush. The air conditioning in our host-ess's small apartment struggled against the heat of a New York City summer. I felt overdressed in my tan shorts and sea blue Spice Isle Bakery T-shirt. Beads of sweat formed on my brow and above my lips. This made me appreciate the tall glasses of pineapple juice on ice that she'd served us even more.

Ena taught high school English. Her summer break had started the Friday before the Caribbean American Heri-tage Festival. She was about my age, maybe a couple of years older. I considered her from the shiny black curls that framed her thin face to the scoop-necked blue, green, and yellow diamond-patterned sleeveless blouse that complemented her warm brown skin. I recognized

Ena. I'd gone to school with a dozen people just like her. Bullies. Angry. Sullen. Taking their disappointment out on everyone around them, regardless of whether the bystander had anything to do with their perceived injustice. My heart battered against my chest in a combination of nervousness and residual anger for all the years of torment from tyrants like her.

I sipped the ice-cold juice and tried to distract myself with a visual scan of her bronze-and-white kitchen. The space was cramped, but clean and sunny. A little oakwood plaque hung on the wall above the entrance. Against a white background, the brown cursive text read: "Bless this House, Oh, Lord, we pray. Make it safe by night and day." My family had a similar prayer in our kitchen. Perhaps like our kitchen, this room was the heart of Ena's home.

Ena kissed her teeth. "And who do you think killed her, then?"

"That's what we wanted to ask you." Bryce returned Ena's intense stare as he flipped to a blank page in his notebook. I wondered if I should start carrying one. Despite his dark blue jacket, cobalt blue tie, and tan collared shirt, he seemed as cool and calm as an ocean breeze. Not a bead of sweat on him. Maddening. "Do you know if Camille had had disagreements with anyone recently?"

"Camille and I, we were in a band together. We weren't friends." Ena searched Bryce's face. Beneath the irritation in her eyes, I recognized a glint of interest. I told myself I wasn't jealous. But I knew I was lying.

"That's strange." I angled my chin. "Miles said the band members were all friends."

"That's not surprising." Ena's scowl deepened. "Miles is delusional. Everybody knows that."

I nodded as though I understood. I didn't. I faked a

smile for the backup singer. "You have a beautiful singing voice. Did you sing in your church choir?"

"Thank you." The tension around Ena eased a bit. "And yes, I sang in my church choir for years." Her eyes took in my T-shirt and shorts with blatant skepticism. "Is that some kind of new detective uniform?"

I ignored her question. "It must've upset you when the band sided with Miles to make Camille their new lead singer and you her backup."

"Of course it upset me." Sparks glittered in Ena's wide dark eyes. "How're they going to replace me? I was with the band since before we had a band, *a whole year* before Camille. And after all that, they shoved me to the back like I'm not good enough? Like I don't have any feelings? Chutz."

"So you *did* resent her?" Bryce sat still and attentive for her response.

"Not enough to kill her." Ena glared at him. Every hint of interest in him had faded from her eyes. He had that effect on people. "The last time I saw Camille, she was alive." Ena's voice broke. "We were putting the equipment back in Earl's van."

Bryce wrote in his notebook. "Where were you between one thirty and three last Saturday?"

Ena used her fingertips to surreptitiously dry her eyes. "Detective, I don't keep track of where I am every minute of every day. Do you?" She moved her shoulders in a quick, jerky shrug. "After our set, we packed our equipment and instruments into Earl's van. Then I walked around the festival for a while until I left around dinnertime."

Bryce tapped his pen against his notepad. "Can anyone corroborate that?"

Miles and Ena had similar timelines. But Miles's interview and photo session with the reporter gave him an alibi from approximately one o'clock until a little after three.

Ena kissed her teeth again. "I need alibis now?" She paused as though thinking. "I was with Horace and Geoff right after we packed up the van."

Horace Bond was DragonFlyZ's bass guitarist and Geoff Rolle played rhythm guitar.

Bryce wrote that down. "And the three of you were together until three PM?"

"I *said* I don't *know* the exact *times,* Detective." Ena glared as she watched Bryce add information to his notebook. "I walked with them for a while after our set. Then I walked on my own until I ran into Earl and his girlfriend. I was with them when we . . . when we heard about Camille."

I frowned as I remembered Camille telling Manny she was going back to speak with her bandmates. "Are you sure you didn't see Camille again before you left the park?" From the corner of my eye, I saw Bryce give me a quick look before returning his attention to Ena.

"That's what I said, isn't it?" Ena shared her scowl between me and Bryce. "I don't know why you're spending all this time looking at me. Are you going to question the other members of the band like this?"

Ena's tone was acidic. In the past, she would've intimidated me, stripping off at least one layer of skin. But not anymore. The successes of the past year—launching a bakery, catching two murderers, and defending myself and my grandmother against killers—had given me more confidence. Ena could continue her angry bear impersonation. I wasn't going to back down from finding justice for Camille.

I held her eyes. "If we need to."

Bryce intervened. "This is a murder investigation, Ms. Sorter. We're going to follow up on every lead."

Ena's eyes narrowed with suspicion. "What *led* you to me?"

Bryce searched Ena's face. "How badly do you want your spot back as lead singer of DragonFlyZ?"

"Miles was a fool!" Ena flung the words at Bryce. "It was obvious Camille was only interested in him because she wanted him to make *her* the lead singer. As soon as she got what she wanted, she wasn't interested in him anymore."

That didn't sound right. "Camille had been the lead singer for two years. She and Miles broke up just six months ago."

Ena shook her head, setting her curls bouncing around her cheeks and chin. "She still used him."

Bryce lowered his notepad. "That doesn't change the fact that with Camille gone, you'd be the logical choice to take over as DragonFlyZ's lead singer again."

"You can't be serious." Ena's frown drew shadows around her eyes and creased her brow. "We've had three CDs, including the charity one. Camille was the lead singer on *two* of those, the benefit and the one before that. I can't stand up in front of the microphone now like a dog, taking Camille's scraps."

When she put it that way, I could see her point. Still . . . "You'd really rather a *new* singer join the band and take the lead while you remain as the backup?"

"Who said I was staying with the band?" Ena raised her chin. Her voice was cooler than her air-conditioning system.

I searched her eyes. "Are you thinking of going solo?"

"Yes." Ena shrugged a shoulder. "So was Camille."

Bryce exchanged a confused look with me. "How did you know that? The only person Camille told outside of her family was Miles."

"Are you kidding?" Ena laughed. "Miles can't keep a secret. Everybody knows that. When Camille told Miles she was leaving DragonFlyZ, she told the band."

Well, Ena had taken the wind out of our sails. If she was telling the truth, we had to either remove her from our suspect list—or determine whether she had a different motive.

"Who else knows you're thinking of leaving the band?" Bryce's expression and tone were unreadable.

"I'm not *thinking* of leaving. I'm leaving." Ena crossed her arms and legs. "But I haven't told anyone I've made a decision yet, so you can't, either. All right?"

"All right." Bryce nodded.

"I promise," I said.

Ena hesitated as though she didn't believe us. "I'm sick of being a member of a band. I want to be in the spotlight. I want to make my own decisions on my career instead of putting what everyone else wants above what I want."

Bryce drained his drink. "Will you ask Karlisa Trotter to be your manager?"

"Karlisa?" Ena rolled her eyes. "No. Camille was right. I want a manager who does more than book nightclubs and collect money. Besides, when I told her I was thinking of going solo, she tried to talk me out of it."

I frowned. "Why?"

"I don't know." Ena shrugged. "She and Camille were butting heads more and more. The final straw was the charity album. I think she thought Camille would get rid of her if she didn't get Camille out first."

Really?

Bryce and I looked at each other. I saw the gleam of curiosity in his hazel eyes. Ena had given Karlisa another motive to kill Camille.

CHAPTER 14

It had been a long day, between managing the increase in customers at the bakery and investigating a murder. Spending quality time with my family always reenergized me.

We'd gathered around the combined tables Friday evening for our dinner meeting. Everyone had pitched in to clean up after our meal of stew chicken, coo-coo, and garden salad that Mommy, Daddy, Dev, and I had prepared. By "everyone," I meant Manny, Reena, Uncle Al, Aunt Inez, Uncle Roman, *and* Bryce. The detective had rolled up his sleeves to load the dishwasher. It seemed only fair to invite him. I wanted there to be transparency and full disclosure with our investigation. I also wanted to loan him my copy of DragonFlyZ's benefit CD so he could familiarize himself with their work.

Whenever we got together as a family, we discussed our days, current events, and New York sports. It was only after we'd relaxed, caught up with one another, and finished our meal that Bryce and I provided an update on the investigation.

"Are you learning a lot working with Lynds?" Granny sat beside Bryce. Her expression was earnest.

Oh, brother.

My neck muscles knotted. I rolled it to release the tension. I didn't want Bryce to be uncomfortable in my family's company. Would he realize Granny was teasing?

Was she teasing?

Uncle Roman's boisterous laughter cut off whatever response Bryce would've made. "Of course he is." He leaned into the table to look past Granny seated between the two men. He gestured toward Bryce. "How much you wanna bet she solves the case before you? Again."

"This isn't a competition." Bryce smiled with confidence.

Uncle Roman snorted. "Says you."

Bryce continued. "I'm grateful for Lyndsay's help and insights on this case."

"Thank you, Bryce." I jumped into the discussion before it got any further out of hand. From where I stood in front of the tables, I gestured toward the presentation board to my right and the names I'd added across the top. "So far, we have three possible suspects: Miles Tosh, Camille's ex-boyfriend and songwriting partner. He's also the lead guitarist for DragonFlyZ."

Bryce scanned the open page in his notebook. "His motive could be jealousy. Camille had broken up with him. It also could be jealousy over Camille getting more credit for their songwriting. She wrote most of the songs the band recorded, which meant she made more money than him."

"Camille said they'd broken up around January." Manny glanced between his parents seated at the foot of the table and Reena on his left. "That was before they'd started recording the benefit album. Her family said she thought he was too controlling."

Bryce met my eyes. "Miles still had feelings for Camille.

He claimed he wouldn't have killed her for breaking up with him. He was convincing."

I gave Manny an uneasy look as Miles's words repeated in my mind, *Not angry enough to push Camille. I might have pushed Manson.*

"He could've been faking." Reena crossed her arms over her warm gold sleeveless cotton blouse.

"I don't think he was." Tapping my chin, I let images of Camille, Miles, Ena, and Karlisa play across my mind. "Manny, you said you'd felt tension in the band during the recording sessions. Did you sense any specifically between Miles and Camille?"

Manny started nodding before I finished speaking. "He'd been cool to her, like he was sulking."

Bryce braced his elbow on the table as he rubbed his chin. "That tracks. He seems like a sulker."

Manny shifted to face the detective. "Camille said they'd been drifting apart for a while."

I gestured again toward our makeshift murder board. "Ena Sorter is the former lead singer. The band voted to replace her with Camille. Now she's its backup singer. And there's a period of time when she was walking alone at the festival."

Bryce turned the page in his notebook. "Obviously, her motive could be that she wants her position as lead singer back."

"But." I raised my right index finger. "We learned today that Ena knew Camille was leaving the band, so that blows our theory."

Manny's brow furrowed with confusion. "Her family said, outside of them, the only person who knew she was leaving was Miles."

Bryce turned to Manny. "Ena said everyone knows Miles can't keep a secret."

"Really?" Mommy's eyebrows leaped up her forehead. "Then did Camille tell Miles so he would tell the band and Karlisa?"

Bryce cocked his head. "That's a good question, Ms. Murray."

Manny dragged both hands over his hair. "But why would she do that? Why wouldn't she just tell the band herself?"

We all looked at Manny and one another. The confusion in the room was thick enough to slice with a serrated knife.

"Maybe she wasn't as certain about leaving the band as her family thought." Ideas were flooding my mind. "Maybe she wanted to know how the band would react before she made a final decision. Depending on their reaction, she could claim Miles misunderstood her, then she could stay with the band without being embarrassed."

"What kind of reaction did she want?" Aunt Inez leaned forward on Manny's right, folding her arms on the table. Like Uncle Al, she'd come to the bakery straight from work. She wore a pale gold shell blouse with black slacks. Her deep emerald jacket hung on the back of her chair.

"I don't know." I shook my head. "Maybe if the band was upset about her leaving, she'd use that to push them into firing Karlisa in exchange for her staying."

Bryce's deep-set eyes glinted with admiration. "That's a good hypothesis."

Granny nudged him with her elbow. "You're learning a lot, eh?"

Dev gestured toward the board. "Tell us about Karlisa Trotter."

I inclined my head in gratitude for his changing the subject. Granny was incorrigible. "The band's manager had a tense relationship with Camille."

Manny nodded. "That's true."

I continued. "Camille was trying to convince her bandmates to fire Karlisa. We also suspect Karlisa was taking money from the band, based on the parts of the argument between them that we overheard at the festival."

Bryce wrote something in his notebook. "We need to check Ena's and Miles's alibis."

I made a note on my to-do list. "Miles said he'd been doing an interview with the *Beacon* when he'd heard about Camille's accident. I'll ask José to verify Miles's alibi with his colleague."

Bryce interrupted me. "I can do that."

Startled by the tension in his voice, I looked at him. "The reporter's José's colleague. It won't be any trouble for him to ask. And he'll be here tomorrow morning with the Saturday breakfast crowd. He's a regular."

Bryce didn't look up from his notebook. "I'll be at the bakery tomorrow, too. I should verify Miles's alibi myself, not José. So I'll speak with him. You don't need to."

Reena and Granny snickered. I ignored them.

Shrugging, I made a note that Bryce would follow up with José. "Fine. I'll verify Ena's alibi with a friend at the gym. She's dating the drummer and can tell me whether Ena was with them when they learned Camille had died." I glanced at Bryce. "Unless you're also going to be at the gym?"

The chuckles rose from the tables again. Everyone turned to Bryce.

Uncle Roman threw back his head and laughed. "Oh-ho. Are you sure you're up for the challenge of crossing words with Lynds?"

Bryce smiled, meeting my eyes. "I'd appreciate it if you could verify Ena's alibi, and I'll check Miles's."

Snatches of conversation I'd heard between the manager and Camille sounded in my ear, *You* knew*! . . . borrowed . . . cheated us!*

I searched out Manny, Reena, Dev, and Granny at the table. "Camille had argued with Karlisa during the festival. Do you remember?"

Dev frowned. "But there was a significant gap of time between the argument and news of Camille's accident."

Reena narrowed her eyes, perhaps picturing the circumstances around the two events. "Karlisa could've run into her a second time and they'd started arguing again."

Granny scanned the room. "One of the CAAS board members has known Karlisa since school days. She said in high school there was a rumor Karlisa was arrested for assaulting another student, someone who'd lived in her neighborhood."

Mommy's eyes grew wide. Her lips parted with surprise. "Karlisa Trotter has a record?"

Uncle Roman leaned forward to look at Bryce. "How come you didn't know that?"

Bryce seemed disconcerted. Uncle Roman had that effect on people who didn't know him. And some people who knew him. "Juvenile records are sealed."

Granny grinned at Bryce beside her. "So you learned something today."

Bryce's lean cheeks turned pink, yet his full lips curved in a good-natured smile. "Yes, I did. This explains how you've been able to solve these cases. You have great connections in the community."

Uncle Roman leaned back against his chair. "And common sense."

I struggled not to laugh at Granny's and Uncle Roman's self-satisfied expressions. I didn't want to add to Bryce's discomfort. I caught his eye. "I think we should speak with Karlisa tomorrow."

He nodded his agreement.

I knew better than most that an argument didn't necessarily lead to murder. But Karlisa had a history of violence. Had history repeated itself, this time with deadly consequences?

"She hit me first." DragonFlyZ's manager glared at Bryce and me with righteous indignation. Her Bajan accent snapped in her words. "That part of the story always gets lost in the telling of my fight with my classmate."

Karlisa might be in her forties. She looked professional in a deep citrus orange skirt suit that she'd accessorized with a chunky gold necklace and matching earrings. Her jacket hung over the back of her chair at the head of the table. In four-inch gold stilettos, she was almost as tall as Bryce's six-foot-plus height. Bryce and I were meeting with Karlisa late Saturday morning at Caribbean Tunes. The recording studio where Manny worked had made a small conference room available for us. Our meeting here seemed odd. Did Karlisa work out of a home office? If so, was it by choice or because her business operated on a tight budget?

Manny had been excited to have landed a job with the up-and-coming studio five years ago. It was his dream come true and our families couldn't have been prouder of him. He'd given us a tour of the facility shortly after he'd been hired. Caribbean Tunes was making a name for itself with a growing number of local recording companies as well as individual artists. Manny loved working with the talent. His enthusiasm had grown as he'd advanced in his career.

When we'd first entered the conference room, Bryce had seemed mesmerized by our surroundings. Vivid album covers from various reggae, soca, ska, and calypso artists were framed and displayed around the room, providing waves of color to break up the plain foam white walls. Recessed lighting focused on the images, seeming to bring them to life.

Six dark wood chairs ringed the matching rectangular table. The chairs were simple but sturdy with soft gold-and-crimson pillows on the seats and against the backs. Lavender candles scented the air. Their aroma was meant to enhance creativity.

At the gym this morning, I'd asked Rocky about Ena's whereabouts after the band's festival performance. Ena had told the truth about being with Rocky and Earl when they'd learned Camille had died. And Bryce had verified that Ena had toured the festival with Horace and Geoff right after packing the van. However, the backup singer had been on her own for a period of time before joining Rocky and Earl. Bryce also had checked Miles's alibi. The *Brooklyn Daily Beacon* reporter had confirmed she'd interviewed Miles for more than an hour, then taken several photos of him.

Bryce continued. "You don't deny that you've been known to have violent outbursts."

Karlisa's professionally plucked eyebrows strained toward her hairline. Her makeup was a little heavy-handed. "When I was a *child*. Now that I'm an adult, I don't conduct myself like that. Past experience taught me violence isn't worth it."

"All right, Karlisa." I held up my hands, palms out, hoping to ease the manager's anxiety. "But you and Camille had argued during the festival. What was that about?"

"Don't you work at that bakery on Parish Avenue?" She

looked suspiciously from me to Bryce and back. "Why's a baker here with the bo-bo, questioning me?"

Self-conscious, I touched my plantain green Spice Isle Bakery T-shirt. I started to speak, but Bryce answered first.

"Ms. Murray has agreed to consult with us because of her connections with the Little Caribbean community." His tone was firm, leaving no room for additional questions. I was both flattered and embarrassed by the admiration in his voice.

Karlisa gave him a mocking smile. "You mean because she was able to solve two murders before you? I can see why you'd want her help." She turned back to me. "Who told you Camille and I had words?"

"My family and I saw you arguing with her. We also heard you." I watched Karlisa, searching for a reaction. "I heard Camille say you knew about something. She accused you of cheating 'us.' I think by 'us' she meant the band. And you were asking her to listen to you. What were you talking about?"

Karlisa kissed her teeth. She crossed her legs and looked away.

Bryce's expression was as solemn as a priest on Palm Sunday. "Ms. Trotter, we need you to answer the question. You can either give us your answer here or I can escort you through the studio to the station for obstructing a homicide investigation."

Sparks shot from Karlisa's eyes. "Camille accused me of cheating the band on payments from their appearances at Nutmeg's. All right? It was all a foolish misunderstanding."

I blinked at her. The thought of having a manager I couldn't trust with my money triggered my temper, but I forced myself to set those emotions aside and focus on Karlisa's explanation.

"Did you?" Bryce spoke without inflection.

Karlisa threw up her hands. "Chutz. It was an honest mistake, eh. I tried to explain that to Camille, but she wouldn't *listen*."

Skepticism was hard to shake off. "Was this the first time you'd made this type of mistake?"

Karlisa looked at me as though I'd slapped her. "You're acting like I *stole* the money. It was an *accident*. I told her I was going to make it right, you know. But, again, she wouldn't *listen*."

I pressed my lips together, shaking my head. "Ms. Trotter, you're talking about people's livelihood. DragonFlyZ worked hard for that money. Surely you can understand why she'd be upset—"

Karlisa bounced on her chair. "But, eh, you don't think *I* worked hard?"

I laughed my surprise. "Not as hard as the band. They're the ones writing the songs, performing—"

Bryce interrupted. "Ladies, could we get back to the investigation, please?"

Karlisa rolled her eyes at me as she turned her attention to Bryce. "What do you want to know?"

Bryce wrote something in his notebook. "Where were you between one and three PM during the festival?"

"I don't know. I wasn't studying the time. I was just wandering around, taking everything in." Karlisa twisted her neck, trying to read what Bryce was writing.

Bryce pulled his notepad closer to him. "So you were walking around at the time Camille was murdered, but you don't have anyone who can corroborate that?"

Karlisa's eyes shot to his face. Color drained from her brown cheeks. Her voice trembled. "That doesn't mean I killed her." She switched her attention to me. "Do you know how many people were at the festival? There must have been hundreds of people there. I never touched Camille."

I returned Karlisa's frightened stare. "Did the other band members know about the mistake you'd made with their money?"

Karlisa's throat muscles worked as she swallowed. Her voice was subdued. "I don't think so. Camille said she wanted to speak with me about it first."

The cold hand of foreboding gripped my shoulder. "Have you paid back the band's money?"

Karlisa's eyes wavered, then dropped. "Not yet."

I exchanged a look with Bryce, then met Karlisa's eyes again. "And now Camille's dead. There's no one to hold you to your promise to pay back the money you owe. Today's a week since her death."

Blood rushed back into Karlisa's cheeks. Her tension battered me like a windstorm. "Well, excuse me, yes. I've had a little bit more on my mind. I've been mourning Camille's death with her family and the rest of the band. There are appearances to cancel, events to reschedule. We were in the middle of contract negotiations with a new record company. But I'm going to pay them all the money I *mistakenly* kept from them by *accident,* including giving Camille's share to her parents."

I'd believe that once it happened. "But the money wasn't the only thing you and Camille had argued about. You knew she was trying to get the band to fire you."

Karlisa's jaw clenched. "I've been with the band from the beginning, longer than Camille had been with them. DragonFlyZ has five other members: Miles, Ena, Geoff, Horace, and Earl. I had the support of every other band member. Camille's the only one who ever complained about the way I was doing my job. Like she knew anything about it." She kissed her teeth again.

"Ms. Trotter." Bryce waited for her to pull her glare from me and give him her attention. "What were you wearing the day of the festival?"

Karlisa frowned. "What kind of cheeky question is that?"

Bryce sighed. "Ma'am, I understand the question may seem strange, but it's part of our investigation. What did you wear to the festival?"

I sensed her reluctance to respond. I didn't remember what Karlisa had worn while she was arguing with Camille. My muscles tensed as I waited for her answer.

Karlisa arched a condescending eyebrow. "I wore a short-sleeved pink blouse and black pants. The festival is a celebration, but I was there representing DragonFlyZ as its manager. I had to present myself accordingly."

So according to Karlisa, she wasn't wearing anything blue in color. I considered her narrowed eyes and tight lips. She was defiant. Could we believe her?

"Do you have any other questions, Lyndsay?" Bryce's question drew me from my speculations.

"No, thank you." I rose from the chair.

Karlisa stood, too. "Camille and I had our differences, but she didn't deserve to die like that, pushed down stairs like trash. I want you to find her killer, but it wasn't me. So don't waste your time looking in my direction."

I considered the band manager's stiff features. "Who do you think would have a motive to murder her?"

Karlisa narrowed her eyes. "Camille wasn't the sweetheart she wanted everyone to believe. She was always fussing at someone."

"Like whom?" Bryce asked, standing across the table from me.

Karlisa cut him a look. "The list is long."

Bryce held his pen above his notepad. "Is there one name that stands out?"

Karlisa crossed her arms over her bright white poly-ester shell blouse. "Sheryl Cross. She was very upset when Camille threatened to pull out of the festival if the Caribbean American Heritage Festival Association didn't pay DragonFlyZ more money."

I tried to hide my shock. This was news to me. Could that be the real reason the association president didn't want me investigating Camille's murder? How do we ask Sheryl about Karlisa's claim without upsetting my client?

CHAPTER 15

Manny's tension hovered over us like a duppy as he stood with Bryce and me in the alley between the recording studio and a sandwich shop late Saturday morning. I wanted to offer him encouragement. I wanted to reassure him we were close—so close—to identifying the person who'd killed his friend. But honestly, I'd be lying if I said anything like that.

The humidity wasn't helping my thought processes. It was the second day of July. The temperature hovered around unbearable. Typically, July's the hottest month in Brooklyn. I could co-sign that. The asphalt beneath my feet seemed to soak up the heat and spit it back up at me. Sweat pooled in my bra and trailed down my back. I wiped a few beads of perspiration from my forehead.

"How'd it go?" Manny's eyes swung from me to Bryce and back. His loose-fitting soft lilac short-sleeved jersey looked cool and comfortable.

Bryce stood beside me. His lightweight teal blue suit and navy tie were crisp and fresh. There wasn't a drop of sweat on him. Did he have a personal air conditioner? "Karlisa denied any involvement in Camille's death."

"Do you believe her?" Manny shoved his fists into the front pockets of his cotton khaki pants.

"No." Bryce shook his head.

"I'm not sure." I spoke at the same time.

"What d'you mean? She has motive and opportunity. Why're you hesitating?" Manny's brow furrowed with impatience and confusion. If we didn't solve this case soon, that frown would become permanent.

"I don't know." Perhaps a glass of ice water would help me think. "She didn't deny that she'd argued with Camille or downplay her resentment toward her. And she admitted she owed the band money."

Bryce was more confident in his position. Perhaps overconfident? "She has multiple motives, including the fact Camille was trying to get her fired, but she doesn't have an alibi for Camille's time of death."

I drew a breath, picking up the stench of exhaust fumes from the nearby traffic and asphalt from the alley. "Would she have admitted to those things if she was guilty? I don't think so. And she said she wore a pink blouse at the festival. The cloth the medical examiner found in Camille's fist is blue."

"She could be lying, Lynds." Manny stroked his chin. The look in his dark eyes was distant as though he was deep in thought.

I pulled my car keys from the front pocket of my navy walking shorts. I had to get out of this heat. "Did Camille say anything about the contract DragonFlyZ had signed with the Caribbean American Heritage Festival Association? Karlisa said Camille and Sheryl Cross had argued about it."

Manny was shaking his head before I'd finished speaking. I sensed him searching his mind for any hints of memory about the topic. "She didn't say anything to me about it. I never heard the band discussing it, either."

"That's all right." I held up my hand, palm out. "I'll check with the other band members."

Bryce corrected me. "*I'll* check with the other band members. I'm the lead detective on this case, remember? I appreciate your help, but I'll do the follow-up interviews."

"Yes, of course. But you'll let us know what they tell you, right?" While he spoke with the band members, maybe I'd call Sheryl Cross. Or maybe not. Sheryl was pretty ticked with me right now.

His hazel eyes glinted. "Yes, of course."

Was he mocking me? I couldn't tell. "I'm serious, Bryce. My family and I are committed to finding Camille's killer."

Bryce raised his hands in surrender. "I promise to keep you in the loop."

Manny's frustrated tone reclaimed my attention. "I didn't think it would take this long."

My eyes widened in surprise. For a moment, I forgot the heat. "Manny, it hasn't even been a week. Don't you remember how long the other cases took?"

"You're right." Manny scrubbed his face with both hands, then dropped his arms. "It's just you've already spoken with the top three suspects: Miles, Ena, and now Karlisa. I was sure it would be one of them, but you don't think so. Where does that put us?"

Bryce glanced at the studio behind my cousin. "I think it *is* one of those three. We have to find the evidence to bring them in."

I tensed as I sensed Bryce trying to rush the case. Seeing the hope in Manny's eyes, I couldn't bring myself to challenge the detective.

I put my hand on Manny's upper arm. His muscles were

tight beneath my fingertips. "Don't forget to eat the lunch Mommy prepared for you and all of it or the next phone call you get will be from Granny."

"I'll call to thank her as soon as I get back inside." Manny leaned closer to kiss my cheek before turning to Bryce. "Take care of my cousin." He matched his firm tone with an intimidating frown.

Bryce held his eyes. "I promise."

Oh, brother. The last two times, I'd taken care of myself. No one had ridden to my rescue. But I didn't bother to remind these two. They were having too much fun with their role-playing.

I gave Manny a final wave goodbye, then turned to walk with Bryce back to my car parked on a side street a couple of blocks away. Parking was no joke in Little Caribbean. We wove our way through the late-morning pedestrian traffic. We were so close, sometimes my shoulder rubbed against his upper arm. A few times, the backs of his fingers grazed mine.

Finally, my little orange four-door sedan came into view. I exhaled and activated the keyless entry. I waited for Bryce to buckle up on the front passenger seat before merging with traffic and steering my car in the direction of the police precinct.

"You're doing the same thing to Miles, Ena, and Karlisa that you did to me and my mother." Checking my rear mirror, I noted the tailgater behind me. Rolling my eyes, I tightened my grip on the steering wheel. The other driver would just have to deal with it. I wouldn't drive above the speed limit. Traffic tickets weren't in my budget.

Bryce's seat rustled as he shifted to face me. "What do you mean?" He didn't sound defensive, just curious. That was encouraging.

In return, I kept my tone even. "I felt you and Stan tried

to fit the crime to the suspects instead of the other way around. Neither of you was looking at the cases critically, which meant you missed a lot of questions."

Bryce hesitated. "What questions do you think I should be asking?"

Several questions popped into my mind. I picked a few of them. "Was the push that caused Camille's death an accident or was it deliberate?"

"What does that matter?" There was a shrug in his question. "Either way, it's murder."

I braked at a stop sign. "It speaks to the killer's motive. If it was an accident, there wasn't a motive. But if it was deliberate, then what benefit had the killer been after?"

"Of course, I knew that." Bryce's words came a little too quickly. "I just meant, whether or not the act was deliberate, it's still a crime."

That went without saying. Ignoring his comment, I eased my car forward, making sure the path was clear for me to cross the intersection. The tailgater blew his horn. Again, I refused to accommodate him. Car *maintenance* was in my budget. Car *collision repairs* were not. "Karlisa has a couple of strong motives, but she'd been wearing a pink blouse, not blue."

"Manny's right. She could be lying." Bryce's words were wry. "The killer would know Camille had torn their clothes as she fell. It's a good bet we'd have that piece of evidence. So when asked what were you wearing, you'd say your blouse was pink instead of blue."

"I think Ena's motive is the weakest." Reassured the intersection was clear, I drove through. "She's leaving DragonFlyZ because she was tired of being in a band. So she wouldn't have a reason to kill Camille."

"She could be lying."

Oh, brother.

I gave him the side eye. "You're beginning to sound paranoid."

"People do lie occasionally, Lyndsay, especially when they're guilty." He sounded amused.

"We don't know whether Ena, Miles, or Karlisa is guilty. Innocent people don't need to lie. My mother and I never did." I let a pointed pause linger.

The rustling sound came again. Bryce had shifted on his seat. "For the record, I never thought your mother was lying."

For pity's sake, had he thought *I'd* been lying? What was I supposed to do with that?

I shook off my irritation and unclenched my teeth. "We're missing something, Bryce. I can feel it."

"We'll figure it out." He paused. "You called me Bryce."

Frowning, I drove around a car that had double-parked illegally, then stopped at a red light. "When?"

"Just now." He caught my eyes. "Does that mean I'm forgiven for including you and your family on the suspect list of those two homicides?"

Forgive Bryce Jackson? "Not quite."

I tore my eyes from his and let them drift back to my view of the traffic signal through my windshield. I had a feeling forgiving Bryce would be like taking a gateway drug to distractions and other problematic behavior. I could only handle one dangerous situation at a time.

Saturday's lunch crowd had been another stressful, hectic, wonderful experience. The sweet scents of baked fruits, confectioners' sugar, melted butter, and fresh breads embraced us. Diners had been in a good mood, too, enjoying the afterglow of the Caribbean American Heritage Festival and the DragonFlyZ music flowing from our sound system. Several guests sang along with the recording.

Others danced as they waited in line. A few did both. It felt like a party. Most of our patrons had taken their purchases home to eat, but our dine-in customers were growing in number. It felt good knowing people enjoyed our shop enough to want to linger.

By late afternoon, customer traffic had slowed to a trickle. Granny, Mommy, Daddy, Dev, and I had time to catch our breath, and I was able to tell them about this morning's interview with Bryce and Karlisa.

"Manny called just before you returned from the studio." Mommy smiled at the memory. "He thanked me for making his lunch and promised to eat it."

"I'm glad." Before now, I hadn't realized how worried I'd been that my cousin wasn't eating. "I need to ask Sheryl Cross whether she and Camille had argued about Dragon-FlyZ's contract for the festival. Everyone Bryce and I've interviewed said there'd been tension between Karlisa and Camille. That makes Karlisa a very strong suspect. But Karlisa mentioned Camille arguing with Sheryl the day of the festival."

Daddy's eyebrows stretched toward his chef's hat. "You want to interview *Sheryl Cross* for murder?"

Granny harrumphed. "The woman who threatened to smear our shop if we investigated Camille's murder? *That* Sheryl Cross?"

"Don't you think that's suspicious?" I waved a hand toward my grandmother. "Maybe that's the reason she warned me away from investigating Camille's murder."

Crossing her arms, Mommy leaned back against the counter. "That's a good point."

Dev arched a thick dark brown eyebrow. His tone was skeptical. "How are you going to approach her? She's already angry with you. She thinks investigating the murder will make the festival look bad."

"I know." I rolled my eyes. That had to be the silliest reason anyone's ever been angry with me. "Getting her to talk about Camille's death is going to be tricky. But it's Saturday afternoon. I'll leave a message on her voicemail. Hopefully, she'll call me back Monday and by then I'll have a strategy for getting her to talk."

Leaving the customer service area in my family's more-than-capable hands, I went to the bakery's office and closed the door to call Sheryl in private. To my dismay, she answered the phone on the third ring.

"Caribbean American Heritage Festival Association. President Sheryl Cross speaking. How can I help you?"

Uh-oh. Now what do I do? "Good afternoon, Ms. Cross. It's Lyndsay Murray. I wasn't expecting you to be in the office today."

There was a brief hesitation before she responded. Her voice was sharp and curt. "I'm balancing the accounts from the festival last week. Are you calling to gloat?"

What was she talking about? "Excuse me?"

"The police ruled Camille's death a homicide." Tension rose in Sheryl's voice. "You were right, but now the festival is permanently marred by the fact that a *murder* happened in the park during the event."

My marketing-training response to Sheryl's panic was like a reflex. "You need to get in front of this, Ms. Cross, and control the narrative. Yes, someone was murdered during the festival. It's a terrible tragedy for Camille's friends, family, and the community as a whole. But don't let people stop there. Let everyone know you're helping the police with their investigation."

This time, the pause was more pensive than resentful. "I like that plan, but how do I get our narrative out?"

"I can help you with that. Draft a statement for the association. I'll review it and get it to José Perez, the *Bea-*

con's crime beat reporter." I was certain José would love to work at least part of the statement into his next update on the investigation into Camille's murder.

"That's very generous of you." Suspicion dripped from Sheryl's words. "You must want something in return."

The offer to help Sheryl frame the association's defense had come naturally to me. I hadn't expected anything in return. But I wasn't opposed to a quid pro quo. Maybe that's why I had that queasy, guilty feeling. "I'm on your side, Ms. Cross. I love the festival and don't want this tragedy to hurt its reputation. I didn't know Camille Abbey, but I can't imagine she'd want that, either."

"You're right. She wouldn't." Sheryl's heavy sigh carried down the phone. "I'll take you up on your offer of help, if you don't mind. That would be one less thing from this nasty murder business for me to worry about."

Her words stoked my curiosity. "Of course I don't mind. Send me your statement whenever you're ready. What else are you worried about?"

"Suppose we're sued?" Sheryl almost shouted the words. I pictured her throwing up her hands in agitation. "People are so ready to jump up and file lawsuits, oui. Suppose her family sues us for not having security at the festival?"

An image of Camille's grieving family came into focus in my mind. "I don't think Camille's family's going to sue your association. I think they have other things on their mind right now. But if something does happen, I know an exceptional corporate lawyer who could help you."

"You do?" Hope sprang into Sheryl's words.

I smiled. "Yes, he's my brother. I don't think you'll need him, but if you do, you could reach him at this number."

Her sigh of relief rolled into my ear. "Oh, thank you, Lyndsay. I really appreciate your help and advice. If I need a lawyer, I'll call your brother. And I'll send over a statement for you to review in the morning, if that's OK?"

"Of course. That'll be fine." I sat straighter on my chair, tightening my grip on the telephone receiver. "Ms. Cross, I'd actually called to ask you something. Is it true DragonFlyZ wasn't satisfied with your festival contract?"

"Who told you that?" Once more, her tone sharpened with suspicion.

I had to think fast again. I needed to protect my sources, even if that source was a suspect in Camille's murder. Little Caribbean didn't think kindly of people who gave up their informants. No one in the community wanted to lose access to the fertile grapevine. "Word on the street's that you and Camille had argued about the contract."

Sheryl grunted. "Karlisa didn't show the band the contract until Friday night. Camille was surprised that the amount was so low, but I told her that was the amount Karlisa had agreed to."

I frowned my confusion. "Didn't Karlisa and the band agree to the amount before she signed the contract?"

"Apparently not." Her tone was dry. "But I had the emails Karlisa and I had exchanged to negotiate the amount. And why would she wait until the night before to show the band the amount? That didn't make any sense. But when Camille told me she was disappointed, I told her to speak with Karlisa."

My shoulders slumped with disappointment. Karlisa hadn't told us that.

CHAPTER 16

"Do you know what happens when the douens come out to play?" Granny asked Reggie and his little sister, Rita.

The siblings were casually dressed in bright T-shirts and dark shorts. They'd joined Granny at her dark wood folding table just after the lunch rush Saturday afternoon. Rita sat on the chair across from my grandmother. Her brother stood behind her.

Reggie was the older sibling. I was pretty sure he was starting his second year of high school in the fall. His younger sister, Rita, looked to be nine years old. They were both slender with dark brown skin and wide ebony eyes. Their family resemblance was strong, especially when they smiled, as they were doing now.

Reggie and Rita lived within walking distance of my family. They were on summer break but still came into our bakery several times a week. They always purchased enough pastries or hot meals to bring home to their family, but I suspected the real attraction was my grandmother's storytelling. I understood the appeal. I loved my granny's stories. She'd entertained Dev and me with them every year when we'd visit her in Grenada and when she'd come to Brooklyn to stay with us. Dev and I had heard all of her adventures, some more than once. But we never grew tired of them.

Mommy, Daddy, Dev, and I lingered around the counter, waiting for today's tale. But Granny's mention of the douens transformed my excitement into dread. The douens were characters from Caribbean folklore. They lived in the forests and wooded areas and were said to be the spirits of babies who'd died before their baptism. Just from that description, you know nothing good can come from these beings.

Their most notable features were their straw hats and backward feet. That's right: their feet faced backward. And their faces were blank except for their mouth. They didn't have eyes or a nose. Who told children stories with creatures like that?

I'd been Rita's age when Granny first told Dev and me about her and Great-aunt Winnie encountering a douen. That had led to weeks of troubled sleep, jumping at every creak and bump in the night. Twenty years later, I still shivered at the memory.

Even if nine-year-old Rita could handle the story, I couldn't. "Granny, could we hear the story of Papa Bois? That one has more adventure."

Rita beamed with excitement. "Ooh! I'd like to hear an adventure. Could you tell us the one about Papa Bois?"

I leaned against the customer counter, almost weak with relief. Dev and I exchanged hand slaps. Mommy and Daddy exhaled.

"Of course." Granny's expression grew serious. "Forests are dangerous, dark, mysterious places, you know. Hungry animals lurk in the trees and behind the bushes. Vicious snakes slither in the grass. And spirits—good and evil—are everywhere."

With every syllable Granny spoke, Rita's eyes grew

wider. Reggie leaned closer as though to catch Granny's every word.

Granny's hypnotic tone kept her audience's attention. "But it's not just wild animals, venomous reptiles, and treacherous ghosts that all you will find in the forests. Papa Bois lives there, too."

"Who is he?" Rita's voice squeaked with impatience.

"What does he look like?" Reggie's words were low and grave.

"Papa Bois is the Father of the Forest. He has the head and torso of a man. He's older, but still tall and muscular." Granny straightened her shoulders and flexed her biceps. "His eyes are big and round. And his hair is long, thick, and curly. But from his hips down, Papa Bois's shaped like a goat—"

"What?" Rita's jaw dropped. Her eyes were wide and staring.

Granny nodded. "Yes, nuh. His hips and legs are just as a goat's. His legs are bent and his feet are cloven hooves. He has two horns growing from his head." She used her fingers to sketch the horns above her silver bun. "He's covered head to toe with short, brown, coarse hair. And he smells *bad*."

"Like garbage?" Rita's words floated on a breath. Her lips barely moved.

"Or rotted meat?" Reggie offered that comparison with a suspicious amount of glee.

"Worse." Granny was emphatic.

Reggie frowned. "What's worse than rotted meat or garbage?"

Granny raised her eyebrows. "Papa Bois."

Reggie and Rita laughed. Mommy, Daddy, Dev, and I chuckled, too.

Granny continued. "Now, Papa Bois is the Father of the

Forest. He protects all the animals and plants in all the forests."

Rita interrupted. "Even Prospect Park?"

The little girl's question impressed me. Granny seemed impressed, too.

Her dark eyes gleamed. "*All* of the forests. It's a *big* responsibility and one he takes *very* seriously. If you cut down a tree or a bush, or you take any of the plants from the forest, Papa Bois will come for you."

"And do what?" Reggie asked.

Granny looked at him in surprise. "People disappear all the time in the forest, oui. If you cause harm to anything or anyone in the forest, Papa Bois will get you."

Reggie and Rita exchanged uneasy looks. Humph! If they think this is bad, they def couldn't handle the douens.

Granny leaned into her table. "Papa Bois carries a horn that he blows to warn the animals when hunters are near. He can outrun any animal in the forest, even deer. And he's a shape-shifter, you know. He can turn himself into any animal: bear, snake, bird, wolf. Anything. That's how he lures hunters deep, deep into the woods so they will never be heard from again."

Reggie studied Granny with narrowed eyes. "Ms. Bain, have you ever seen Papa Bois or are you just telling us what you've heard?"

Granny leaned back against her chair and pressed a hand to her heart as though the young man's question wounded her. "I've seen him with my own eyes." She used the index and second fingers of her right hand to point to her dark brown eyes. "How else d'you think I know how he smells?"

Her young audience gaped at her before recovering their speech at the same time.

"When did you see him?" Rita demanded.

"What happened?" Reggie asked.

The look in Granny's eyes grew distant as though she were no longer in our cheerful little bakery with its gold, green, and red décor and blond wood furnishings. Instead, she'd settled into happy memories of her childhood in Grenada. When she spoke, her tone was almost wistful. "You remember I told you about my older sister, Winnie?"

The siblings glowed as though Granny had admitted to being related to the pop singer Rihanna. Granny's stories of her adventures with her older sister were making Great-aunt Winnie a celebrity posthumously. Granny's sister had died a few years ago of ovarian cancer. I knew my grandmother mourned her passing every day.

Granny seemed to collect her thoughts. "One day, when we were about your age, Rita, Winnie decided to build a tree house."

Mommy, Daddy, Dev, and I exchanged looks. That couldn't be true. For one thing, that's not the way Granny had told us this tale. In our version, she and Great-aunt Winnie together had made the decision to build a tree house. For another thing, Great-aunt Winnie had told us on more than one occasion that she was terrified of heights. Not just afraid; terrified. Once again, Granny was revising history and Great-aunt Winnie wasn't here to defend herself.

"So Winnie took my daddy's axe and led me into the woods behind our home." Granny paused. I sensed she'd allowed her memories to carry her decades into the past. She was a little girl again, back in Grenada, embarking on another adventure with the older sister she loved. "The woods were darker than I'd thought they'd be. But I wasn't scared. And neither was Winnie. Birds were singing in the trees above us. A soft breeze rustled the leaves in the bushes around us. Everything seemed fine—until we crossed deeper into the woods."

"Then what happened?" Rita seemed breathless with excitement and impatient with the suspense.

"Everything stopped." Granny swept one hand across the other in a cut-off gesture. "The birds stopped singing. The breeze stopped blowing. The leaves stopped rustling. Everything was silent. All we could hear was our own breathing and our hearts beating. And you know what that means, don't you?"

Rita shook her head. Her eyes were wide, more with wonder than from fear.

"No. What does it mean?" Reggie was still as a statue as he waited for Granny to answer.

"It means *something* has entered the forest and the animals sense danger." Granny's voice was low. "And then we smelled it. The odor was strong and sour, more powerful than garbage or rotting meat." She sniffed the air as though the stench had followed her across time.

"Eeww!" Rita squeezed her eyes shut and wrinkled her nose.

"It made our eyes sting and our nostrils burn. It smelled so bad, tears streamed down Winnie's and my faces. I looked at Winnie." Granny turned her head to the left. "She looked at me." She turned her head to the right, then looked back at Reggie and Rita. "We were both frozen with fear. What had made the birds stop singing? What had caused the wind to stop blowing? And what smelled so bad? And then he stepped from behind a tree—"

Reggie interjected. "Papa Bois?"

"Yes, man. It was Papa Bois. He stood closer to me than where that door is to me now." Granny pointed to the bakery's entrance twenty feet away.

Reggie and Rita glanced at the front door. They turned back to Granny. The blood had drained from their faces.

"What did you do?" Rita's voice was high and thin. I hoped the little girl would be able to sleep tonight.

"We screamed. Winnie and I screamed so loudly I'm sure some of the animals screamed back. My whole body went cold and numb. I couldn't stop shaking. The axe dropped from my hand. I don't remember turning or even starting to run. It's like the fear just took over. The next thing I knew, we were yelling and racing from the woods. We didn't stop running or shrieking until we reached home." Granny smiled as though the memory was more of an amusement than a scare. "Our parents had to calm us down before we could speak. When we told them we'd seen Papa Bois, they forbid us from ever going into the woods without one of them ever again. Ha! We were happy to give them our word. To this day, I've never gone into any forest, woods, or even a park by myself. There are too many dangers lurking in there, you know. Some of them you can see and some you can't."

Granny's words reminded me of Camille's murder. She was right. There were dangers lurking in forests, woods, and parks. When those dangers were unknown, how do you go about identifying them?

"You don't like my douens story?" Granny's dark eyes were shadowed with bewilderment. Reggie and Rita had just left.

I blinked. "Granny, your douens story still gives me nightmares."

Her lips parted with surprise. "But, eh, after all these years? You're grown now."

Standing beside me, Dev snorted. "Douens are creepy at any age."

"He's right." My parents spoke in unison, but their words were almost drowned out by a rumble of agreement from the handful of guests in our dining area.

I turned back to our matriarch. "You see, Granny? It's unanimous."

"Chutz." She rolled her eyes. "All you forming the fool. Besides, everybody knows there aren't any douens in the U.S." She gave us the side eye. "Or are there?"

Daddy sighed, shaking his head. "Now I'm sure I'll have bad dreams tonight."

Mommy put her hand on his shoulder and rose on her toes to kiss his cheek. "I'll protect you."

I was contemplating sleeping with the lights on when the bell above the shop's entrance chimed.

Belle Baton, president of the West Indian American Relief Fund, entered the bakery with a thin woman who appeared to be a few years younger than Belle and me. She gave us a shy look before her wide brown eyes fastened onto our pastry display. I smiled at the compliment.

Stepping up to the cash register, I gave both women a welcoming smile. "Good afternoon. It's good to see you again, Ms. Baton. How can I help you ladies?"

Beneath the counter, I crossed my fingers, hoping Belle was here to discuss Spice Isle Bakery catering the aid society's holiday event. I'd emailed her to request an appointment to review her catering needs. She still hadn't responded.

"Good afternoon." Belle addressed my family. "How're all you doing?"

After everyone had exchanged greetings, Belle turned her attention to me. "This is my assistant, Cynthie Biggs. I'd like your bakery to cater our holiday reception, but I'd also like you to cater an event we're hosting in honor of

Camille Abbey. It would be a small gathering, perhaps fifty people, at my home."

I didn't have to ask whether my family would be interested in this new opportunity. Their eyes twinkled with pleasure.

"We'd love to." I pulled my rose-colored cell phone from the front pocket of my grass green shorts to check the time. We had two hours or so before our evening customers would start arriving. Putting away my phone, I gave Belle and Cynthie my most professional smile. "Would you like to fill me in on some of the details now?" *Before you change your mind?*

Belle nodded. "That would be fine."

Trembling with excitement, I pulled a writing tablet from one of the drawers beneath the counter and snagged a pen from the holder beside the register. I glanced at the jug of paper butterflies on the counter.

Thank you for bringing us good luck.

Curious stares from the few customers who lingered over their late lunches and afternoon snacks followed us as I led Belle and Cynthie to a table in the far corner of the bakery's dining area. If our catering business continued to grow ahead of schedule, my family and I would need to figure out a more private space to meet with our clients. Perhaps we could use the floor above the main bakery. We were using it as extra storage space now, but we could renovate it to add a conference room and perhaps an event space. Until then, I'd have to focus on tuning out my audience.

I stopped beside a table for four and gestured for Belle and Cynthie to sit. "A celebratory event in honor of Camille is such a thoughtful gesture."

Belle hooked her purse on the side of the chair before

taking the seat across from me. "DragonFlyZ's benefit CD has brought in a great deal of money for the agencies the West Indian American Relief Fund supports. These groups provide assistance and services to communities on the islands struggling to recover from the devastation brought on by natural disasters." She inclined her head toward Cynthie. "It's DragonFlyZ's CD, but we know Camille was the driving force behind the project. This is just a small way for us to recognize her generosity."

Cynthie's voice was a reverent whisper. "The whole band, including Camille, came to our offices a bunch of times to plan the project launch. They called me Cynthie."

I blinked. Wasn't that her name? "It's sad that we're only realizing now *after* her death how many people Camille touched while she was alive."

"You're right." Cynthie brushed away a tear. "Her songs were so great and her voice was so beautiful. But she didn't just reach people with her music. She touched people with her heart."

Belle blinked rapidly, perhaps to hold back tears of her own. "Camille would be glad to know her generosity continues even after her death."

With a flash of insight, I realized Belle and Cynthie might be able to help identify possible suspects and maybe even motives for Camille's murder. "Did you know Camille well?"

Cynthie shook her head, pulling a tissue from a packet she'd fished from the navy purse on her lap. "No. I'm sorry. I don't mean to fall apart. I just loved her music so much."

"There's no need to apologize, Cynthie." Belle patted the other woman's shoulder. "We all miss Camille. It's hard to accept that she's gone. Then to learn someone killed her . . ." Belle closed her eyes and shook her head. "I can't believe it."

"Neither can I." My mind searched for ways to ply Belle and Cynthie for information. "Had either of you heard of any trouble Camille may have had?"

Belle shook her head. "None at all. Everyone loved her."

Cynthie wiped her runny nose. "Ms. Baton's right. Everyone loved her. Whoever pushed her down those stairs at the park is a monster."

Yes, a monster. Just like the douens. I shivered. "I'd heard rumors that there'd been tension between the band members. Did you notice anything like that during your meetings with them?"

Belle's eyes stretched wide. "You think someone in the band pushed Camille? But why would they do that?"

"That's crazy." Cynthie shook her head vehemently. Her thick, curly dark locks bounced around her dark diamond-shaped face. "They couldn't hurt each other. They're a family. They love each other."

Or perhaps they wanted fans to think that. I kept that thought to myself, though. Cynthie probably wouldn't appreciate it. "Was Karlisa at those meetings also? Did you sense any tension between her and the band?"

Belle braced her elbow on the blond wood table and cupped her chin. She seemed to be searching her memory. "Well, yes. Karlisa didn't approve of the project, you know. All the band members were excited about the album, but Karlisa thought it would hurt their negotiations with bigger recording companies."

"Ms. Baton's right." Cynthie shifted on her seat. Why did she keep referring to Belle as "Ms. Baton"? They seemed to be close in age. "Karlisa was kind of cool toward

Camille, but Camille didn't let it get to her." She sounded proud of Camille for that.

This was another strike against Karlisa. Belle's and Cynthie's recount of the tension between the band's manager and Camille corroborated what everyone else had said about Karlisa's deteriorating relationship with the lead singer. Camille was pressuring the band to fire Karlisa and convincing other members to support projects Karlisa didn't think were in their best interest. This gave the manager the most compelling motive to date for Camille's murder.

Although I was anxious to tell Bryce about the insights Belle and Cynthie had shared, I had to focus on the details Belle was sharing about the event she wanted to host in Camille's honor: the number of guests, the buffet-style setup, and the date.

"Your event is July 11. That's less than two weeks from today." It was actually ten days away. Thanks to my years of experience with unreasonable deadlines imposed by inconsiderate bosses during my former marketing career, I managed to keep the panic from my voice. "I'll have to add a rush charge to our estimate. It's standard for events with such a quick turnaround."

"Of course." Belle rose to leave. "I don't want to wait too long before hosting this event. It's my hope that by then, the police will have arrested the killer."

Cynthie stood, once again blinking back tears. "You're working with the detectives, right? From what Ms. Baton tells me, I'm sure with your help, they'll solve this case quickly. Camille's murderer has got to be brought to justice."

I gave the other woman a noncommittal smile. I wasn't feeling confident about this investigation. Granted, I hadn't felt confident about the other two, either, but Karlisa stumped me. She may have motive, but did she have the temperament? Camille complained Karlisa wasn't assertive enough to take their band to the next level. Was she aggressive enough to shove someone down a flight of stairs to her death?

CHAPTER 17

Sunday mornings, all roads lead to church—and then to the bakery. We were minutes from opening for one of the bakery's busiest days of the week. Since we were closed Mondays and Tuesdays, our regular customers stocked up on enough of our baked goods to keep them satisfied until we reopened Wednesdays. But the headline in today's *Brooklyn Daily Beacon*—"Band Manager Person of Interest in Singer's Murder"—brought my baking to a screeching halt.

"I can't believe it." My voice snapped with impatience. "When I called Bryce yesterday to tell him Karlisa had misled us about Camille's argument with Sheryl about DragonFlyZ's festival contract, I didn't think he'd tell José that Karlisa was a person of interest."

"The fact Karlisa omitted that she'd lied to the band members about how much they were going to be paid for the festival is a pretty big deal." Dev stood to my right at the top of the long center island in our state-of-the-art kitchen. "The DA could argue it shows consciousness of guilt."

Like the rest of us, he was wearing a black chef's hat. But whereas Mommy and Daddy were wearing matching black chef's smocks, like me, he'd slipped on a red apron with a yellow, green, and red Spice Isle Bakery logo. The apron protected his baggy bronze shorts and blue Spice Isle Bakery T-shirt.

Dev was combining ingredients for our hard dough bread. His movements were smooth and easy as though he were conducting a band. I smelled the butter and flour as he worked the dough in the large mixing bowl.

The air in the kitchen was full to bursting with the scents of cane sugar, warm fruits, melted butter, nutmeg, ginger, cinnamon, coconut oil, as well as spices and sauces from entrées we were preparing for our morning guests. The aromas floated past me and through the air vents in search of hungry neighbors. Many of our patrons were regulars who'd come to feel like extended family.

"Or maybe she lied about an argument between Camille and Sheryl because she was afraid." My pulse quickened with nervousness.

Daddy stood across from me. He grunted as he kneaded the dough for the coconut bread. "If she was innocent, she wouldn't have anything to be afraid of."

I folded the newspaper. "I was afraid when the police were investigating me for a murder I hadn't committed."

Silence dropped into the kitchen. I could feel my family being pulled back in time to those desperate weeks when we struggled to prove my innocence.

"What's wrong, Lynds?" Mommy asked. "You don't think Karlisa's the killer?"

I crossed the kitchen, pausing to drop the newspaper in the office before continuing on to wash my hands at the sink. "Karlisa wanted to give us another suspect to investigate. I've been where she is. I can understand that."

Granny set her hands on her slim hips. A scowl furrowed her brow. "But, eh, you've never lied about another person's motives, though."

My grandmother's hair was covered by an orange, red, and brown headcloth. The bakery's red apron protected a slim bronze-and-green ankle-length dress. She'd accessorized with chunky bronze matching earrings and necklace.

"That's true and I never would." I returned to my position at the center island and spread the currant roll filling across the flattened rectangle of dough. "But what's Karlisa's motive? Money? She's going to repay the band members the money she owes them. And about her being replaced as band manager, Camille hadn't convinced the other members to fire her."

Daddy looked up at me from across the island. "So who do you think is the killer?"

I considered the currant rolls I was preparing for the oven. "I don't know yet. I haven't taken Miles or Ena off our list. And there may be others we haven't considered."

"You and I know what it's like to have our names appear in the newspaper as a person of interest in a homicide." Mommy stood beside Daddy, slicing green plantains. Her voice was low. "It's not nice. I don't know whether Karlisa is guilty, but it does seem as though the police are anxious for people to believe they're making progress in the case."

Granny had pulled a tray of fresh currant rolls from the industrial oven behind us. Wielding her serrated bread knife, she portioned the logs, each cut freeing the sweet, buttery aroma. The temptation was too strong for me. I snatched a roll from the tray and bit into it. The hot, flaky crust melted in my mouth, releasing an explosion of cinnamon, sugar, and sweet currants against my taste buds. I hummed my pleasure.

"Mind you." Granny frowned at me. "You're cutting into our profits, you know."

"I was hungry." I covered my full mouth as I protested her scold.

Granny rolled her eyes and carried the tray of currant rolls toward the kitchen door. She set the platter on the counter. "Let's say a prayer before opening the bakery."

My family and I joined hands and waited for Granny to lead us in prayer before Dev, Granny, and I walked out to the customer service area to greet our guests.

Almost two hours later, our order line was finally down to a few people. Everyone seemed to be in a good mood. Dev and I processed our patrons' orders at a brisk pace. Mommy and Daddy served the hot plates. Granny continued her running commentary, and DragonFlyZ's benefit CD kept customers dancing in the line.

The crowd dwindled to our last customer, Karlisa Trotter. She was wearing a wide-brimmed hat and oversized dark sunglasses. If that was a disguise, it was an epic fail. I wasn't the only one who'd recognized her right away. People kept glancing back at her in the line. I was sure her appearance was the reason more people than usual lingered in our dining area. No one confronted her, but everyone wanted to know why she was here.

I hoped my smile appeared natural. "Good morning. How can I help you?"

"Lyndsay, it's me." She briefly tipped down her sunglasses before readjusting them. "I need to speak with you."

I glanced toward the dining area. At least a dozen people were staring at us, openly trying to read our lips. We couldn't expect any privacy there.

Reaching under the counter, I pulled a plastic hair cap from one of the supply drawers. I held it out to her. "You'll have to wear this."

She gave me a dubious look but accepted the item. Removing her hat, she fit the cap over her thick ebony curls without a word.

I turned to Dev. "Can you take the counter for a few minutes?"

He glanced at Karlisa before catching my eyes. "Of course." His unspoken message was clear: *Be careful.*

"Thank you." I hoped my expression was also easily understood: *I promise.*

I led Karlisa past curious eyes, including my grandmother's and my parents', into the bakery's office. Before closing the door, I gestured toward the green padded cloth chair in front of the desk while I took the matching seat on the other side. "How can I help you?"

"Did you see today's paper?" Karlisa hissed the question through her teeth as she removed her sunglasses. She probably feared her voice would carry into the kitchen or, worse, out to the main bakery area.

I wouldn't put it past Granny to be listening at the door even though we all knew I'd tell them everything Karlisa and I discussed as soon as we had a lull in customer traffic.

"Yes, I read it." I winced in sympathy. "The detectives consider you a person of interest in Camille's murder. The article said they brought you in for questioning."

Her brown eyes filled with tears. She wiped them away with the backs of her hands. "They found a torn blue blouse in my trash bag. They showed it to me. It's my size, but I'd never seen it before. I swear it."

A torn blouse. Camille had a piece of cloth in her hand when the emergency medical team had found her.

I slid the box of tissues on the desk closer to her. "Why did you lie to us about the festival contract? You told us Camille had fought with Sheryl about the band's payment. But the truth is she'd fought with *you,* hadn't she?"

Karlisa pulled a tissue from the box and wiped her eyes again. "Yes." The word expressed relief and regret. "I'm sorry, but I was afraid. I thought if you'd known Camille and I had argued twice in one day, you'd think I'd killed her, but I didn't. I swear. I didn't kill Camille."

"But you lied and now the detectives think you *did* kill her."

Karlisa's chin quivered. "This is like a nightmare. I don't know what to do." Her words were choked.

"You'll make things right with the band." I held Karlisa's eyes with a steady, pointed gaze. "You'll be the best manager they could ever hope for: honest, punctual, transparent."

Karlisa gave me a hasty nod. "Of course."

I arched an eyebrow. We wouldn't be having this conversation if her professionalism was unquestionable.

I pulled up Alfonso's work number on my cell and drew the notepad beside the office phone closer to me. "In the meantime, I know an excellent defense attorney. You should call him."

Karlisa accepted Alfonso's phone number with one hand while she dried her tears with the other.

I considered the band manager. Were her tears real? Her fear was generating a chill in the office. Either Karlisa was innocent or she should give up her managing job and pursue a career in acting.

But her claim that someone planted a torn blue blouse in her trash had me curious enough to take a second look at our other suspects—with or without help from NYPD's finest.

"Congratulations on solving another case." José smiled with satisfaction as he approached the bakery's customer service counter late Sunday afternoon. "I knew you would."

His voice carried into the dining area where a dozen or so customers had gathered for lunch. Most of today's diners seemed to be couples and friends. There were a few families and some single diners. A few were dressed in Sunday service finery.

Mommy, Daddy, and Dev were in the kitchen, cooking a variety of our signature menu items for our customers. The steam rose from the pots and pans on the stove and drifted into the customer service area, reminding me that I'd skipped lunch. The air conditioner was a quiet, expensive hum beneath DragonFlyZ's "Love Is Like Rum"

I matched my voice to José's volume so our guests could hear my response. "All the credit belongs to the detectives, but we're not sure we're done with this case."

Surprise replaced José's confident expression, stealing his smile and widening his eyes. "Why not? Wait." He pulled an audio recorder from the front pocket of his dark brown straight-legged pants. "Mind if I record this?"

I hesitated. Did I really want to give José an interview? I glanced at Granny. She was crocheting another afghan square. Seeming to feel my eyes on her, she looked at me over her shoulder and nodded. She was right, of course. Past experience had proven it was better to get our story in front of the public before the police took control of the narrative. From the beginning, José had warned me that could cause problems.

Turning back to him, I took a deep breath. The aromas of stew, curry, and jerk seasonings made my mouth water. The scents of cinnamon, ginger, and nutmeg soothed me. "All right."

He flashed a grin as he activated the recorder and laid it on the counter beside me. He held up a pen and notebook that he'd pulled from his faux leather satchel. "Back up. The detectives said Karlisa Trotter doesn't have an alibi for the time of Camille Abbey's death and that they think Karlisa killed her because Camille was trying to convince the band to fire her. Why do you think Karlisa's innocent?"

Good question. My gut feelings weren't going to persuade anyone.

Granny's voice interrupted my thoughts. "That didn't change the price of cocoa."

Silence dropped into the bakery. A few customers chuckled. All were waiting for Granny's next words.

José's thick black eyebrows knitted. He sent my grandmother a puzzled look. "What do you mean, Ms. Bain?"

Granny kept her attention on her afghan squares. "What did Camille's death change for Karlisa? Karlisa wanted to stay with the band, but the band's not together anymore. Camille's dead."

It felt like someone had turned on the lights. Granny's words untangled my thoughts. "DragonFlyZ's successful because of their talent and Camille's songs. The band was going to ride that success all the way to the top. Just like any manager, Karlisa wanted to get to the top with them. But with Camille's death, the band will have to rebuild. They may still call themselves DragonFlyZ, but they won't be the same band."

One of our patrons called out from the dining area, "But maybe she didn't mean to kill the singer. Maybe it was a crime of passion."

I glanced over my shoulder to see who'd spoken. A middle-aged man met my eyes with a steady, expectant expression. He sat at a table with two young children and a woman close to his age. They appeared to be a family who'd just left a church service.

Nodding, I faced him. "The medical examiner said whoever pushed Camille used a lot of force. Based on the angle of her body and where it had been found in relation to the steps, it wasn't an accidental or spontaneous push. It was deliberate."

The man's eyes widened. Forcing a smile, he looked back at his young children. He seemed desperate to distract them. "So, is everyone enjoying their food?"

Their enthusiastic responses warmed my heart and made me smile. I turned my attention back to José. "Charging Karlisa with Camille's murder seems logical on the surface, but I think we need to dig a little deeper."

Granny hummed as she added more chain link stitches to the lavender-and-white pattern. "I agree. Something doesn't seem right."

I watched José's hand speed across the formerly blank sheet of paper as he took notes on our interview. "I'd caution the public not to rush to judgement. The police consider Karlisa a person of interest, but as my grandmother pointed out, we don't have a compelling motive. We all want justice for Camille. Her murderer stole a lot from our community. But we need to make sure the *right* person's punished."

José nodded. "So if you don't think Karlisa is the killer, who do you think killed Camille?"

My eyes bounced from the pen and notepad in the reporter's hands to his recorder on the checkout counter, back to his piercing dark gaze. "I don't know."

José raised his eyebrows. His eyes gleamed with anticipation. "Have you shared your doubts with the detectives?"

"Yes, I have." Even I heard the bite of irritation in my words.

Humor flashed across José's elegant tanned features. I had no idea why. Nothing about this was funny.

"What did they say?" He held his pen poised above his notepad, waiting for my reply.

I blew out a breath. "They're convinced they have the right person, but my family and I don't believe the motive fits the crime."

José leaned closer as though eager for my next response. "So what're you going to do to find the killer?"

Granny called over her shoulder, "We can't tell you that. The bush has ears."

I inclined my head toward Granny. "As my grandmother said, we don't want to share our next steps with the media right now. We don't want to risk the real killer finding out about our plan."

More importantly, we didn't have a plan. Not yet anyway.

CHAPTER 18

The chime above the bakery's entrance sounded as José wrapped up our interview for his *Brooklyn Daily Beacon* story late Sunday afternoon. As he turned toward the door, Bryce's hesitation on seeing me speaking with the crime beat reporter was almost imperceptible. Time stood still as I took in the detective's appearance in his casual outfit. A tight cream T-shirt molded his muscular torso. Baggy navy shorts exposed his powerful runner's calves. No one could accuse Bryce Jackson of going easy on leg days. I tugged my tongue off the roof of my mouth.

"Ah, Detective Jackson." José grabbed his audio recorder and strode to Bryce. "We were just talking about you. Lyndsay gave me an interview, explaining why she thinks you're wrong about Karlisa Trotter being Camille Abbey's killer. I'd like to include a quote from you as well."

Bryce's frown moved from José to me and back. His hazel eyes were clouded with disappointment and suspicion. Was that jealousy I sensed from the detective? That was ridiculous. We weren't dating. But then neither were José and I. Absurd.

Bryce shoved his hands into the front pockets of his

shorts. "I've already given you the reasons we consider Ms. Trotter a person of interest in this case. I don't have anything to add."

José gave a careless shrug. "If you're sure, then I'll work my story around Lyndsay's quotes." His dark eyes sparkled as he caught my attention over his shoulder. "I'm sure people will be interested to know that the Grenadian Nancy Drew has doubts about the NYPD's case."

I unclenched my teeth. "Stop calling me that."

Ignoring me, José gave a triumphant wave before sailing through the exit.

Bryce pulled his hands from his shorts pockets and paced to the customer counter. His lips curved into a half smile. "Don't you like the nickname?"

Irritation was like itchy powder against my skin. "I'm a real-life, grown woman who's trying to build a business. If they keep referring to me as a fictional, adolescent amateur sleuth, no one will take me seriously."

He rested his hands on the counter between us. "Well, I have a solution to your problem. Stop interfering in police investigations."

Granny grunted. "And who's going to solve them, then?"

I fought not to laugh as I held Bryce's eyes. To his credit, Bryce's face lit with amusement.

"Point taken, Ms. Bain." He returned his attention to me. His expression became guarded again. "You let José interview you? I thought you didn't like speaking with reporters."

"I don't, but why shouldn't I? You did." Folding my hands on the counter between us, I gave him a pointed look. "My family and I read your interview in this morning's paper."

"This is a high-profile case for this community. The

public deserved an update." He inclined his head toward the door as though José still stood there. "Are the two of you friends . . . or something?"

His sudden change of topic caught me off guard. The ground shifted beneath my feet. My brain felt sluggish. It took a moment to collect my thoughts.

Granny took advantage of my hesitation. Dropping all pretense of crocheting, she shifted on her chair to face us. "Why're you asking?"

Was she kidding me right now? "Granny."

"I'd like to know why he's asking, too." Mommy's voice carried across the pass-through window. With the automatic dough mixer whirring and DragonFlyZ's "Midnight Magic" bouncing through our sound system, how could she possibly hear us?

Daddy and Dev chuckled. My skin grew warm as every cell in my body filled with embarrassment. I squeezed my eyes shut. Could someone die of shame? I could see that happening.

"I was just curious." Bryce's shrug was more of a stretch as though his back muscles had tensed. "You told him you disagreed with our focus on Karlisa."

"I do." I straightened. "I wish you'd given me a heads-up before you spoke with José. I thought we were working on this case together."

"We are." He leaned into the counter. I captured a whiff of his cologne through the scents of confectioners' sugar and cinnamon. "It was the tip you gave me that Karlisa had lied to us about the conflict between Camille and Sheryl Cross that prompted Stan and me to get some officers together to help search her trash. You helped us break the case."

Man, he really could be clueless sometimes. "The fact that the information *I* gave you allegedly helped you break the case didn't make you consider calling me with an update? Instead, you called José and thought it would be all right for my family and me to read about it in the *Beacon* this morning?"

Bryce's brown cheeks darkened with a blush. "I'm sorry, Lyndsay. I got busy with the search and paperwork."

"Mmm." I gave him a look that said he needed to do better. "Of our three main suspects, Karlisa seems to have the strongest motives, but I feel like we're missing something."

"Like what?" Bryce spread his hands. "Occam's razor: The simplest explanation is usually the right one. Camille was trying to get Karlisa fired and Karlisa wanted to keep her job as DragonFlyZ's business manager."

Granny grunted. "Killing Camille wouldn't get her what she wanted. Camille was the lead singer, but there were still five other people in the band. What makes all you think the band would drop Karlisa just because Camille said so? Did she have magic powers?"

Bryce shifted his posture to face Granny. "But Ms. Bain, when we searched Karlisa Trotter's trash, we found a torn blue blouse."

That posed a problem. "Karlisa told us about the blouse. She said it wasn't hers."

"Are you sure it's the same blouse?" Dev's disembodied voice carried through from the kitchen.

"Sounds like a frame-up," Daddy added his opinion. I agreed.

Bryce massaged the back of his neck. "The crime lab's comparing the material from Karlisa's blouse with the cloth we found with Camille's body."

I studied his face, noting the tension around his lips and eyes. "What will you do if it's not the same blouse?"

Bryce drew his hand over his tight curls. He looked at

me as though he was at a loss as to how to respond to my family's questions and insights. "What do you want to do?"

I raised my eyebrows. "Oh, so now you're asking my opinion?"

Granny laughed.

"Lynds." Mommy's tone chastised me. "Be nice."

Mommy was always trying to make sure I made it into heaven.

I shrugged in resignation. "I gave Karlisa Alfonso's phone number."

Bryce nodded. "He's a smart defense attorney."

"Yes, he is," Dev called out.

I continued. "But Karlisa doesn't want to stand trial for a crime she didn't commit." I gave him another pointed look. "I don't blame her. My family and I want to make sure the right person is tried for killing Camille. We're holding one more family meeting to review what we know about the case and the people involved."

"When?" Bryce asked.

"Tonight." I pulled my cell from my pocket to check the time. "As soon as the shop closes."

Bryce checked his watch. The broad, bronze band looked solid on his thick wrist. "May I join you?"

As I struggled to mask my surprise, my family showered him with a chorus of approvals.

"Of course!" Granny stood to join us at the counter.

"Please do." Mommy almost sang her response.

"Sure!" Daddy's answer mingled with Mommy's.

"The more the merrier." Dev's reply sounded a little too casual.

Bryce flashed a grin. His even, bright white teeth were a dentist's dream. "Great. I'll see you then." There was a bounce in his step as he turned to leave the bakery.

I was fifteen again, watching my high school heartthrob

walk away. His strong calves flexed with every stride. The muscles in his back rippled beneath his shirt. Then I realized Bryce had stopped by the bakery but hadn't bought anything. What did that mean?

Sigh. He was getting to me.

"What's on your mind, love?" Granny's voice was almost a whisper.

I hesitated, bringing my thoughts back to the case. "Granny, I don't know whether I believe Karlisa's innocent or if I'm defending her because of what happened to Mommy and me."

Granny cupped her soft, warm hand around my forearm. Her eyes were warm with sympathy. "You've always had a soft heart. Trust your instincts. You were right about the bakery."

I arched an eyebrow. "Deciding to go into business with my family is a little different from helping a killer escape justice." The thought of making such a colossal mistake stole my breath. "Bryce is right. Karlisa's motives are strong, at least on the surface. And now the police have found a torn blouse in her trash. What if I'm wrong? I mean, can I be objective?"

Granny's grip tightened on my forearm. She shook her head. "It won't get that far. We're just asking a few more questions. There's nothing wrong with that. Lynds, you have to trust the truth will out."

Nodding, I took a deep, calming breath. There's nothing wrong with asking a few more questions. And my family firmly believed the only stupid question is the one you *don't* ask.

"Lynds, the phone's for you." Daddy's voice came across the pass-through window early Sunday evening. It carried over the sounds of the commercial mixer, patrons' conversations, and DragonFlyZ's "Sing Up Your Name (for History)."

Bryce had left a couple of hours ago, but I was still having trouble concentrating. "Thank you, Daddy."

Granny emerged from the kitchen where she'd been helping my parents replenish our inventory to replace me behind the customer service counter.

I stepped aside to let her walk past me. "Thank you, Granny."

She waved a dismissive hand. "Don't mind."

Business was always brisk on Sundays, but there were more customers than usual because of the long Fourth of July weekend. I was grateful for the sales, but Belle's reception in honor of Camille was a week away. Between the increased orders at the bakery and the investigation, I hadn't had much time to plan for it.

Tossing a smile toward my parents, I stripped off my black nitrile gloves as I hustled into the office. The number on the identification screen was familiar. Why was the Caribbean American Heritage Festival Association calling? I took a calming breath before answering. "Spice Isle Bakery. This is Lyndsay."

"Lyndsay, this is Sheryl Cross." The association president's tone was uncharacteristically tentative. I sensed her tension across the phone lines. What was going on?

I lowered myself onto the green cloth cushioned executive chair behind the office desk. "Good evening, Ms. Cross. How can I help you?"

"Call me Sheryl. Please." She cleared her throat. "I wanted to thank you for your help with the association's statement and talking points about poor Camille Abbey's murder."

I frowned. Was that it? Thanking me made her uncomfortable? My muscles relaxed. "You're welcome, Ms.— Sheryl. It wasn't any trouble. Before opening the bakery, I worked for a marketing agency. I used to write crisis talking points all the time."

"Well, you're very good at it. I'm sure that company wishes you were still there."

I swallowed a burst of laughter. That was doubtful. Anyway, *I* was glad I'd left the agency. I couldn't be happier than I was working in the bakery with my family in our community. Once we repaid our business loan, everything would be perfect. *Please, God.*

"Thank you." Sensing her hesitation, I waited for her to say more.

My eyes dropped to the black metal framed family photo we kept on the desk. Reena had taken it. It showed Granny, Mommy, Daddy, Dev, and me holding on to one another, grinning into the camera as we posed in front of the bakery the day before we opened. I loved that picture.

Sheryl broke the brief and awkward silence. "I wasn't comfortable being interviewed, but the quotes the *Beacon* reporter used in his article read well, I thought. It reestablished the association as a vital and active part of the community instead of just being a site of a criminal act, you know."

"The article was able to do that because you'd prepared for the interview. José Perez's a good journalist, but he was using your words." I had to give the reporter his due.

I didn't like the way he'd focused on my mother and me when we'd been "persons of interest" in those previous homicide cases. But he was diligent and determined to provide his community with as much information as possible on events that affected us and our neighborhood.

"I couldn't have done it without your help." Sheryl's

voice was stiff. She was like a penitent forced into reconciliation. "Your family was right from the beginning. I can see that now. Camille was a member of our community. As such, the Caribbean American Heritage Festival Association should have been leading the charge to find out who killed her."

I shivered as a chill moved through me. "I pray that nothing like this ever happens again, but I appreciate what you said."

"I'm praying for the same thing." Sheryl exhaled a heavy breath. "Lyndsay, I have to ask you something."

"What is it?"

"Why did you help me?"

I blinked. "Because I could."

There was a pause before Sheryl spoke again. "That's it? I tried to have your family pulled from the festival. When I learned you were investigating Camille's death as a murder, I withdrew my request for you to cater my daughter's wedding."

As she reminded me of the mean and petty ways she'd treated my family, my temper stirred. A deep, calming breath scented with cinnamon, sugar, ginger, and nutmeg helped me keep the situation in perspective. This experience was bigger than Sheryl and me.

"The festival is important for our community and for the city. It helps West Indians keep our culture and traditions alive. It also reminds the city of the close ties it has to Caribbean nations. You were right that Camille's murder could have a devastating effect on it. I didn't want that to happen. By helping you, I was helping the festival."

"You're a smart young lady. I can see that your bakery's going to be a very successful business." Sheryl's chuckle sounded like relief. "And I want you to cater my daughter's wedding and the association's holiday party, please. Not because you helped me with the newspaper, but because I want both events to be outstanding."

"Thank you. We would be honored." I smiled. "And both events will be exceptional."

"I'm sure they will." Sheryl sighed again. "We've already started planning next year's festival. We'd love for Spice Isle Bakery to be a vendor again. We received very high marks for your bakery from attendees who responded to our survey. Your application for next year will just be a formality."

I was momentarily speechless. "That's wonderful news. Thank you."

"It was all your hard work." Sheryl's tone was dismissive. "And now that the murder has been solved, people's attention will move from the festival to the trial. But I'm surprised to hear it was Karlisa."

My interest perked up. "Why does that surprise you?"

"Because Karlisa is a professional." She made the statement as though that personality trait alone should absolve the band manager of guilt. "I knew she and Camille had had their disagreements. Camille felt Karlisa could be doing more things for the band. But let me tell you something. Karlisa is one cool customer. I've known her for many years. I've seen her get into disagreements with plenty of people. She never let her anger get the better of her, you know. She's always very restrained."

Then what would make her lose control of her temper now? Unless Karlisa's telling the truth. I was even more convinced that someone was trying to frame her—and getting away with it.

CHAPTER 19

"Karlisa's guilty." Manny gestured toward Bryce seated at the other end of the combined tables in the bakery's dining area. His tone was curt and inflexible. "You said the evidence pointed to that."

I rubbed my forehead with three fingers of my left hand. This wasn't going as well as I'd hoped. In fact, it was going very badly.

I'd called for a family meeting. We'd gathered Sunday night after the bakery had closed for the long weekend. Bryce was the first to arrive. So it was technically a family meeting plus Bryce. Uncle Roman had announced he was hungry as soon as he'd walked through the door. He was dressed in a blinding lemon yellow T-shirt and lime green shorts. Reena kept glancing at his outfit in disbelief. She'd driven to the bakery with Uncle Al, Aunt Inez, and Manny.

We'd pushed several tables together to accommodate the eleven of us. After our dinner of stew chicken, rice and peas, and salad, we cleared the table and set the dishes to wash. I brought the whiteboard from the front of the customer service area with me when we returned to the dining room. Setting up at the foot of the tables, I prepared to address the lingering questions that cast doubt on Karlisa's guilt.

"Evidence? What evidence, eh?" Uncle Roman relaxed back against his chair. He was seated between Daddy at the head of the table and Dev on his left. "Your granny's already poked so many holes in it, it's more like Swiss cheese." He laughed at his own joke.

"Don't study him." Granny made a vague gesture across the table at Uncle Roman before giving Manny, seated beside her, her full attention. "On the surface, Karlisa seems to have reason to want Camille gone, but that reason doesn't hold up to tough, tough scrutiny."

Reena shifted to face Manny on her left. "She says she was walking around the festival by herself when Camille was being murdered. She can't prove that's what she did, but we can't prove she's lying, either."

Bryce sat across the table from Manny. Before moving to the whiteboard, I'd been sitting in what was now the empty seat between him and Dev. "We found a torn blouse in Karlisa's trash. We're comparing it to the material Camille had been holding."

Mommy interrupted. "Someone else could've put that blouse in with her trash."

Dev nodded his agreement. "Everything hinges on that scrap of cloth. Unless the police can tie it without question to the blouse found in Karlisa's trash, their case is sunk."

Manny's eyes burned with frustration as he turned to me. "So what do we do now?"

My heart was hurting for him. Camille had been dear to him and he wanted justice for her. He wanted whoever had hurt her and ended her life so prematurely to be punished for their actions. That's what we all wanted, for Camille and for Manny. But it had to be the right person.

I took a breath, easing the tightness in my chest and drawing in the lingering scents of onions, peppers, and sugar from the stew chicken. "For now, Alfonso has agreed to represent Karlisa if her case should go to trial—"

"Alfonso?" Manny's eyes were wide with disbelief. He looked at Reena. "Do you think it's a good idea for your boyfriend to represent Karlisa? Suppose she killed Camille?"

Aunty Inez's gentle voice claimed his attention. "But, Manny, suppose she didn't?"

"Manny, I'm sorry. *I'm* the one who gave Karlisa Alfonso's number." My stomach muscles knotted. "I didn't think about how hurtful it would be if Karlisa was guilty." And then Reena's boyfriend would end up defending the person who'd killed someone Manny had cared for so deeply.

"Manny, I think we're looking in the wrong direction." I gestured toward the whiteboard on which I'd written Karlisa's name as well as the names of DragonFlyZ's band members. "I don't think Karlisa or anyone in DragonFlyZ had a motive to kill Camille. Whatever resentment the backup singer, Ena, may have had toward Camille for replacing her as the lead singer wouldn't have been a motive for Camille's murder. Ena's leaving the band. The drummer, Earl, and the guitarists Geoffrey and Horace got along well with her."

"And they have alibis for the time of the murder." Bryce gestured toward the whiteboard. "Geoffrey and Horace were together, and Earl was with his girlfriend. Miles Tosh, the lead guitarist and co-songwriter, also has an alibi. An entertainment reporter with the *Beacon* was interviewing him."

Manny glared at the board. "Well, if you've taken all the band members and their manager off the list, who's left?"

Uncle Al sat beside Aunty Inez at the foot of the table closest to me. "That's what we need you to tell us."

I nodded. "Uncle Al's right, Manny. You spent almost the entire day with her. Did she have any tense interactions with anyone? Did anything unusual happen? Maybe it didn't seem strange at the time, but in retrospect maybe it stands out?"

Manny was shaking his head as I spoke. "She spoke with Karlisa briefly right before the performance. They were both kind of curt with each other. But things were always tense between them, even at the studio."

"But did they ever get violent?" Mommy asked. She sat with Daddy at the head of the table.

Manny narrowed his eyes as though he was searching his memories. "No, never. They never even raised their voices."

I tilted my head, questioning him. "They never, ever shouted at each other?"

Manny faced me. "No, never."

I frowned. "Then who was Camille shouting at during the festival?"

Silence dropped into the bakery. From their startled expressions, I could tell that, like me, Granny, Manny, Reena, and Dev recalled the heated argument we'd overheard between Camille and someone else.

"What are you talking about?" Bryce looked from me to Manny and back.

Reena answered him. "After DragonFlyZ's performance, Manny and Camille came back to the Spice Isle Bakery truck for refreshments. Then Camille left. A little while later, we heard her and someone else shouting at each other. They were standing maybe fifty feet from us, but we could hear them. And we could see Camille. The other person was standing behind a tree."

Bryce pulled out his pen and notepad. "You didn't recognize the voice?"

"No, I didn't." Manny's voice was clipped with frustration. "The voice sounded female. At the time, I thought it could've been Karlisa, but the voice was different. And like I said, Karlisa never raised her voice."

That was in keeping with what Sheryl Cross had said about Karlisa.

Bryce glanced up from his notepad and caught my eyes. "Do you remember what they were talking about or what they said?"

I looked away, trying to think. "We weren't able to hear every word, only snatches of the conversation. Camille shouted, 'You knew!'"

Granny leaned into the table. A frown furrowed her brow. "The other person said, 'Something. Something. Borrowed.'"

I picked up the reenactment. "Camille interrupted her, 'And take care of it.'"

Granny warmed to her role. "'Something. Something. Listen . . .'"

I concluded the reenactment. "'Something. Something. Cheated us!'"

Dev looked at us in amazement. "That's what I remember."

"Me, too." Reena sounded impressed.

Manny's words were heavy with grief. "Shortly after that, we learned someone had shoved Camille down the stairs about five hundred yards from that tree."

Cold seeped into my skin. I wrapped my arms around my waist. "Camille's killer may have been standing behind that tree."

"I came as soon as I could." I crossed the threshold into the Abbey family's foyer late Monday morning. It was the Fourth of July. The drive from the bakery to their residence had taken maybe half an hour. Most of that time had been spent looking for a parking space.

Their home was similar to my family's. It was a brown-and-black stone, three-story, single-family dwelling with a narrow, shared, and gated driveway.

I'd been working alone on the accounts when Camille's middle sister, Viola, had called. I'd insisted Granny, Mommy, Daddy, and Dev take today and tomorrow off. It had been a crazy busy week. They needed the break, especially since next Tuesday we were catering Belle Baton's reception. That meant they'd only have one day off next week.

Viola had sounded anxious and angry over the phone. Not angry with me, thankfully. That one seemed to have a temper. It had been hard to follow her disjointed account of a break-in at her family's home. She'd spoken so fast. Her words had tumbled over one another, and she'd repeated herself several times. The only thing I'd been able to understand had been her pleas for me to come speak with them in person. There was something I had to see for myself. The Abbeys were a grieving family. I didn't have the heart to say no.

Although Viola had called, it was Camille's mother, Lynne, who welcomed me. Her Haitian accent was both friendly and formal. "Thank you for coming, dear. We didn't know who else to call. Come. We're in Camille's room."

She led me through the bright, cozy foyer. Her sleeveless brown-and-purple abstract print blouse billowed around her. Her long legs, exposed beneath tan shorts, moved quickly. I hurried to keep up.

The home's interior had spacious rooms with high ceilings. The hardwood floors were polished to an almost glass-like shine. Vivid area rugs were centered across the surface, a different one in each room.

The living room featured a thick red floral sofa with matching love seat and armchairs. The maple wood table and chairs seemed almost too big for the dining room. I barely glimpsed the white-and-orange kitchen before Lynne guided me down a flight of gray wooden stairs to the basement. This must be Camille's room.

I was struck again by the similarities between our homes. My room—I preferred to think of it as a suite—was in my parents' basement as well. Camille had organized her space similar to mine. The sleeping area was in the back of the room. There was a desk and chair where she must have worked and studied in the center section. A sitting area with a love seat, armchair and ottoman, and television was arranged at the front of the room. That's where Camille's father, John; middle sister, Viola; youngest sister, Gwen; and brother, Benedict, waited for us. Their combined tension pulsed in the air around us.

"Good morning." I was growing more confused and uncomfortable by the minute. Why was I here?

The room carried a faint floral scent that reminded me of the fragrance Camille wore during the festival. I looked at brown-paneled walls that displayed colorful plaques with religious texts, including Psalm 23, the Serenity Prayer, and the Beatitudes. The nearby dark wood bookcase was stuffed with fiction and nonfiction books. Biographies and autobiographies of recording artists and executives were shelved beside poetry collections. University textbooks stood beside romance novels. Framed photographs were set on every available flat surface, including her desk, her nightstand, on top of the television, and beside her laptop.

"We're so glad you came." Viola wore a black-and-pink belted romper. She tugged me toward the center of the room where Camille had set up her black mesh computer chair, black-and-white metal-framed desk, laptop, and printer. "Someone broke into my sister's room in the middle of the night."

"I'm so sorry." Putting myself in their position, I was battered by combined waves of anger and sorrow. They shattered my heart and dropped its pieces into my gut.

Who would be so cruel as to break into this family's home and steal the treasures of the loved one they'd just lost?

I surveyed the surroundings. The bed was rumpled and a pillow was missing. An indentation toward the center of the mattress lingered as though someone had knelt on it. On the far side of the bed, items had fallen to the carpet in front of the natural wood grain nightstand. On the opposite side of the room, the top two drawers of the matching chest were open and clothes had been tossed to the floor. My fists clenched at my sides.

Lynne's voice penetrated the screams of outrage in my head. "Camille was very neat. Her room never looked like this." She swept a hand across the space. The motion was jerky with anger. "Since we have the day off, I came down this morning just to . . ."

John stepped forward and wrapped an arm around her shoulders. His crimson cotton short-sleeved shirt complemented his dark skin. His words were tight. "This is a place where we can still be with our daughter. We can feel her with us. And someone has violated that."

"I understand." My voice sounded thick with tears. I

took a breath. "About what time do you think the break-in occurred?"

"I was the last to go to bed." Benedict wore a blue-red-and-gray New York Yankees T-shirt and dark blue baggy shorts. He gestured toward the youngest Abbey daughter. "Right after Gwen. It was around midnight. Neither one of us heard anything before that."

I glanced at Gwen and waited for her nod of agreement. "And the thief only entered Camille's room?"

"That's right." Viola jabbed her index finger toward the ceiling. "We were all asleep upstairs. None of us heard anything." Murmurs of agreement from her family broke the somber silence. She marched to the bedroom door and pointed to the back of the basement. "The thief must've come through the exterior door to the basement. I checked. The lock's broken."

The implications of Viola's statement gave me chills. "You think whoever broke into your home knew this was Camille's room?"

"That's not all we're saying." John rubbed his wife's shoulder. I didn't know whether he was giving comfort, taking it, or both. "We believe whoever broke into her room killed her."

My eyebrows stretched toward my hairline. "Why do you think that?"

"Cam's fans didn't know where she lived." Dressed in cut-off blue denim shorts and an oversized white cotton short-sleeved shirt, Gwen seemed to shake with temper. "Even if they did, they wouldn't know which room was hers. This was personal."

Benedict gave a stiff nod. "It can't be a coincidence. Whoever killed my sister knew her. Whoever broke into her room knew her. The thief and the killer are one and the same."

Lynne leaned against her husband's side. "If one of her friends had wanted something, they would've just asked for it. They wouldn't have had to do all this." Her arm swept the room again.

"Do you know the police suspect Karlisa Trotter of Camille's death?" I waited for their nods of affirmation. "Did Karlisa know which room was hers?"

Even if she did know, would Karlisa risk breaking into the Abbeys' home while she was under suspicion? That would be so unwise. What if she'd been caught?

Benedict crossed his arms over his chest. "Karlisa rarely came to the house and when she did, Cam met with her in the dining room."

"I know the police think Karlisa killed my sister." Gwen's voice broke. Her throat muscles flexed before she continued. "They didn't like each other. But I can't imagine Karlisa pushing Cam to her death. She didn't have it in her."

Viola snorted. "She's too lazy. If she was going to kill someone, she'd do something that took less effort, like poison."

The She's-Too-Lazy-to-Commit-Murder defense was interesting. It was both exonerating and insulting.

Benedict shifted his stance. "Miles and Ena have been in Cam's room a bunch of times."

"What did the police say about the break-in and your theory about the theft and murder being connected?" I assumed they'd called the police before calling me. At least, I hoped they had.

"Detective Jackson's off today." Viola marched back across the room. I could almost see the smoke coming out of her ears. "The officer we spoke with didn't seem interested in what we had to say."

"Could you get in touch with Detective Jackson?"

Lynne's dark eyes pleaded with me. "Get him to at least consider what we've said."

First Manny and now the Abbey family were asking me to speak to Bryce on their behalf. I was beginning to feel like the NYPD Homicide Hotline. "Do you have any idea what was stolen?"

Gwen crossed to the natural wood chest. She gestured toward it without touching anything. "She always kept her perfume here. Now it's gone." She pointed to the wall beside her. "A framed copy of the band's first album cover. They'd all signed it." She moved to Camille's desk and pointed to a spot beside the pen-and-pencil holder. "The recorder she'd used when she was working on lyrics." She waved a hand toward the wall next to the desk. "And a plaque she'd made with the phrase 'Everyone has a right to decide their own destiny.' It's based on a Bob Marley quote, but she changed it."

"I recognize it." I frowned, considering the places Gwen had pointed to.

"What are you thinking?" Benedict asked.

"The thief had been in this room before while Camille had been working." I looked from the chest to Camille's desk. "That's how they knew to take her recorder. I understand why they took it and the autographed album cover. I can even understand why they'd take the plaque Camille had made herself. With her death, those items would be worth a lot."

Benedict fisted his hands at his sides. "Those filthy snakes."

I silently agreed with him. "But why would they take her perfume? Was there something special about it?"

"No." Gwen shrugged. "She bought it at the Bronze Mixer." She named the small neighborhood pharmacy on Parish Avenue.

It was a puzzle. "I'm so sorry this has happened. I'll speak with Detective Jackson about your theory that Camille's murder is connected to this break-in. That makes sense to me. It's an angle we have to consider. But I don't know whether I'll have any more luck with him than you had with the officer."

The family followed Lynne and me out of Camille's room. The silence surrounding us was thick as we climbed the steps up from the basement. I couldn't stop thinking about how the break-in had tainted one of their last remaining connections with Camille forever. Someone had touched Camille's belongings. They'd taken her things. That was bad enough. It would be unforgivable if the killer and thief were the same person. They would've taken the family's loved one and stolen their mementoes of her. This family needed justice. They'd called me for help. I wanted to do all I could for them—and my cousin—but I was at a loss. How could I find the killer if I couldn't identify their motive?

CHAPTER 20

"I thought you were going to take today off." I smiled at Dev as he came through the bakery's rear door Monday afternoon.

"I am. I came in to watch you work." As he strode toward the center island, he raised the white plastic bag he was carrying chest high. "And I brought food. Granny fixed us each a plate of fried fish, callaloo, and rice and peas."

He placed the bag on the center island, then turned to give me a bear hug. He smelled like soap and peppermint. Just like Daddy.

"Fantastic. Thank you. I just realized I'm hungry." I pulled two tall glasses from the cupboard and filled them with cold mauby tea from the fridge.

"Granny said you'd forget to eat." Dev pulled the wrapped plates from the bag and set one in front of me. "How can you own a bakery where you're surrounded by food and forget to eat?"

"I get busy." My stomach growled.

Dev shook his head. "You have to keep your strength up, especially while you're training for your kickboxing exhibition."

"I promise." After saying grace, I gathered a forkful of

the fried fish. Steam wafted up to me, carrying the scents of scallions, onions, allspice, salt, and pepper. "Seriously, it's good to see you, and I appreciate your bringing me food, but why are you here? Is everything OK?"

"Everything's fine." He took a deep drink of mauby. His pose seemed relaxed, but his dark eyes were watchful.

I swallowed a sigh. We'd been best friends my whole life, twenty-seven years. Didn't he realize I knew when he was lying?

"Good. I'm glad." Now we were both lying. But if he wasn't ready to tell me what was on his mind, I couldn't force him.

"How did things go with Camille's family?"

I'd texted Granny, Mommy, Daddy, and Dev before going to see the Abbeys, then again when I'd returned to the bakery. After giving them a brief summary of what had happened, I'd explained details would have to wait until I got home. There was too much to text. But since Dev had made a special trip, I told him everything now.

Finishing the update—and my lunch—I waved my empty fork toward the office. "I left a message for Bryce. Hopefully, he'll return it today. I'm sure the thief stole those items from Camille with the intent to sell them. The perfume puzzles me, though. I wonder if any of the band members are having financial problems."

Dev drained his glass of mauby. "That's a good question."

My shoulders lifted, then dropped with a sigh. "I'm not looking forward to questioning them again."

"Then don't." He shrugged. "Let Bryce do it. It's his job."

"I can't walk away from this, Dev." I drew my fingers down the side of my glass. It was cold and damp against my skin. "I feel invested in this case. It started as a way to help Manny get through his grief. But as I got to know more about Camille and her family, it's become important to me to get justice for them."

Was I betraying my family by staying on this case? They worried about my safety and I hated that. But I wanted to see this investigation through to the end. I wanted to help catch Camille's killer.

"I can understand how you'd feel that way. You've always had empathy for other people." Dev held my eyes. "Camille seemed like a good person. Her death was a great loss to her family as well as the community. I'm sorry Manny won't get a chance to know her better."

"So am I." I allowed a few moments of silence before addressing the elephant in the room again. "Are you ready to tell me what's bothering you?"

Dev shook his head at me. His lips curved into a reluctant half smile. "How do you do that?"

I rolled my eyes. "I've known you my *entire* life."

"All right." He shoved aside his empty plate and glass, then met my eyes again. "I haven't told anyone else yet. I'm still processing it. Dexter, Trainor, and Scott want me back, Lynds." He named his former law firm. "The senior partners called me this morning. They said my clients are insisting I return to the firm. They won't do business with anyone else. The firm's offered me a promotion and more money."

"Dev, that's amazing." My heart was pounding against my chest. "I knew you were an excellent lawyer, but I had no idea you inspired that kind of loyalty in your clients. That's incredible. I'm so proud of you."

"Thank you." He sounded dazed. "I knew my clients respected me, but I had no idea they'd have this reaction to my leaving, either."

"That's really impressive, big brother. When do you

return to the firm?" As soon as the words left my mouth, my heart dove into my stomach.

Dev would be leaving the bakery. The whole family wouldn't be working together anymore. He wouldn't tease me in the kitchen as we prepared to open the shop. He wouldn't dance with me behind the counter as we served our guests. And he wouldn't be there to brainstorm ideas for growing our business. Yes, we could definitely use his help in the kitchen and at the counter since business had picked up, but it was more than that. I enjoyed his company. *We* enjoyed it.

But being a lawyer had been his dream since he was a child. His happiness was important to me. If that meant he would be returning to Dexter, Trainor & Scott, PLLC, then I'd throw him a huge celebration before sending him on his way. And I'd cherish the time we'd had with him in the store. I was certain that's what Granny, Mommy, and Daddy would want as well.

"I don't know whether I'm going back." Dev drew his hand over his tight dark brown curls. "I'm flattered that my clients want me to return and I'm glad the firm finally sees my value. They apologized for demanding we close the bakery, by the way. And you impressed them by identifying Claudio Fabrizi's and Emily Smith's killers."

"That's nice." I'll probably feel more charitable toward them tomorrow. After all, their mistake in firing Dev had benefited my family.

"But I've loved working here with you, Gran, Mom, and Dad."

"And we've loved working with you." *Don't go!* "But, Dev, you've wanted to be a lawyer for as long as I can remember."

"I know." He stood and paced the kitchen. "And I loved it. I loved the research, the investigations, the strategy. I didn't like the hours, though. Long days, late nights, weekends. Do you know what I did last Fourth of July?"

Of course I did. "You worked."

He stopped on the other side of the center island and gestured toward me. "This Fourth of July, I'm having lunch with my sister at our bakery. And tonight, Joymarie's making dinner for me."

"Must be nice."

"Yes, it is." He returned to his seat.

"Granny, Mommy, and Daddy are probably researching wedding venues and selecting playlists." Reaching across the center island, I squeezed his forearm. "Dev, this is a big decision that'll affect the rest of your life. The partners only called you this morning. Maybe you should think about it for a day or three." *Don't go!* "We all want you to be happy, whether that means you stay with us at the bakery or return to the firm. I don't want you to have any regrets. Neither would Granny, Mommy, or Daddy."

"I won't." He leaned into the center island. "I'm happier now than I've been in a long time."

"That's what you think *now*." I released his arm. "But will you feel the same next week or next month? The selfish part of me wants to work with you. I won't lie. Having you here feels right. But for our shared peace of mind, I want us both to know that if you stay with the bakery, you're making that decision because it's what's best for you, not because you think it's best for us or because you want to spite the law firm. Although I wouldn't blame you."

"This is what's best for me, Lynds. Working with my family at the bakery. I'm sure of it. But if my taking a few days to think about it will make you feel better, fine. I'll tell the partners I'll give them my answer next week."

"I appreciate that, Dev."

"But I won't change my mind."
Promise?

"I still don't understand why the Abbeys think the killer and the burglar are the same person." Bryce sat on the opposite side of the table in the bakery's dining section late Monday afternoon. The bakery was closed. My family had the day off, so we had the space to ourselves.

Bryce wasn't working the holiday. Instead of one of his smart business suits, he was wearing a navy T-shirt and gunmetal gray knee-length shorts. He still looked good. He'd probably look just as attractive in sackcloth and ashes.

I'd poured us each a mug of ginger tea. I wasn't certain he liked it. He was nursing it a bit longer than I thought was necessary.

I took another sip from my mug before repeating myself. "Their instincts and deductions. Whoever broke into their home knew Camille well enough to know where she slept."

Bryce spread his hands. "That doesn't mean the killer broke in. She could've told people she'd converted her family's basement into a bedroom."

"What about the missing items?" I cupped the mug between my hands and rested it on the table in front of me. "How would the thief have known about those things unless they'd seen them in Camille's room? I spoke with Karlisa earlier, by the way. She confirmed that she'd never been in Camille's room."

Bryce nodded, staring into his still-full mug of tea. "That's a good point, but again, I can't take it to a judge for a search warrant or a prosecutor for charges."

Frustrated, I lowered my mug. "I understand, but could you at least return the Abbeys' call? Camille was their daughter and sister. They should know how the investigation into her death is going."

"I will." Bryce leaned into the table, bringing his face closer to mine. A trace of his cologne teased me. "You think this break-in is evidence that Karlisa's innocent, don't you?"

"It could be." I paused, remembering Granny's story about the origin of her animosity toward Tildie. "My grandmother had a childhood friend who betrayed her."

"I'm sorry about that."

"So am I, but my point is my grandmother was furious with her friend because of her betrayal, but she didn't attack her. Instead, she walked away and didn't speak with her for decades. That's why I can believe Karlisa walked away from Camille after their argument."

"All right. Maybe she did walk away from Camille— the first time." Bryce sat back on his chair. The look in his hazel eyes was distant as though he was imagining the scene. "But then she thought about their argument and became angrier so she went to find Camille a second time. Or maybe she wanted to warn Camille against telling the other band members about their missing money."

"I suppose that could've happened." It was plausible, but I still had doubts. So did the Abbey family. They couldn't picture Karlisa shoving Camille. "What about the person who'd been arguing with Camille beside the tree?"

"We can't confirm it was a different person." Bryce shrugged. "Just because Karlisa hadn't raised her voice in the past doesn't mean she didn't raise it that day. And remember, she has a history of violence."

"That one encounter in high school." I spread my arms. "And she said it had been a bad experience for her. That's the reason she learned to control her temper."

"She could be lying." Frustration eased into his tone. "You don't think it's Karlisa, but you don't have a stronger suspect."

"Not yet." Tension was building at the side of my neck. I stretched those muscles to help ease them.

Bryce studied me for a beat or two in silence. "The court set a date for the trial to begin for Emily Smith's murder."

I closed my eyes briefly in dismay. "I know. I read about it in the *Beacon* this morning."

I hadn't had a chance to discuss this latest update on the pending trial with my family. In fact, I was doing my best not to think about the situation, but it wasn't going away.

"Listen, Lyndsay, just because the court set a date doesn't mean the trial will happen." Bryce's tone was earnest. "The prosecution and defense could still come to a plea agreement."

"Or they might not." I let my eyes drift away from his.

"There's no reason to be nervous if you have to testify." He leaned forward into the table again. I could feel him trying to recapture my eyes. "I'm sure your whole family will be there. Stan and I will be there, too."

It made me smile to think of the detectives who'd investigated my mother and me for murder coming to court on one of the trial dates to give us moral support.

"I'm not afraid to testify. Well, actually, I am. Kind of." I paused to gather my thoughts. "I'm concerned about how the defense is going to approach the case. The fact that they keep turning down the plea deal makes me think they're going to bring up other suspects, including my mother, to try to give the jury reasonable doubt. I don't want her to go through that again."

Bryce reached out, cupping his hand over mine as I fisted it on the table. "I don't want you or your family to go through that, either. It's true there will always be people who're quick to tear others down especially when they're as well regarded as your family. But remember, Lyndsay, the vast majority of people in Little Caribbean—your customers, neighbors, and of course your family and friends—know your mother's innocent."

"You're right." I drew a calming breath. The air teased me with the scents of the hot ginger tea in our mugs and Bryce's cologne. "I have to be positive."

And I was. I was absolutely positive that I didn't want this case to go to trial.

CHAPTER 21

Granny made a face. "You've got some real work ahead of you."

She crossed to the large trash container in the rear of the bakery's kitchen early Tuesday morning and threw away my latest coconut drops effort. I followed, regretfully adding the one I'd sampled to the pile. It had been tough, dry, and dusty. It stung to have my grandmother throw out my baking efforts, but she was right. My latest attempt wasn't good enough for our bakery.

My sigh rose from the pit of my stomach. "I don't understand. The batch I made yesterday was great. You said so yourself." It was a strain keeping my disappointment from my voice.

I returned to the blond wood center island and dropped onto the nearest barstool. I needed a moment—or ten—to clear my thoughts. Rubbing my temples beneath the band of the black chef's hat that covered my hair, I let my restless eyes sweep our state-of-the art kitchen. They skimmed the shiny silver refrigerator, oven, and dishwasher before landing on the vivid splashes of color on the far-left wall.

Mommy had painted and framed portraits of Caribbean music greats Buju Banton, the soca star; Harry Belafonte, the King of Calypso; and Bob Marley, the reggae pioneer. Centered below their images was a large rendering of the flag of Grenada. Its red border stood for courage. Yellow triangles denoted warmth and wisdom while the green ones symbolized the island's vegetation. The nutmeg was its most famous produce. The large star in the center represented its capital, St. George's. Six smaller stars signified the parishes: Saint Mark, Saint Patrick, Saint Andrew, Saint John, Saint George, and Saint David.

"Remember, nothing beats a failure but a try." Granny pressed her lips to my forehead.

With that single, simple gesture, she healed my battered heart. I straightened my back and took a deep breath, filling my lungs with air scented with nutmeg, sugar, ginger, cinnamon, warm butter, and baked raisins.

Exhaling, I rose to my feet. "You're right. Third time's the charm." *I hope.*

Granny replaced me on the barstool. Beneath a red Spice Isle Bakery apron, she wore a plantain green two-piece shorts set. Her matching hair wrap was knotted above her right shoulder.

Adjusting my apron over my white T-shirt and black walking shorts, I crossed to the drainboard. I collected the recently washed mixing board and baking utensils. On my way back to the center island, I preheated the oven and plucked an egg from the fridge.

I put on fresh gloves, then measured the whole-grain flour and poured it into the mixing bowl. After adding the softened butter, I used a fork to combine the butter into the flour.

"Don't mash it so." Granny gently touched my left arm. "Use the tines to cut the butter into the flour." She mimicked the motion with her right hand in the air.

"Yes, Granny." After a few minutes, I'd cut all the butter

into the flour. I added the sugar, salt, nutmeg, cinnamon, and baking powder to the bowl.

"Take your time. Relax." Granny's voice was low, almost hypnotic. "This isn't a race."

I paused, making the effort to focus on the moment and my movements. After thoroughly mixing the ingredients, I beat the egg. Granny stood from the stool and selected a baking pan from a cupboard.

"You seem to be getting along with Bryce." Granny greased the pan. Her tone was a little too casual.

I went on mild alert. "I'm surprised by how well we seem to work together." I mixed the egg and vanilla extract into the bowl.

Granny gave a noncommittal hum as she returned to the stool. "Do you think you can forgive him for putting you and your mother on his murder suspect lists?"

My cheeks heated with discomfort. "I already have. He apologized to me privately and to our family. I accepted both."

I sprinkled the ginger, grated coconut, and raisins into the bowl, then combined these latest ingredients with the others.

Granny nodded with silent satisfaction. "But if you've forgiven him, what's keeping the two of you from going out? The man keeps asking you to lunch and dinner and drinks and such. He's not going to wait forever for you to say yes."

"Granny, I don't have time for a relationship right now." Walking past her, I carried the mixing bowl to the oven where she'd left the greased baking pan. "The bakery has to be my priority. We've just opened. I have to remain focused on our goal." Using a tablespoon, I scooped spoonfuls of the batter onto the pan, spacing them several inches apart.

Granny folded her arms and set them on the center

island's blond wood surface. "The bakery's been open for three months. In all that time, you haven't taken a single day off."

"There's a lot to do." I concentrated on spacing out the drops of batter onto the pan. *Please let this batch be exceptional.* "Besides, you know the saying: 'When you love what you do, you never work a day in your life.'"

"There's also a saying that all work and no play stunts a person's growth." Her voice was as dry as sand. Or my last batch of coconut drops. "And you can't count your murder investigations as a hobby. Those are work, too. Dangerous work."

Of course, she was right. Those cases weren't hobbies. Hobbies were supposed to be relaxing.

"Things won't be like this forever. Once I figure out an efficient, productive routine, I'll schedule days off." I slipped the pan into the oven and set the alarm on my cell phone for twelve minutes.

Granny tsked. "It's been *three* months. If you haven't found a way to balance work and days off, then it's time to ask for help. There's no shame in it, you know."

"It would take time to find someone and then train them. Time I don't have." I washed the mixing bowl and baking utensils. Normally, I'd pack them into the dishwasher, but these were just a few items, not enough to run the machine.

"Invest the time now. Save more time later."

I turned to face her, crossing my arms. "And where would I find these trainees, Granny?"

She chuckled. "I have teenage godchildren, and friends with teenagers and college students who could use some extra cash. You can train them to manage the inventory, schedule the marketing, or clean the bakery on the weekend. You'd be surprised how much free time you'll have if you give someone else one or even two tasks to take off your shoulders. Learn to ask for help."

I loved taking care of the bakery, but the thought of having a few free waking hours was appealing. Still . . . "I don't know, Granny. Even if you picked the person, it'll still take a lot of time and effort to train them."

Granny considered me in silence for several moments. Her sigh was a thin thread of frustration. "Lynds, when I was younger, I worked hard all day, every day, to help my parents and to raise my two children by myself after your granddad died."

I dried my hands on a towel, then took the barstool on the opposite side of the center island from Granny. "I remember your telling Dev and me about that."

These were stories she'd told us when we'd visit her in Grenada and when she'd visit us in Brooklyn. She'd never make the memories seem sad, though. Granny wasn't one to feel sorry for herself—or "poor me one," as she'd say. Instead, she used those accounts to encourage us with our dreams. They illustrated that we could be successful and achieve our goals if we put in the effort and worked hard.

She continued as though I hadn't spoken. "I worked hard so Al and Della would have a better life. Della and Jake worked hard so you and Dev would have a better life." She pinned me with haunted brown eyes. In their depths, I saw the pain and uncertainty she'd never shared. "Love, I didn't work that hard to now watch my granddaughter work herself to death."

Message sent and received, but asking for help was harder than I'd imagined. I wanted to be able to handle all these tasks on my own. But my grandmother was right. I didn't want to burn out before the bakery had barely begun.

I took a shuddering breath, then reached across the center island to squeeze my grandmother's hand. "Granny, could you help me, please?"

She shifted her hand to hold mine. Her bow-shaped lips curved into a faint smile. "Of course, love. I'll make some calls."

"Your shop had long lines before the festival, but they're even longer now, oui. All you managing OK?" Tildie had stopped by the bakery late Wednesday afternoon, claiming she wanted to check on us. I think she was continuing her campaign to rebuild her friendship with Granny.

"We're fine. Thank you, Ms. Robinson." I served Granny and Tildie each a coconut bread and glass of iced mauby tea. "We've been crazy busy the past week and a half and that's just the way we like it."

"Thank you, love." Granny had set aside her crocheting to accept the snacks. "Yes, it was packed this morning. You'd think people hadn't seen sweets in weeks instead of days."

"Oh, I'm so glad the festival went well for you and brought in extra business." Tildie sipped her tea.

"How are things with your store, Tildie?" Granny's words came reluctantly, but I was proud of her for making the effort.

Tildie's eyes widened with surprise. I sensed her tension ease with relief as she smiled at Granny across the small folding table. "It's going well, Genevieve. Thank you for asking. It's going well."

I smiled as I carried the tray back to the customer counter. It didn't seem like they'd need a referee this time. My grandmother's gesture had seemed small, but it couldn't have been easy. Tildie's past actions had been selfish and cruel. But she'd been reaching out to Granny, trying to make amends. As Granny had said, it was time to leave the past behind and move forward. It was another example of her being a strong role model for me.

I went back to cleaning the dining area: straightening the seating arrangements, wiping down the tables and chairs, and sweeping while the sun was still out. If I waited until closing to sweep, I'd risk Granny's lecture about stirring up duppies. Considering the murder investigations the bakery's been involved with, perhaps she was right to be concerned about our attracting ghosts.

Tildie's voice carried to me as I emptied the dustpan into the trash bin at the edge of the section. "Speaking of sales picking up, orders for DragonFlyZ's benefit CD were through the roof. And that wasn't just in my shop, but all the businesses carrying it saw a strong surge in sales after poor Camille's death. May she rest in peace."

Granny pinched off another bite of her coconut bread. She seemed deep in thought. "I suppose that's to be expected. It's human nature to put more value on people and things once they're gone. All those sales are going to support groups that are doing the work she believed in. But it's too bad she won't get to celebrate her accomplishment."

Tildie grunted. "But that's the thing. Those organizations aren't getting the money."

Granny's eyes jumped up to meet Tildie's. "What d'you mean?"

I froze on my way back to the kitchen. "Why aren't they getting the money, Ms. Robinson?"

Tildie seemed to enjoy our shocked reactions. She swallowed more of her coconut bread, then washed it down with her iced mauby tea. "I've been getting calls from organizations that are contracted to receive proceeds from the CD. They say they haven't received any money since the project started."

Granny's jaw dropped. "What? But they were supposed to be receiving it since June 1. It's July 6."

This was a serious problem. Setting the broom and dustpan against the dining room wall, I crossed to the pass-through window to call Mommy, Daddy, and Dev to join us. They needed to hear this, too.

"What's going on, Lynds?" Dev held the swinging door open for Mommy and Daddy as they joined us in the customer service area.

My heart squeezed every time I looked at my older brother and thought about his leaving the bakery to return to his former law firm. Dev and I hadn't discussed the firm's offer since he'd told me about the partners calling him on the Fourth of July. I was pretty sure he'd told Granny, Mommy, and Daddy, too. They'd seemed a little quieter this morning as we'd prepared to open the bakery. Had he also told Joymarie? If so, how had she taken it? Did she want him to stay with the bakery or return to the firm? I really couldn't guess. The only thing I was certain of was that he'd promised to give it serious consideration before making his final decision next week. The suspense was killing me.

I gestured toward Granny's table in front of us. "Ms. Robinson said the aid organizations that were supposed to receive funds from the DragonFlyZ benefit CD still haven't received any money."

"How can that be?" Mommy stood beside Granny's chair. "I bought six copies."

"But it's July." Daddy came to a stop behind Mommy. "Weren't they supposed to have received two disbursements by now, one in June and one at the beginning of this month?"

"That's right." Tildie nodded. "Camille took the initiative with the project. Set up the account for the organizations to get monthly payments based on the percentage they'd agreed to. But remember, neither the band nor Karlisa nor any of the shopkeepers selling the CDs get a dime. All the money goes to the aid agencies."

I remembered reading about the terms of the charitable project in different news media outlets. Some of the aid agencies selected for the project were much larger and provided more assistance programs than others. The more programs the organization provided, the greater its share of the proceeds. It seemed like an equitable arrangement.

Dev came to stand next to me. "So what happened to the money? Is there a problem with the accounting process?"

"I have no idea." Tildie spread her arms. "I was just telling Genevieve that my phone's been ringing off the hook. People are calling me and the other store owners selling the CDs because they can't get a straight answer from the West Indian American Relief Fund. They're threatening to go to the media."

"I don't blame them," I muttered. This wasn't what Camille had wanted. Her spirit must be restless. "Have *you* tried calling Belle?"

Tildie kissed her teeth. "I left a message for her the other day. She hasn't called me back. One of the shopkeepers said Belle told her she's waiting for the bank to release the money. I don't know what would be taking the bank so long. They should've released the May proceeds last month, but there's always so much red tape."

Red tape was one theory. My mind was racing with other possibilities. "Hopefully, everything will work itself out soon. The aid organizations have a right to be upset, but I'm sure you, the other store owners, and DragonFlyZ are upset, too."

"Yes, it's very concerning." Collecting her purse from the back of her chair, Tildie got to her feet. "But speaking of stores, I'd better get back to mine. It's been nice visiting with all you." She smiled at Granny before looking at me. "Thank you as always for the refreshments."

I inclined my head. "It's our pleasure. Thank you for stopping by."

Tildie had an extra spring in her step as she left the bakery. She seemed happier. I was so pleased the tension between her and my grandmother had eased.

"Are you thinking what I'm thinking?" Granny's question came from behind me.

I turned to face my family. "We have a new suspect to look into: Belle Baton."

"Hi, Karlisa. It's Lyndsay Murray. How're you?" I'd hurried into the bakery's office late Wednesday afternoon, hoping to squeeze in a call with the DragonFlyZ manager before our evening customer traffic got into full swing. Dev, Granny, Mommy, and Daddy could probably handle the orders without me for a little while, but that would make me feel as though I was shirking my responsibilities.

"I'm fine, thank you, Lyndsay." Karlisa sounded surprised to hear from me. Familiar music played in the background. It sounded like one of the songs on DragonFlyZ's benefit CD. A weird coincidence. She lowered the volume on the recording before continuing. "Well, maybe 'fine' is an exaggeration. I'm scared almost out of my wits. I've lost my appetite and I'm having trouble sleeping."

I closed my eyes as her words snatched me back to when Bryce and Stan had suspected me of killing Claudio Fabrizi, and when they'd suspected my mother of killing Emily Smith. I hadn't been able to sleep or eat, either. If it weren't for my family's love and support, I would've lost every cell of my mind. Did Karlisa have family nearby?

I swallowed, trying to remove the knot of emotion from my throat. "I know what you're going through. My family and I went through the same thing. The police had also suspected my mother and me of committing murder."

"I know." Karlisa's voice was low. "I read about both cases in the *Beacon*. I'm ashamed to admit I'd thought the police were right. I thought you'd killed Claudio Fabrizi. It never occurred to me that the police could make a mistake. And then when they suspected your mother of killing Principal Smith, I didn't think they could make the same mistake twice."

I'm not going to lie. Knowing Karlisa had suspected my mother and me to have been guilty of murder stung. To make things worse, I was certain she hadn't been the only person to believe that. For all I knew, there were still people who thought we were guilty. Perhaps that's why Emily Smith's killer hadn't accepted the prosecution's plea deal. Was the defense trying to cast reasonable doubt on their client's guilt by implying someone else could have murdered the principal? Were they going to imply my mother was responsible?

I couldn't think about that now.

I sighed to ease the tightness in my chest. "My mother was the victim of bad timing, and someone had tried to frame me."

"I realize that now." The music beneath Karlisa's words had stopped. She must have turned off the CD player. "I'm really sorry and ashamed I ever doubted your innocence or your mother's. You and your family are being so kind to me. It's hard for me being so far from my family. They're all in Florida. I'm the only one in New York.

They've been calling, but talking on the phone's not the same."

"No, it's not." I don't know what I would've done if my family had been so far from me while I was dealing with Claudio's murder investigation. "Do you have friends nearby?"

Karlisa hesitated. Her voice was heavy with sorrow. "I work all the time. The only people I'm really close to are the members of DragonFlyZ and they've been avoiding me. I think they think I killed Camille." Her breath caught on a sob.

"I'm so sorry, Karlisa." My heart broke for her.

She gave a shuddering sigh. "I spoke with Alfonso Lester yesterday. He's very nice."

"Yes, he is." I smiled at the mention of Reena's boyfriend. "He's also a really smart lawyer. Dev mentored him."

"Really? Alfonso's very lucky, then." Karlisa blew her nose. "He took a lot of time reassuring me and telling me, step by step, what usually happens in a situation like this. I feel like I know what to expect. That's very comforting."

"I'm glad." I glanced at the time on my cell phone. I needed to redirect the conversation to the murder investigation so I could get back to work. "Karlisa, what can you tell me about DragonFlyZ's benefit CD project and its sales?"

She sniffed a few times. I imagined her using her free hand to wipe her nose and dry her tears. This was a stressful time. I didn't blame her for getting emotional. "Nothing really. Camille and other members of the band took care of setting up the project: recording studio, distribution, the online accounts, physical stores, partnership with the West Indian American Relief Fund, bank account. Everything."

I was afraid of that. "Did the band members tell you how the participating aid agencies were supposed to receive their donations?" If not, I'd have to ask the band members directly. That would have to wait until the bakery closed, though. I needed to get back to work.

"Yes, they did." Karlisa paused. I sensed her gathering her thoughts. "People can download the music from an online account. But there are four physical stores in Little Caribbean where people can buy the actual CDs. Either way, money from the purchases is transferred electronically to an account Camille opened for this project."

"And the agencies are supposed to receive money from this account?" I tried to visualize the process and possible pitfalls.

"That's right. The money was supposed to be transferred the first weekday of June and July. Camille insisted on that. The CD's a limited-time offer. Sales would stop at the end of Caribbean American Heritage Month, June 30." Karlisa sighed. "I've heard demand has been incredible, even greater than we'd hoped. Camille would've been so proud. I was wrong to try to talk them out of the project. And one of the side benefits is that it's increased sales of the band's other CDs. I wish Camille had lived long enough to see how successful it's been."

"So do I." I wished that for so many reasons. "I understand each aid agency receives a percentage of the month's proceeds. Does the bank make the distribution?"

"Oh, no." Karlisa chuckled with surprise. "They would've charged way too much to handle the distribution. Camille gave access to the account to the president of the West Indian American Relief Fund. Why're you asking?"

The answer snatched my breath. I struggled to sound nonchalant. "I was just curious. The owner of one of the stores that sold the CDs is a family friend." I winced. That excuse was so flimsy. Would Karlisa buy it?

Apparently, she did. "Oh. That's interesting. Well, Camille asked the president of the relief fund to handle the distribution since she has long-standing relationships with all of the agencies."

Shock temporarily cleared my thoughts. "Thank you for your time, Karlisa. Listen, have faith. Everything will work out. I'll be in touch again soon."

"I appreciate everything you and your family are doing for me. Alfonso Lester said if anyone could uncover the truth, you could."

That was a lot of pressure. "I promise to do my best."

"I know you will." Karlisa sighed again. "Thank you for calling, Lyndsay. It was good to talk with you."

We ended the call and I took a moment to pull my thoughts together. Belle had access to the benefit CD project's bank account. Agencies were claiming they didn't receive their distributions in June or July. Belle wasn't returning anyone's calls.

Why was Belle ducking calls?

What had happened to the proceeds from the CD sales?

Was Belle the person Camille had argued with near the tree?

I sprang from the desk chair and hurried to the customer counter. I had to bring this new information to my family for their input and feedback. But first, there were pastries to sell.

CHAPTER 22

"So Sheryl, I was wondering why the Caribbean American Heritage Festival Association doesn't work on projects with the West Indian American Relief Fund. It seems like the perfect partnership." Granny sipped her sorrel as she waited for Sheryl Cross's response. She looked almost regal in a floral-print melon maxi dress that skimmed her slim figure.

My family and I had invited Sheryl to the bakery under the pretense of discussing her association's holiday reception before providing her with an estimate. In reality, we hoped Sheryl could provide information that could help us better understand why Belle might steal money from the benefit CD project and kill Camille to prevent the singer from exposing her theft. We needed a strong motive before bringing our new theory of the murder to Bryce and Stan.

It was late Thursday afternoon. The weekday lunch crush had dwindled to fewer than a handful of guests in the dining area. Mommy, Daddy, Dev, and I had gathered extra chairs around Granny's dark wood folding table, doing our best to look only casually interested in the conversation. Inside, I was anxious for Granny and Sheryl to start dishing some dirt.

My impatience was one of the reasons I'd asked Granny to lead the interview with Sheryl. She was the best actor in the family.

Sheryl looked smart in her dark mustard sheath dress. Her sniff was sharp with disdain. "That young woman is too irresponsible. I won't risk my association's reputation by collaborating with someone who's so undependable."

"Is that so? Hmm." Granny feigned confusion. "I'd heard you two don't work together because she thinks you're too cheap."

I stiffened. Granny was making that up. I was almost certain no one had said that to her. The accusation must be a ploy to get Sheryl to discuss what, if anything, she knew about Belle's money situation.

Good job, Granny!

I turned with studied nonchalance to survey our patrons in the dining area. The movement was meant to reinforce the impression that I was only half listening to Sheryl and Granny's conversation. I also wanted to see if our customers needed anything. Two or three of them watched us with open curiosity, but most of our guests were involved in their own conversations, books, or newspapers.

"*I'm* cheap?" Sheryl's reaction was a harsh whisper. Her eyes stretched wide with outrage. She looked around the bakery as though checking to make sure she hadn't been overheard. Other than the two or three nosy guests, no one appeared to be paying attention to us. Sheryl leaned into the table and lowered her voice anyway. "*I'm* the one who's cheap? Listen, Belle Baton's the one people should be worrying about. She's left unpaid invoices all over Little Caribbean."

"Uh-oh. But wait." Granny straightened on her chair.

"She hasn't paid her bills? Why haven't we heard of this before?"

Sheryl continued, seeming not to have heard Granny. "I've spoken with some of those vendors. They're talking about suing her, you know."

"She's facing lawsuits?" That would be a motive for stealing money. I kept my voice low also. "Is the relief fund having financial trouble?"

"Lynds." Granny shifted on her chair to face me. "Did we get the deposit check for Belle's event?"

I nodded. "Yes, Granny. I received Belle's deposit check earlier in the week and deposited it the same day." I turned back to Sheryl. "Is the—"

Granny interrupted again. "Did it clear?"

I returned my attention to my grandmother. "Yes, Granny. Belle's check cleared."

She exhaled. "At least we'll have that money."

Sheryl grunted. "That one's got champagne tastes with mauby pockets."

I smiled at the saying. If Sheryl was right, Belle sounded like she was trying to carry on an expensive lifestyle without the means to pay for it.

The association president wrinkled her nose. "She had the nerve to invite me to the reception. Can you believe it? She wants people to link my organization with hers. As long as she's a part of the fund, that will *never* happen. I'm not going."

I tried again to get answers from Sheryl. "Is the fund having money trouble?"

Sheryl's expression grew pinched as though she'd sucked a lemon. "Her parents built that agency because they saw a need for it. They each had two jobs while working to get the relief fund on its feet. It took them a lot of years and even more hard work. It was solid and well respected while they were alive. Her parents have been gone less than a year—God rest their souls—and the fund's reputation has already been damaged beyond repair."

Dev frowned. "Is it just the unpaid vendor bills or does the fund have other issues?"

Disgust tightened Sheryl's round features. "Belle has made a mess of her family's legacy, eh. Staff quit. Their nonprofit status is in trouble. It's a shame."

"Yes, it is." Mommy sighed. "Did her parents prepare her to take over the agency?"

Sheryl shrugged. "Apparently not well enough. They listed her as a member of the administration, but they didn't count her responsibilities."

Daddy folded his arms. "Did she actually work for the fund or was her name just on some documents?"

Sheryl gave a reluctant smile. "Well, you know, Jacob, they put her name on the papers because she's their daughter. They spoiled her. They gave her everything she wanted. She never heard the word 'no.' And she never learned to manage money."

There we have it, a motive for Belle to steal the benefit CD proceeds. And if Camille had confronted her about her embezzlement, they would've argued and Belle may have shoved Camille down the park steps. But that was a lot of "could haves" and "may haves." I'll have a hard time convincing Bryce.

Granny drained her sorrel. "It's such a shame that her lack of preparation could mean the end of the fund after all of her parents' hard work."

"I agree." Sheryl stood, checking her gold-link wristwatch. "I'd better get back to work. Thank you very much for the tea. Good luck with Belle's event. I think you'll need it."

I watched Sheryl march from the bakery. Her steps

seem irritated. It was understandable considering what we'd been discussing. "I wouldn't want to cross her more than once."

"I wouldn't want to cross her at all." Daddy looked from me to Dev and back. "What do you think? Do the fund's financial problems give Belle a strong enough motive for murder?"

"I think it's strong enough for us to speak with Bryce." I looked over my shoulder at Dev.

"I agree." He met my eyes before looking at Daddy, Mommy, and Granny. "It should convince him to interview her at least. I wish we could remember what she was wearing, though. Was it a blue shirt?"

My thoughts were racing. "Do you think Belle is behind the break-in at the Abbeys' home?"

Mommy frowned. "How would Belle have known which room was Camille's and what was in it?"

I couldn't answer that. However, I believed Camille's family's instincts were right. It was too much of a coincidence that Camille would be murdered and then her room burglarized. It made sense that the killer and the thief would be the same person, especially if money was the motive for both crimes.

"For now, let's focus on finding Camille's killer." Daddy offered Mommy his hand to help her from her chair. They were still wearing their black chef's smocks and dark lightweight pants.

"All right." I stood and turned toward the dining area. "I'll ask Bryce to meet with us in the morning so we can update him. We need a plan."

Bryce wasn't alone when he entered the bakery late Friday morning. Stan was with him. I felt a pinch of disappointment. I don't know why. I liked Stan. He was polite and friendly. I loved the way he talked about his wife, and the way he enjoyed my family's cooking and baking.

Oh, who was I lying to? I was disappointed because I'd started looking forward to those times I had Bryce to myself.

I fixed a polite smile on my lips. "Good morning, Bryce. It's good to see you again, Stan. Thank you both for coming. Would you like a snack before our meeting?"

I was managing the customer counter on my own during the lull in activity. Mommy, Daddy, and Dev were in the kitchen preparing for our lunch service. Granny was at her table, crocheting another lavender-and-white afghan square.

"I sure would," Stan responded before I'd finished my question. The older detective looked like he'd dressed in a rush. His hair was pointing in different directions. His silver-and-navy striped tie was askew, and as usual, his brown suit was rumpled. "I'd like a slice of coconut bread and a glass of sorrel, please." He turned to Bryce. "Would you like one?"

"Sure, but I'll get mine. Thanks." Bryce looked striking in a pale brown suit, matching tie, and cream shirt.

Stan waved away Bryce's words. "I'll get his, too."

Granny's chuckle drifted back to me. "All you always fighting over who would pay the bill."

I turned to fill Stan's order. "Congratulations on your upcoming retirement, Stan. Are you looking forward to having more time for yourself?"

"I'm excited about it." Stan sounded uncertain. Was he trying to convince us or himself?

"Will you miss the work, Detective?" Granny continued working on her afghan square, but I sensed she was listening closely for his answer. Had she also heard the tentative note in Stan's voice?

"Definitely, Ms. Bain." Stan faced Granny. "I get a lot of satisfaction in helping to find justice for victims and putting killers in prison so they won't hurt anyone else. I'll miss being a part of that." He smiled. "But my wife's right. I won't miss the hours. She's already making a honey-do list to fill my free time."

Granny chuckled. "Your work is very important and you've been at it a long time. You deserve the rest."

"Thank you, ma'am." Stan inclined his head. "I'll need some of that extra time to work off all these delicious pastries from your bakery."

After pouring myself a glass of iced mauby tea, I led Bryce and Stan to a table for four on the opposite side of the dining area from the guests who lingered over their late-morning snacks. The group—two women and two men—seemed to be in their late sixties or early seventies. They were nicely dressed in short-sleeved muted shirts and blouses and light-colored linen shorts.

From the snatches of conversation I caught, they were locked in a fierce debate over the candidates running for Brooklyn Borough President. How did they know who was winning the argument? They were all talking at once. On the upside, their discussion reassured me they wouldn't pay much, if any, attention to my meeting with Bryce and Stan.

I sat on the side of the table with a clear view of the bakery's entrance. "Have you received the results from the comparison of the blouse found in Karlisa's trash and the cloth found in Camille's hand?"

Bryce took the seat directly across from me. "Not yet. The results aren't due for another day or two."

"Monday on the outside." Stan sat beside Bryce. Ignoring the knife and fork I'd placed on his tray, he pinched off a piece of his coconut bread.

It blew my mind how long it took to get crime scene reports in real life compared to police dramas on film and television. "While we're waiting for those results, I think we should look into Belle Baton. She's the president of the West Indian American Relief Fund."

Lowering my voice, I told the two detectives what my family and I had learned from Tildie, Karlisa, and Sheryl: Belle's financial trouble, the multiple potential lawsuits, her access to the benefit CD proceeds, and the fact that none of the aid agencies had received a dime.

"That's an interesting theory." Stan finished his coconut bread. His brow furrowed as though he was turning the information over in his mind.

"I agree." Bryce drained his sorrel. He stared blindly behind me as though picturing what I'd said. "It would give Belle a strong motive for killing Camille. But, Lyndsay, motive alone doesn't make her the killer."

My eyes stretched so wide, I thought they'd pop out of my head. "You thought *I* killed Claudio Fabrizi based on a much flimsier motive." The one time I'd lost my temper and gotten into a public argument with someone, I ended up on a short list of murder suspects.

Oh, brother.

Bryce shook his head. "You may have been on the suspect list—"

I couldn't let that go unchallenged. "There's no *may have been* about it." I used air quotes around "may have been." "I distinctly remember being on your suspect list."

He continued as though I hadn't spoken. "But we never arrested you."

"Thank you?" I exhaled a frustrated breath. "I'm not asking you to arrest her. But we should search her home."

Bryce arched a thick black eyebrow. *"We?"*

I rolled my eyes. "OK. *You.*"

Stan looked from Bryce to me. "I'm afraid we don't have probable cause, Lyndsay. We don't have any material evidence linking her to the crime scene. Your information gives us reason to believe she's embezzling from the benefit CD fund, but the only thing linking her to Camille Abbey's murder is our gut. That won't get us a warrant."

I exhaled a heavy sigh. "Meanwhile she could be destroying any evidence she might have that would link her to Camille's murder."

Bryce spread his hands. "I'm sorry, Lyndsay, but we can't search Belle Baton's home without a warrant."

I thought for a moment. My tone was tentative. "Can we ask her for permission to search her home?" Not an ideal compromise, but it could do in a pinch.

Bryce was already shaking his head. "If she's the killer, asking her permission to search her home without a warrant would tip her off that we're looking at her for the murder."

Stan nodded his agreement. "Then she'd definitely get rid of anything that could link her to Camille Abbey's death. You can bet money on that."

I frowned. "It's been almost two weeks since Camille's death. She may have already destroyed evidence. There must be something we can do to give us a stronger reason to get a warrant."

Stan ticked off his fingers. "It would be really helpful if you could find someone who saw Ms. Baton with Ms. Abbey arguing or near the steps around the time of her murder. Or if you learn Ms. Baton told someone she'd killed Ms. Abbey. That spontaneous confession could get us an arrest."

Seriously? "If she gave me a spontaneous confession, why would I need a search warrant?" This wasn't working out the way I'd imagined.

Search warrants temporarily override our constitutional protections from unreasonable searches and seizures. Because of that, the reasons to receive a search warrant had to be very, very, very strong. Unimpeachable. I should've realized that while our information showed Belle had a good motive for murder, motive wasn't evidence.

Bryce stood to leave. "Stan and I'll interview the band members, event organizers, and Karlisa Trotter again. See if any of them could verify where Belle was around the time of Camille Abbey's death."

"That's a good idea." Even to my ears, I sounded distracted.

Bryce gave me a sharp look. "Lyndsay, what are you thinking about?"

Surprised, I met his eyes. "Nothing. Just the case. Why?"

"Lyndsay." When I continued to hold his eyes, he sighed. "Don't do anything illegal or rash. OK? You could jeopardize the investigation. Promise me."

"I promise . . ." *Not to tell you what I'm planning.*

I wasn't going to compromise an investigation into Belle. But what I was planning might skirt the edges enough to warrant giving Bryce and Stan plausible deniability.

CHAPTER 23

"Bryce and Stan don't believe we have strong enough cause to get a search warrant for Belle's home." I leaned against the back counter beside the pass-through window.

It was late Friday afternoon. Granny, Mommy, and Daddy were preparing to go home. They worked the early shift. Dev was staying to close the bakery with me. I'd told him a million times I could manage on my own. But I think he was still upset about the night someone had followed me from the bakery. And I didn't mind his company, which showed I wasn't completely over that scare, either.

"They're right." Dev rested his left hip against the counter on the other side of the pass-through window. "All we have are circumstantial evidence and suspicions."

Granny threw up her hands in frustration. "Then why did we bother to tell them anything?"

Dev gave a half smile. Being used to Granny's drama, he didn't take offense. We were too thick-skinned for that. "We want the detectives to question Belle. Get her on the record regarding her relationship with Camille and her alibi for the time of her murder."

Mommy adjusted her purse strap on her shoulder. "And remember, we're supposed to be working with the detectives on this one. Everything we know, they should know, too."

I shared Granny's concern, but Dev and Mommy were right. "The detectives' hands are tied. Without a warrant, they can't search Belle's home. But I can."

"What?" Mommy's eyes flared wide.

"What are you talking about?" Daddy shook his head, seeming to question his hearing.

"No, you can't." Dev stared at me as though the force of his will could get me to change my mind. It couldn't.

Granny smiled. "She's done it before."

Mommy gave Granny a chastising look. "Don't encourage her, Mommy."

My parents and grandmother marched out of the kitchen. They surrounded me at the customer service counter. Mommy was scandalized. Daddy was disapproving. Granny looked ready for adventure.

My grandmother's suggestion that I was developing a pattern of risky behavior made me pause, though. I used to be the conservative family member; the one who was more often than not risk averse. Dev took calculated chances. Reena had never met a gamble she didn't want to dive into. And don't get me started on Uncle Roman. In the past three months, I'd launched a business and investigated three murders. I didn't recognize myself anymore. Was that a bad thing?

I didn't think so.

Daddy frowned at me. "How're you going to break into someone's house and search it? That's a crime, you know."

I straightened from the counter. "I'm not going to break in. Belle's hosting the reception honoring Camille at her home. I'll search it then."

Dev rubbed his forehead with the fingertips of his right

hand. "You're planning on searching a suspected murderer's house. Suppose she catches you?"

Granny raised her arm in my direction. "Belle's not going to harm Lynds when her house is full of people."

"We don't know that, Gran." Dev crossed his arms, looking like the personification of inflexibility. "She might hurt Lynds under the guise of saying she thought she was confronting a burglar. Or she might wait for her to be closing the bakery on her own one night and attack her then."

I scowled at my big brother. "You're determined to make me uncomfortable about closing the bakery by myself at night, aren't you?" Without waiting for his response, I faced my parents and Granny. "The catering is the perfect cover for the search. Belle's giving me a tour of her home tomorrow so that we know where to do the staging. That'll give me a chance to decide which rooms to search."

"And what would you be looking for, if you went through with this foolishness?" Daddy wasn't warming up to this plan.

I forged ahead anyway. "A torn blue blouse. Remember? We think the killer planted the blouse Bryce recovered from Karlisa's trash. Hopefully, I'll find the real one in Belle's bedroom."

Dev dragged a hand over his tight dark curls. "Do Bryce and Stan know what you plan to do?"

My eyes widened with horror. My lips parted in surprise. "No, and we can't tell them. They have to have plausible deniability in case we're discovered."

"I don't know about this, Lynds." Mommy paced away from us to Granny's table and back. "This is exactly what we didn't want when your father and I opposed this investigation in the first place. You're putting yourself at risk. You didn't even know Camille."

My body trembled in reaction. My throat started to close. I wrapped my arms around my waist. I didn't relish putting my life in danger. And I certainly didn't want to upset my family. But neither did I want to disappoint myself.

Looking over my shoulder toward the dining area, I checked on our final three guests, two middle-aged women and an adolescent boy. They were finishing their banana pudding, coconut cake, and beef pattie. Bursts of laughter periodically interrupted their hushed conversation. The trio seemed oblivious to the tension surrounding me at the counter.

I faced my family. "When we first started this investigation, I wanted to help Manny through his grief. Knowing who killed his friend would bring him comfort."

Dev still stood with his arms folded. His stubborn demeanor emphasized his resemblance to Daddy. "And you've helped Bryce and Stan get on the right path to finding Camille's killer."

"But, Dev, this case has become more than that to me." How could I make them understand? "It's more than a way to help Manny or get justice for Camille." I turned to Mommy. "It's also about revealing the truth and preventing what happened to you and me from happening to Karlisa. The thought of her being tried for a crime she may not have committed makes my stomach sick."

The sound of footsteps crossing to the bakery's exit broke the sudden silence. A chorus of voices floated toward us. "Good afternoon."

I looked over my right shoulder again to acknowledge the trio's farewell. "Good afternoon. Thank you for coming."

My family echoed my words. Once our guests had left, my relatives' silence returned. I sensed my parents and

Dev struggling to come up with other arguments to dissuade me from my plan.

Granny stepped toward me. She cupped the left side of my face with her soft palm and kissed my right cheek. "I'm proud of you, love."

Mommy's, Daddy's, and Dev's sighs were quiet surrenders. Dev and Daddy dropped their arms.

"If you're determined we should do this, then *I'll* search Belle's bedroom." Dev's grumpy offer came from beside me.

I turned to him with a dubious look. "And jeopardize your law license if Belle finds you? No, you won't. I've got this."

Stubbornness stamped Dev's features. "And what if she catches *you*?"

Granny waved a hand toward me. "Have you ever seen your sister's kickboxing moves? She can take care of herself."

I smiled at Granny before returning my attention to my overprotective older brother. "Besides, I'm going to arrange to have a couple of people make sure Belle's occupied during the event."

Granny clapped her hands. "I can do it. Let me do it, nuh."

I squeezed her arm with regret. "You'd be perfect for this, Granny, but Mommy, Daddy, and Dev will need your help with the catering while I'm searching Belle's bedroom."

Granny looked crestfallen. "You're right. So who're you going to ask?"

"I have several people in mind, including Manny." I felt good about my options. "Belle invited people from Caribbean Tunes because they produced the benefit CD. He can help keep an eye on Belle." I nodded as I considered my other options. "And there are a couple of other people I have a feeling will be more than happy to help."

DragonFlyZ's "Sing Up Your Name (for History)" swept across the recreation room on the ground floor of Belle Baton's elegant home Monday evening. Camille had written that song specifically for the benefit CD. It was an appropriate choice for the reception honoring the late singer.

Guests were starting to arrive. Despite the somber occasion, many of them were swaying to the beat. I couldn't imagine a better tribute to Camille's talent than letting her music touch you.

But I was a wreck. My neck and shoulder muscles tightened with each passing minute as I waited for Manny to arrive, as well as José and Sheryl, the two other people I'd recruited Friday afternoon to help keep Belle distracted while I searched her room and my family served the food.

My heart had sunk when Belle had given me a tour of the staging area Saturday afternoon. It was the perfect space for a reception. Guests would have plenty of room to socialize despite the tables we'd set up for buffet-style serving. We'd keep the rest of the food warm in the small kitchen at the back of the event level.

For my purposes, the only drawback was that the ground floor where the reception was taking place was two levels away from Belle's bedroom. And—bonus!—the door leading from the stairwell to her private residence would remain locked.

"So what are we going to do?" Dev asked. Again.

I gritted my teeth and forced my lips into a smile. "Well, first, you're going to take that scowl off your face before our host and her guests wonder what we're arguing about."

The spicy aromas of curry and jerk meats and the sweet

scents of fried ripe plantains wafted toward me from the tiny kitchen behind us. There was a lot on the line tonight. If we couldn't find anything to link Belle to Camille's murder, then we would've risked prison, or worse, for nothing. On top of that, if our suspicions were correct and Belle was paying for us with funds she'd stolen from the benefit project, we'd have to return the check, which meant we weren't going to be paid. All I could do was hope and pray that tonight wasn't a complete bust, for either justice or business.

"Is everyone ready?" The sound of Manny's whisper made me weak with relief.

Granny, Mommy, and Daddy emerged from the tiny kitchen to join Dev, Manny, and me. Mommy, Daddy, Dev, and I were dressed in our formal black chef's smocks with our Spice Isle Bakery logo, matching chef's hats, and black pants. There was no reason we couldn't advertise despite the clandestine mission.

My grandmother embraced Manny. "We are now that you've arrived."

Granny, in keeping with her staunch refusal to wear any type of uniform ever again since her retirement from the Grenville Post Office in Grenada, wore a turquoise-and-gold dress that traced her slender figure to her ankles and a scarlet head wrap that complemented her sienna skin and emphasized her wide, dark brown eyes.

"No, we're not." Dev spoke around a stiff smile. "The doors in the stairwell are locked."

"They are?" Mommy gasped. She turned to me, lowering her voice further. "Lynds, I don't think we should go through with this."

"Go through with what?" Out of nowhere, Belle appeared. Her eyes were clouded with suspicion. How much had she overheard?

She looked like a silver screen movie actress in her black ankle-length evening dress that skimmed her full curves. She'd accessorized with chunky sterling silver earrings and matching necklace and bracelets. Her makeup was flawless. The West Indian American Relief Fund might not be doing well, but Belle was, which added to my fears that she was embezzling from the benefit CD sales.

Sheryl stood beside Belle. She seemed anxious and stiff, but at least she'd arrived. Thank goodness. That accounted for two of my three decoys. Where was José? For a newspaper reporter, he was showing a distinct problem with meeting deadlines. This plan was unraveling much faster than it had come together. My pulse was racing like a rabbit at the base of my throat. My saliva dried up. My mind went blank.

And then inspiration crash-landed into my brain. "Go through with asking you if we could use your stove upstairs for one of our bigger pots."

Belle looked from Mommy to me. "I thought you couldn't cook in people's houses because of Department of Health rules. I don't want people getting sick and suing me, you know."

True. It sounds like you already have enough lawsuits pending.

My smile came much more easily this time. "We're not going to cook anything. We need to keep it warm, but the stovetop in the kitchen down here is too small to accommodate it comfortably."

Her confusion cleared. "I see." She pulled a set of keys from a pocket hidden in the skirt of her dress. She held up the larger one. "This is for the dead bolt. The other one goes to the doorknob. Keep both locked at all times, please. I don't want people wandering into my home, but I can trust you."

Sheryl touched Belle's shoulder. She looked cool and professional in a silver short-sleeved sheath dress. "We should let them get back to the food, Belle." She met my eyes. Her smile was tight around the edges. "Everything smells wonderful as usual."

Could Belle sense Sheryl's tension? We all had to act natural or risk raising Belle's suspicions.

I flashed an easy grin. "Thank you for the compliment, Sheryl. I hope you enjoy the food."

Sheryl's features eased. "I always do." She drew Belle away with her.

I turned back to my family. They each looked at me as though I'd climbed out of a spaceship. "What's wrong?" I touched my chef's hat and checked my smock. Everything seemed OK.

"You're so good at this, it scares me." Mommy shook her head.

Granny chuckled. "You're quick on your feet. Just like me."

I didn't have time to process their comments. We had an event to cater, a host to distract, and rooms to search. The reception area was filling with guests. Manny's boss had arrived. Camille's family had gathered together. As I turned to address my relatives, I caught sight of José speaking with Belle. What a relief. Now everyone was in place. I was beginning to believe this could actually work.

I exhaled. "Granny, Mommy, Daddy, and Dev, pretend this is just another day at the bakery. The food remains hot and fresh. The serving platters stay full. OK?"

"OK." Granny rubbed her hands together.

"Got it." Dev still seemed troubled.

"All right." Mommy exchanged an uneasy look with Daddy.

Daddy wrapped an arm around Mommy's shoulders. "Everything will be fine."

From his lips to God's ears. I turned to my cousin. "You're on your own. Granny, Mommy, Daddy, and Dev won't be able to help you. They'll have their hands full, pretending everything's normal."

He nodded. "I understand."

I hoped so. "Act casual. Mingle with the other guests. Your coworkers are here as well as members of Dragon-FlyZ and Camille's family. If you hear anything that could also help us with the investigation, let us know. But most importantly, keep an eye on Belle. If you see her alone, distract her. José Perez and Sheryl Cross are your backups, but don't rely on them. Other guests might pull them away. Above all, don't let Belle come upstairs to check on me."

Manny held my eyes. "You can count on me."

I stepped back and came up against the wall beside the kitchen. "OK. Let's get to work."

CHAPTER 24

I had to stay off the radar. If Belle saw me moving around the reception room, and in and out of the kitchen, before suddenly disappearing, she might come looking for me. That's why I spent most of my time Monday evening in the kitchen, filling salad bowls and platters for Granny, Mommy, Daddy, and Dev to carry to the buffet tables. To avoid seeming as though I was hiding—which I was—I made an unassuming appearance in the reception area, carrying a serving dish of coconut rice.

"Lyndsay, I'm glad we caught you." Viola Abbey, Camille's middle sister, spoke from behind me.

I set the serving dish on the buffet table between the jerk chicken and fried plantains before turning. Her siblings and parents were with her. I shared a warm smile with all of them. "Good evening. How are you?"

Lynne shook her head with a sigh. "We're taking one day at a time. That's all we can do."

I touched Camille's mother's arm briefly before folding my hands at my hips again. "That sounds like a wise decision."

Viola claimed my attention. "Thank you for convincing Detective Jackson to call us. Has he said anything more to you about the break-in? Or my sister's murder?"

I shook my head. "I'm afraid not. Has anything else happened?" I hoped the answer was no. How much more could this family take?

"No, nothing." Viola rubbed her eyes. I couldn't tell if she was wiping away tears or frustration. "I don't think he's taking us seriously, though."

It hurt to hear them say that. "That's not true. Detective Jackson can be methodical and skeptical, but what's important is that he's taking this case very personally. Give him some more time. He'll get justice for Camille. I'm sure of that."

"All right. I feel better after talking with you." Lynne's frown was troubled.

From the corner of my eye, I could see Belle watching us. Could she hear what we were talking about? It was time for me to get out of sight again. "I'm glad I could help. It's good to see you. I'd better get back to the kitchen."

Had Belle broken into the Abbeys' home? If so, what was she going to do with Camille's stuff? Sell it? My mind was spinning.

"Of course, dear." Lynne found a smile. "Thank you for catering this event."

"It's an honor." I'd taken two steps toward the kitchen when a familiar voice stopped me.

"Lyndsay Murray?" Earl Lees, the drummer of Dragon-FlyZ and Rocky's boyfriend, approached me. "I thought that was you."

I was starstruck, just for a moment. "It's good to see you again, Mr. Lees. May I call you Earl? But I wish it was during a happier time. How are you holding up?"

He took my arm, leading me away from the groups of people and to a quieter section of the room. "We're still in shock." He released me and pushed his hands into the front pockets of his dark brown pants. "We can't imagine the band without Camille as our lead singer. And now we're hearing talk about the police suspecting Karlisa for her murder. We can't believe it."

I glanced around the room. Belle wasn't watching me any longer. She was with José and Sheryl again. Manny was nearby, talking with the manager of his recording studio and Miles. I didn't see the band's manager.

"Karlisa didn't come." I made it a statement rather than a question.

"Can you blame her?" Earl shook his head. He seemed sad and a little baffled.

Did he think I could clear up his confusion? Right now, I was bewildered enough for both of us.

"No, I can't blame her. I wouldn't want to attend an event where people thought I was a murderer, either, especially if the victim's family was there." I took a deep breath. Confrontation still made me uncomfortable, but we had to stop dancing around issues. No one had time for that. I needed direct answers to direct questions. "I spoke with Karlisa the other day. She said she hasn't heard from the band. No one has returned her calls. Do you think she's guilty?"

"No! I don't know." Earl flexed his broad shoulders as though trying to remove a weight. "It's hard to imagine Karlisa pushing Camille down a flight of stairs."

I searched his expression for what he might be leaving out. "Why?"

Earl's eyes widened with surprise at my question. "She's been our manager for almost six years. The whole time, she's always been calm and professional. So why would she explode now?"

"I've heard she and Camille argued a lot. Had they ever gotten physical with each other?"

Earl snorted. "They sniped at each other all the time.

But, no, they were *never* violent to one another." He flexed his shoulders again. "That's why we just don't know what to think. It's so confusing." He hesitated, giving me a critical look. "Rocky told me you've investigated other murders. What do you think? Is Karlisa guilty?"

I expelled a breath packed with frustration. "I'm sorry, Earl, but I don't know, either." I stepped back. "I'd better get back to the kitchen. I'm sorry."

His characterization of Karlisa matched Sheryl's: calm, professional, not prone to outbursts. And her motive, killing Camille before the singer could convince her bandmates to fire her, was questionable. Belle had a stronger one: money. But how do we connect Belle to Camille's murder?

The stairwell was paper white and narrow. Very narrow. People would have to climb it single file. I felt I had to keep my elbows tucked at my sides or risk banging them against the balustrade as I carried a large, stainless-steel pot of coconut rice and peas.

The only source of light came from an uncovered high-wattage bulb in the ceiling two stories up. Six scuffed and battered wooden steps led to a faded and scratched side door. It opened onto the street level. A second flight of stairs carried me to the first landing. During the tour of the reception area, Belle had explained there was a comfortable apartment behind the sturdy blond wood door. In the past, her parents had rented it out. At present, it was empty.

The muted sounds of DragonFlyZ's music, conversations, and the aromas of curry, jerk, and macaroni-and-cheese pie followed me up the final steps to Belle's private residence. I was giving myself fifteen minutes tops to get in, look around, then get out. I shifted the large pot to balance in the crook of my left arm and against my hip. This pot had the bulk of the side dish. I'd topped off the serving tray downstairs before leaving on my mission. Worst-case scenario, there was a backup pot on the stove downstairs in case my family ran out before I returned. It was highly unlikely, but I preferred to be prepared.

I unlocked the solid pristine white door to Belle's home. It opened into a cozy dining nook that seemed like it had been redecorated. I smelled fresh paint from the pale pink walls and new wood from the polished oak flooring.

A small oak wood table with four matching chairs stood steps away from the door. Beside it, a window bracketed by pink drapes a few shades warmer than the wall offered diners a view of the side yard. The kitchen was to my right on the other side of the wall from the stairwell. The black-and-pink space was stylish, impeccable, and obviously remodeled. The expenses were adding up.

The new kitchen featured oak cabinets, black-and-pink marble counters, and black appliances against pale pink walls. At the far end of the kitchen was a single window framed with pink curtains. The space appeared so clean it was hard to imagine anyone had cooked a meal or baked pastries here.

How could Belle afford this beautiful renovation if she couldn't pay the relief fund's vendors?

I unclenched my teeth. We didn't *know* she was embezzling from the fund or the benefit CD sales, but circumstantial evidence seemed to be piling up.

I set the pot on the stove before setting the stopwatch on my cell. Fifteen minutes, in and out. I retrieved my nitrile gloves from the pocket of my chef's smock. I couldn't leave any prints. A butcher's block of knives, coffeemaker, and toaster lined up across the counter to my left. The area was so pristine. Did Belle have maid service?

On my way out of the kitchen, an overabundance of nosiness compelled me to check the refrigerator. I am my grandmother's granddaughter. Several bottles of wine, fruit, and cheddar cheese occupied the otherwise empty fridge. Ice cream and frozen meals were in the freezer. What a waste of a beautiful kitchen.

Shaking my head, I turned in the direction I thought would lead to her bedroom. Shadows deepened the farther I advanced down the narrow, hardwood hallway. There were four doors in this section of the house. The first door was thin and seemed like a linen closet. I'd check that last if I had time and was desperate enough. The second one was closed. A peek inside gave the impression the room wasn't occupied. The bed had been stripped. The beige venetian blinds were closed, but the closet doors were open, displaying empty hangers. Had this been Belle's parents' room?

The door at the end of the hallway was open. It led to a full bathroom decorated in strong blues and warm whites. By process of elimination, I hoped the final room beside the bathroom belonged to Belle. I pressed open the door and was struck by Belle's familiar perfume. It was a robust floral scent, heavy on the jasmine. I checked behind me before creeping inside.

This space was twice the size of the one next door. Perhaps Belle had moved into her parents' room after they'd died. It also was chilly as though the air conditioning for this room had been cranked up really high.

Beneath the fragrance of Belle's perfume, I detected the hint of new carpet and fresh paint. My eyes swept the area. Her walls were the same pale pink as the kitchen, but the thick carpet and light drapes were a deep rose. A double bed covered in pale pink sheets dominated the space. I hurried to its far side next to the closet and dropped to my knees to search under it. I faced the front of the room so no one could sneak up on me.

Ha! A large black plastic storage container had been tucked beneath the head of Belle's bed. Could it really be this easy? Reaching beneath the bed frame, I grasped the edge of the case and dragged it out. Keeping as low as I could in the hope of remaining hidden, I unsnapped the lid and looked inside. The items in the container triggered my memory of Camille's youngest sister's words.

She always kept her perfume here. Now it's gone. A framed copy of the band's first album cover. They'd all signed it. The recorder she'd used when she was working on lyrics. And a plaque she made with the phrase "Everyone has a right to decide their own destiny." It's based on a Bob Marley quote, but she changed it.

Everything that Gwen had told me had been stolen and more was in this container.

"Put it back." Belle's voice turned my blood to ice.

I looked up. She stood in the doorway, holding a knife.

Camille's family was right. The killer and the burglar were one and the same.

My eyes dropped to Belle's large carving knife, then flew back to her face. Dropping the storage container's lid to the thick pink carpet, I surged to my feet. A million thoughts screamed in my mind. They were all related to the same thing.

"What have you done with my family?" I struggled against an almost crippling fear. My family hadn't warned me Belle was on her way. Why not? Had she hurt them?

Belle's dark brown eyes were hard with anger and contempt. "Shouldn't you be worried about yourself?"

I fisted my hands at my sides. "*You're* the one who should be worried if you've hurt my family."

Belle's full lips tightened. "I knew something was going on when the person who treated me like a leper suddenly acted like my best friend and a police reporter wanted to interview me for the society page."

What a relief. This explained why my family hadn't warned me. Belle had been on to us. She'd given them the slip. But I was on my own now. I watched Belle with wary eyes. At any moment, she could leap at me and plunge her knife into my gut.

I stepped away from the bed. I needed room to defend myself. "You have a house full of people, including my family. How're you going to explain killing me?"

"I'll tell them the truth." The spite in Belle's words stung. "I found an intruder going through my belongings. I didn't realize it was you until it was too late."

That defense sounded distressingly plausible. Dev had warned me. "My family's not going to buy that."

"How would they prove otherwise?" Belle moved forward, closing the distance between us to less than twenty-five feet.

If she threw that knife, could she hit me?

My body wanted to step back. I forced myself to stand still. Bracing my legs, I prayed the defensive moves I planned to use would work. I didn't want to engage Belle yet, though. It might seem ridiculous, but I wanted to know if we were right. I wanted to know why she'd killed Camille.

I shifted farther from the bed. Belle's eyes tracked me like a cat monitoring a mouse. "Did you kill Camille because she found out you were stealing the benefit CD money?"

Belle's frown deepened. "Who are you, my priest? I don't have to tell you anything."

I ignored her aggression. "She did, didn't she? Camille confronted you about stealing from the project and threatened to report you to the police—"

Belle gestured with the knife. She must have pulled the largest one from the block. "I wasn't *stealing* anything—"

I continued despite her interruption. "You got scared. Your fear turned to anger. The two of you argued. Maybe you didn't mean to push her—"

Belle's face was a mask of disgust. "Yes, I did. I absolutely meant to push her."

I gasped, covering my mouth. "What? Why? Why would you deliberately shove a person down a flight of stairs?"

"I wasn't *stealing* anything." Belle paced to her left toward the black lacquer nightstand on the other side of the bed. She spun on her heels, stomping back to the matching dresser on the opposite wall. Her movements were tight and jerky, like a robot in need of oil. "I was *borrowing* the money. Vendors were threatening to sue me. I had to settle my debts or the court could've forced me to sell my home."

I understood her anxiety at the thought of losing her home. It was her parents' legacy and they'd worked so hard to pass it on to her. But Belle was in a crisis of her own making.

"So instead of selling your home or coming up with an alternative solution, you killed Camille?" Hearing those words made my stomach sick. Camille had created something selfless to help people in need. Belle had made it all about her in the most despicable way.

Belle took another stride forward. We were less than twenty feet apart.

Her scowl deepened and darkened. "She didn't give me a choice. Can't you understand that? She should've minded her own business."

My eyes stretched wide with disbelief. Did Belle really believe she had the right to "borrow" money intended to help Caribbean nations recovering from a pandemic, hurricanes, a volcano, and other natural crises?

"DragonFlyZ's benefit CD *was* Camille's business. It was her idea, her vision, her band. She wrote the songs. Camille was the face of the project. You were supposed to disperse the money to the aid agencies. You broke their trust."

"You aren't listening to me." Belle spread her arms. "Camille was being unreasonable. They were going to sue me and *take my home*."

"So you took her life?" I gestured toward the container behind me. "What were you going to do with her belongings? Sell them? They aren't yours. They belong to her family now."

"I needed the money!" Belle's scream caught me by surprise.

I flinched. "And Camille's family needs their daughter and sister."

She raised her knife in a silent warning. Her knuckles showed white, wrapped around the hilt. "Who are *you* to lecture *me*?"

I stared at her in disbelief. She was like a douen, a soulless, heartless monster. "How did you even know which room was hers?"

Belle's eyes shot daggers at me. "I stopped by Camille's home one day to give her the packet of applications from the aid agencies. She showed me the CD cover comps. She wanted my opinion on the designs." She shrugged. "I asked if I could see them printed, so she took me to her room."

My mind was clear. I had the information I'd needed. I waited for Belle's attack. *Please let these defensive moves work.*

A *snick* cracked the brief silence. Bryce appeared in the doorway. His gun was pointed at Belle.

"Drop the knife. Hands up. Turn around." His voice was cold and steady, dropping the temperature in the room another ten degrees.

Belle's eyes widened in shock, then narrowed in determination.

She wasn't going to drop the knife.

Belle hunched her shoulders, faking compliance. She turned halfway toward Bryce.

She wasn't going to drop the knife.

I dropped to the floor and rolled, sweeping her feet out from under her. The knife fell from her grip. Belle dropped on top of me. I rolled over with her, straddled her back, and grabbed her arms.

Bryce holstered his gun, then rushed to help me. He snapped his handcuffs onto Belle's wrists. "Belle Baton, you're under arrest for the murder of Camille Abbey, the attempted murder of Lyndsay Murray, embezzlement, and breaking and entering." He pulled her to her feet.

Belle's eyes burned into me before she squared her shoulders and turned away.

I looked at Bryce. My smile trembled. My hands shook. "What a way to make an entrance."

He smiled back. "What a way to disarm a threat."

I forced my legs to carry me back to Belle's bed and rescued the plastic storage container. I lifted it, bringing it to Bryce's attention. "Returning Camille's items to her family will make this horrible experience worth it."

CHAPTER 25

"Thank you for texting Bryce." I looked around the tables we'd pushed together in the bakery's dining area to fit the ten of us attending this family meeting late Monday night.

"You're welcome," Granny, Mommy, Daddy, and Dev responded in unison.

It made me smile. Like me, they were still in their catering uniforms. Well, Mommy, Daddy, and Dev were. Granny was still in her turquoise-and-gold dress. She'd removed her scarlet head wrap. Her silver mane flowed over her slim shoulders.

Bryce had told me my family had texted him shortly after the reception had started. While he was grateful they'd clued him into what was going on, he wasn't happy with me. At all. He didn't buy my "plausible deniability" reasoning. Instead, he'd come back with my role as a consultant. By the time I'd finished giving him my statement, we'd both been irritated. He hadn't even thanked me for solving his case for him. Again. I'd left the precinct without a backward glance.

Seated on my right, Dev looked kind of irritated right now, too. "If you're going to put yourself in danger for other people, then you need to let us look after you."

"Your brother's right." Granny was on my left beside

Mommy, who sat at the head of the table with Daddy. She leaned forward to gesture toward Dev on my other side. "I know you know how to defend yourself, but you're not invincible, you know."

"But Lynds had a plan." Reena sat across from me with Uncle Roman on her right. She frowned at her brother to the left of her. "What happened, Manny?"

My cousin spread his hands in front of him. "Sheryl Cross and José Perez said Belle had gone to the bathroom. What was I supposed to do? Follow her in there?"

I lifted my right hand, palm out. My left was wrapped around a hot mug of ginger tea, which Aunt Inez had made for everyone before the meeting started. The sharp, spicy scent soothed me. "It wasn't Manny's fault, or Sheryl's or José's, either. Belle was on to us. Based on their history, I should've known she'd be suspicious of Sheryl's buddy act."

"And I shouldn't've been in such a rush to find someone to blame." Manny held my eyes. "You were right, Lynds. That wouldn't've honored Camille's memory. Thank you for following your instincts and finding the real killer."

Murmurs of agreement and praise circled the table. Reena squeezed her brother's shoulder. Her expression was a blend of sympathy and support.

Granny rubbed my back. "Brave."

Dev's irritation eased enough for him to offer me a half smile. "I'm proud of you. But try not to give me any more gray hairs."

"I promise." I looked around the table. "But I couldn't have done it without all of your support, including that tip from Ms. Robinson. What she'd told us about the aid agencies not getting the money from the benefit CD broke the case wide open."

Aunt Inez's full lips thinned in disgust. "That Belle's a

piece of work, oui. Taking donations meant to help others who are struggling and in pain and using them as your personal piggy bank to spend on extravagance like designer clothes and home remodeling. Can you imagine?"

"No, I can't." Daddy's eyes were wide with amazement.

"She'd killed Camille, then hosted a reception in her honor and invited her family." Uncle Al's face was ashen. I worried that he was going to be sick. He took a drink of his ginger tea. "I can't get over that. She has no heart."

Reena clenched her fists on the table. "That's really next level right there."

Daddy shook his head. "She's a monster and I'm glad she's going to prison where she belongs."

My father was right. Belle was a heartless monster. "I'll never forget the Abbey family's reaction when they saw Bryce taking Belle out of her house and they realized why."

Granny bent her head. She blinked as though forcing back tears. "Oh, Lord, yes."

Lynne's knees had buckled. Benedict had caught his mother just before she collapsed to the floor. John had covered his face and sobbed his heart into his hands. Gwen had stopped Viola from trashing the reception area. I couldn't blame her. I'd probably want to do the same. Instead, the sisters had embraced, crying on each other's shoulder. That image was seared into my brain. I tightened my grip around the hot mug, trying to ward off the chill that was spreading across my chest.

My eyes scanned the dining space. The lights were turned low and the white blinds were pulled shut, isolating my family and me in this safe space. Shadows from the busy pedestrian traffic on Parish Avenue slipped from window to window, like duppies looking for a way in. I turned my attention back to our family meeting.

Reena broke the heavy silence. "Was Belle really going to sell the stuff she'd stolen from Camille's room?"

"Yes, she was." I nodded. "I don't know whether the Abbeys are aware that Camille had taken Belle into her room to show her printouts of the benefit CD cover designs."

Dev expelled a breath. "It makes you wonder whether she'd been planning to kill Camille for a while."

"I don't think so. I believe this started as a tragic accident." I stared blindly into my half-full mug while an echo of my first conversation with Belle sounded in my ears, *I admire you, you know. You're confident and fearless.* "Belle is so used to getting her own way. It's possible she mistakenly tried to assert herself with Camille. That's when everything spiraled out of control, but she just kept justifying her behavior to herself. When Belle confronted me in her bedroom, she didn't have any remorse or guilt or shame over what she'd done and what she was continuing to do. She couldn't understand why Camille wouldn't let her use the donations or why I wanted to expose her as a murderer."

"Wow." Manny's thick dark eyebrows rose in amazement. He shifted his attention to Dev. "Do you think she'll try for an insanity defense?"

"I hope not." Dev's features were tight with anger. "She's hurt a lot of people, families, communities, countries. She deserves a long jail sentence."

Uncle Roman grunted. "She should be locked up for life." He found a smile for me. "So you're three-for-three, undefeated. Are you going to continue the streak?" His generous smile and teasing words eased the cloak of grief from my shoulders.

I laughed as he'd meant for me to. "No, Uncle Roman. This is it." I looked at my wonderful, supportive relatives and felt their love surrounding me. "No one else in our family will be suspected of murder, and I pray no one else we love will be hurt. So there won't be any need for me to get involved in any more murder investigations."

Dev arched an eyebrow. "So the Grenadian Nancy Drew's retiring?"

Laughter exploded from the table.

I winced at the ridiculous nickname. "That's right. No more dead bodies for me. From now on, the only cases I'm taking on will be the ones carrying cooking supplies."

"You know, Lynds, working on those investigations has been good for you." Granny stood at the counter behind me, transferring another batch of fresh currant rolls from a baking pan to the pastry tray early Wednesday morning.

The scent of warm, melted butter, brown sugar, and cinnamon drifted back to me, reminding me that I needed to get something to eat before the bakery opened.

The kitchen was bursting with the sweet scents of fresh pastries, spicy aromas of fried dishes, and the sharp fragrance of bush teas. DragonFlyZ's "Uprising," another original song from their benefit CD, bounced from our sound system. Mommy, Daddy, Dev, and I synced our movements to the driving beats. We were trying to sing along with the recording, but no one knew all the words. The result was almost tragic. Still we needed this outlet. It had been thirty-six hours since the harrowing events that had led to Belle Baton's arrest Monday evening, not that I was counting. Channeling our residual stress and fear into the music helped.

Standing at the head of the center island, I wielded a rolling pin over my latest currant-roll-in-progress. "You really think so, Granny? Why?"

"I disagree." Mommy was on my right. She looked up

from the yellow plantain she was slicing in preparation for frying. "Those investigations scared me to death. I'm glad we're done with all that."

Granny joined us at the center island. I shifted to give her more room. Today, she'd made the concession of wearing a chef's hat. Beneath her red bakery apron, she wore a bronze shorts set. Chunky gold jewelry dressed it up.

"I'm not saying they weren't dangerous, Della, but I enjoyed the challenge." Granny shrugged. "More importantly, they helped build your daughter's self-confidence. Before the investigations, she was like a turtle always hiding in her shell." She hunched her back and raised clenched fists. I suppose that was her turtle impersonation. It was less than flattering. "The investigations took her out of her comfort zone and tested her. Each time, she passed. The first test was Claudio Fabrizi. She had to do that investigation to prove her innocence."

Daddy stood to my left, mixing the batter for the fish bakes. "She investigated Emily Smith's murder to clear your name, Della."

Granny pointed to me. "But you chose to continue this investigation even after the police thought they'd solved it because it was a case *you* believed in. This is the first time you found the courage to step out of your comfort zone for yourself, not for family."

"I hadn't thought about it like that, but you're right." I didn't know which was more disconcerting: the ways in which I was changing or that Granny had noticed before I did.

In the past, I'd been afraid to try new things or meet new people unless it involved my family, like this bakery. Camille's case had been full of new experiences, people, and places. In the end, I hadn't stuck with the investigation because of Manny. I'd done that for myself.

"Both the bakery and the investigations have helped you come into your own, Lynds." Dev kneaded dough for coconut bread at the opposite end of the center island. Joymarie requested one every morning. Granny wasn't the only observant one.

I see what you're doing there, Dev. And I approve.

My brother continued. "The bakery's good for me, too. I'm happier and more relaxed now. I'm even sleeping better. For the first time in years, I feel like I have a healthy balance in my life. That's why I'm declining the senior partners' invitation to return to the firm. I'm staying here at the bakery."

I stared at him, wide-eyed and slack-jawed. "Are you sure, Dev?" Was I dreaming?

He laughed. "Absolutely. The bakery's not an obligation to me, Lynds. It's what I want. I'll keep my law license in good standing. That way I can represent the shop if we ever need legal representation. And I might do some work with other local businesses, but the bakery's my main focus."

I followed Mommy, Granny, and Daddy as we converged on Dev to wrap him in a family hug.

"I'm so happy you're happy." Granny's voice was muffled against Dev's back.

"This is wonderful news." Daddy stepped back to pat Dev's shoulder.

"I was hoping you'd stay." Mommy leaned back to study Dev's face. "Joymarie must be glad for your decision, too. This way, you have more time to spend together."

My silent look mocked him. *Told you. They're researching wedding venues and selecting playlists.*

His shrug said, *Let them.*

I mentally patted myself on the back. I knew Joymarie was The One for Dev. She was smart, kind, fun, and hardworking. I couldn't be happier.

Yet there was a wisp of a cloud hovering over me. I hadn't seen Bryce since giving him my statement Monday night. That hadn't ended well. We'd parted with testy words. We'd exchanged olive branches through texts. Maybe I'd feel more settled if we'd spoken to each other. Or maybe Detective Fine had decided dating a baker who moonlighted as an amateur detective was a little too extra.

I set the next batch of currant rolls in our commercial oven. "Are we ready to open? Granny, can you lead us in a prayer?"

We held hands and bowed our heads as Granny gave thanks and asked for grace and blessings. Then she led Dev and me into the customer service area. I stood with my brother behind the counter while Granny unlocked the bakery door. Once again, we couldn't see the end of the line. I thought I'd burst with excitement.

Tanya and Benny were the first through the door. Granny's friend opened her arms with a dramatic sweep. "Congratulations, Murray family! You solved another murder."

Benny grinned. "We never had any doubt you'd do it."

Other patrons poured in, applauding, whistling, and cheering as they shouted compliments, questions, and commentary. Always with the commentary.

"All you should stay open every day," Grace Parke called from near the center of the customer service line. It continued out the door. "We can't wait days to get the real insider knowledge on these investigations, you know."

Dev's look of surprise added to my amusement. Though I noticed he didn't have a response for the older woman. He stood in silence behind the register, waiting to cash out the orders.

"On behalf of my family, I apologize for your inconvenience, Ms. Parke." I arranged Tanya and Benny's fish bakes and fried plantains on a tray for them to enjoy in the dining area. "Thank you so much, Ms. Nevis, Mr. Parsons. We hope you enjoy the food."

"We know we will, dear." Tanya gave Dev and me a cherubic smile.

I returned my attention to Grace. "José Perez did an excellent job, wrapping up the investigation for the *Beacon*."

José had interviewed my family and me after we gave Bryce and Stan our statements.

The reporter stepped out from behind D'André, who was next in line. "That's very nice of you to say. Thanks, Lynds."

"We're still not there, José," I corrected him in a singsong voice.

"Are you sure?" He gave me a winning smile. It had no effect on me.

D'André pulled out his wallet. "Lemme get a couple of beef patties and a sorrel. What about the information that *wasn't* in the article?"

I turned to fill his order. "Like what?"

From the middle of the line, Carole, the Bubble-Gum-Chewing College Student, waved her hand. She must still be on school break. She wasn't carrying her overstuffed backpack. "Like if you used your kickboxing moves to subdue the perp?"

"Did Belle Baton attack you?" another guest called out.

"Was the catering job a cover to get close to the killer?" yet another asked.

Overwhelmed, I stared at the crowd. I couldn't fill all their orders and answer their questions at the same time. I needed a new plan.

"No." Granny's voice silenced our audience. "The catering job was not a cover. It was a real job with real food."

Several guests chuckled at her response. "Detective Jackson showed up before Belle could hurt my granddaughter. Thanks be to God. Any other questions?"

To my relief, the rest of the orders continued smoothly as Granny fielded our patrons' barrage of questions.

The breakfast rush had drained to a trickle by late morning. Granny had returned to crocheting her lavender-and-white afghan. Dev was helping Mommy and Daddy clean the kitchen while I bussed the tables and swept the customer service area.

I looked up as the bakery door chimed. I felt a twinge of disappointment that it wasn't Bryce, but a pleased smile eased my expression at the sight of Miles, Ena, Karlisa, and John and Lynne Abbey. Granny set aside her afghan.

Leaning the broom against a nearby wall, I turned to the pass-through window to ask Mommy, Daddy, and Dev to join us. I was certain they'd want to greet our visitors.

Granny stood. "Would you like to sit in the dining room?"

We pushed two tables together to accommodate the ten of us. The few customers already seated looked at us with open curiosity. I was tempted to take bets on how soon our meeting would make the rounds on the Little Caribbean grapevine.

Karlisa was seated between Miles and Ena. "The members of DragonFlyZ and I thank you from the very bottom of our hearts for helping to catch Camille's killer." She pressed her hand to her chest. "I'm especially grateful, of course. You believed in my innocence even when the evidence was against me, and I was sabotaging myself with lies that I thought would protect me. You kept investigating. I don't know how I'll ever repay you."

I gestured toward my family beside me. "We just wanted the truth."

"That's what we all wanted." Miles's voice was subdued. "Thank you. We needed—I needed—to tell you that. The band, we met yesterday and agreed we're going to stay together. Ena and I are going to try writing the songs together."

Ena looked at Camille's parents, seated at the foot of the table. "And we're going to make the benefit CD an annual project in Camille's honor."

Lynne hurriedly pulled a tissue from her oversized black handbag. She dried the tears rolling down her round cheeks. "She would've loved that. She'd be rooting for you."

"My family and I are so very sorry for your loss." I scanned the faces of the grieving family members and bandmates seated around the table. Their heartache over Camille's death was evident and tangible. What was that saying? "You never get over the passing of a loved one; you can only get through it."

John covered Lynne's hand, which lay on the table between them. "Thank you. It doesn't bring her back, but it helps to know who killed our daughter and why. My family and I are grateful to you and your family for getting those answers for us. Without them, we surely would've gone mad."

Lynne took a shuddering breath. "Now at least we can have a little peace and closure."

Karlisa pursed her lips in a wry expression. "The West Indian American Relief Fund is looking for new leadership. Imagine that."

Lynne linked her left fingers with her husband's. Her right hand gripped her tissue in a fist. "We're going to reinvest Camille's album and songwriting royalties, and create scholarships for young songwriters."

"That's wonderful." Granny smiled at the grieving

mother. "It helps to turn heartache into something positive."

John nodded. "And yes, the West Indian American Relief Fund's looking for a new president. I've heard very few people have applied. Our daughter Gwen wants the job. I don't know why she'd want any part of that messy business."

Mommy inclined her head. "Because she knows the fund does important and necessary work. I hope she gets the job."

Daddy put an arm around Mommy's shoulders. "My wife's right. And with the benefit CD becoming an annual project, your daughter would make sure the money was transferred to the aid agencies properly."

The tension eased from John's face. "That's true. She'd be protecting Camille's legacy."

I shared a look between Camille's parents. "Once Gwen gets the job, we have a check for the fund. It's the money Belle Baton paid us for catering her event. We believe she took it from the benefit CD. We want the fund to distribute it to the aid agencies as Belle was supposed to."

John gave a sharp nod. He seemed too upset to speak.

Lynne dried more tears. "Thank you."

The chime drew my attention to the bakery's entrance. Bryce crossed the threshold. His eyes went straight to me. How did he always know where I was, even in a crowd?

Excusing myself from the table, I crossed the store and greeted him with a smile. "What can we do for you, Detective?"

He smiled back. He looked photo session ready in a midnight blue tapered-leg suit and plantain green tie. "Are we back to 'Detective'?"

"Bryce."

"This is one of the rare times I've come to you with good news." Whatever it was, he seemed to be savoring it.

"What is it?"

His hazel eyes twinkled at me. "You'll probably read this in the *Beacon*'s breaking news report, but I wanted to tell you personally. Emily Smith's killer has accepted the plea deal. The case is *not* going to trial."

I lost my breath. My mind blanked and my jaw dropped. "Oh, my goodness!" I was bouncing on my toes without even realizing it. Grinning, I turned to my family. "Emily Smith's murder case isn't going to trial! The defense accepted the plea deal." My fists shot into the air. I tossed back my head and laughed.

My family surged to their feet with shouts of joy and relief. The bakery erupted into applause and cheers.

I threw my arms around Bryce and held him tight. "Thank you so much. This is the *best* news."

He hugged me back. "This calls for a celebration."

"I'll tell you what." Stepping back, I grinned up at him. "Let me take you to lunch. I know the perfect place."

RECIPES

Coconut Pudding

Dry ingredients
- ½ cup cornstarch
- ½ cup sugar
- ¼ teaspoon salt
- ½ cup toasted coconut flakes
- ¼ cup ground cinnamon

Wet ingredients
- 1 teaspoon vanilla extract
- 4 cups coconut milk

Utensils
- Saucepan, small
- Whisk
- Dessert cups, 4

Instructions
- In a small saucepan, combine cornstarch, sugar, and salt.
- Add vanilla extract.

- Whisk in coconut milk. Over low heat, allow the mixture to simmer, stirring constantly until the contents thicken (approximately 6 minutes).
- Remove the saucepan from the heat. Pour the pudding into dessert cups.
- Place the dessert cups in the refrigerator to cool (approximately 1 hour).
- Garnish cooled pudding with toasted coconut flakes and ground cinnamon.

Baked Sweet Potato Pudding

Dry ingredients
>2 tablespoons sugar
>4 cups grated sweet potato
>1½ cups grated coconut
>2½ cups sugar
>1½ teaspoons cinnamon
>½ teaspoon salt
>1 tablespoon ginger
>½ teaspoon nutmeg
>½ cup grated taro

Wet ingredients
>¼ cup water
>2½ cups milk

Utensils
- Medium mixing bowl
- 9″ × 13″ baking pan

Instructions
- Grease the baking pan, then set the pan aside.
- Combine the water with 2 tablespoons of sugar, then set it aside.
- Set the oven to 350 degrees Fahrenheit.
- Combine all of the ingredients in the mixing bowl.
- Pour the mixture into the greased baking pan.
- Cover the surface of the mixture with the sugar-and-water combination.
- Bake the mixture for 1½ hours.
- Allow the baked sweet potato pudding to cool at room temperature for 20 minutes.